MIDLIFE BATTLE

DRUID HEIR BOOK 7

N. Z. NASSER

Midlife Battle: Druid Heir Book 7
Copyright © N. Z. Nasser 2022
Published by Hanora Sky Press

eBook ISBN 978-1-915151-16-2
Paperback ISBN 978-1-915151-17-9

THE PLAYERS

Alisha Verma - Druid Heir
Echo - Alisha's leopard sidekick
Mirabel (sometimes known as Bel) - a fairy
Marina Ambrose - Alisha's best friend
Ezra Neuhoff - half-werewolf, half-wizard Minister for Justice
Orpheus Might - Vampire, Minister for History and the Today
Robert Jameson - Detective, Shadow Squad
Fei Yen and Faeza - hu hsien, shapeshifting foxes
Joshi Verma - Alisha's father
Sahil Verma - Alisha's brother
Alma Bluejay - Flour seer and Joshi's love
Rajiv Chawla - Rajika Verma's brother
Gaia - Goddess of the Earth
Lavinia Drach - Witch, Prime Sorceress
Isadora Drach - Witch Headmistress of Wildwoods and
Minister for Education
Flinar - Elf, Defence Minister
Calypso Archer - The Custodian of the Celestial Library
Helio Woodwink - Fairy, Bestiary Master
Cillian O'Meara - Leprechaun, Minister for Finance
Erelim - Angel, Minister for Diplomacy

Phinnaeous Shine - Shapeshifter, former Prime Sorcerer
Margola Silver - Selkie, Minister for Information
Pan - God of Shepherds, Goats and Pastures
Meriel Naehorn - the former elf queen
Mammatas and Rhokon - sphinxes
Nightfall - a horse in the Celestial Library
Ignacio - rat familiar
Tielbu - a dragon
Ra - the Sun God
Pan - God of Shepherds, Goats and Pastures
Hermes - the Messenger God
Mami Wata - Water Goddess
Cardea - Goddess of Door Hinges, Thresholds and Health
Morpheus - God of Dreams
Death - a goddess

1

W inter closed in, bringing with it snowstorms and the promise of renewal. All across London, children trampled the blanket of white and left sludge in their wake. At the cottage, Ezra, Mirabel and I prepared for our first Christmas together. Fairy lights roped around the bay window. The scent of mulled wine lingered in the air. Echo cheerfully murdered the tunes of Christmas classics on the radio. A bare fir tree waited for our attention.

Tonight, we invited our nearest and dearest over to decorate it.

Blame Ezra. It was his suggestion. He said traditions brought families closer together.

With Mirabel in our lives, a new chapter had begun. Once, we'd fiercely protected our privacy at the cottage. Now, we drew loved ones closer into our orbit. Some days, it seemed like there was a revolving door between the pack farmhouse, Wildwoods, Baba Yaga's Gym and our cottage.

Ezra's yearning for close-knit family ties meant he glossed over the truth: having everyone under one roof spelt disaster. Family celebrations could be as fraught as they were fun. Jostling for respect. Careful tiptoeing over sore points.

Fights over the last Yorkshire pudding. Silenced protests when more food landed on your plate, though you had already burst a seam.

Little wonder that I checked my supply of paracetamol before our guests arrived.

Sometimes, when all was quiet—when Mirabel was asleep, the day's work was done, and we had slipped into a comfortable silence—I found Ezra's grey eyes on me. I didn't tell him how the Book of Names hadn't let me rest since we had buried it in the garden. How its whispers tornadoed through my head, a shadow life. An intrusion at all times, whether I was deep in conversation or in his arms. Whether I was curled up on the sofa with Mirabel and Echo, training with my sword, showering, or resting my head on my pillow at night.

I didn't tell him, but maybe Ezra knew. Just like I could tell from the slightest change in the shade of his eyes or the set of his shoulders when something bothered him. Maybe that was why he insisted on having a party and living in the moment.

In case we didn't have many moments left.

After all, the goddess of Death could not be cheated twice. It was only a matter of time before she came for me. Everyone knew it. My hair greyed quicker than before, as if Death already had a grip. But life couldn't stop. Not when you were in love. Not when you had a daughter to care for. Not when the alternative didn't bear thinking about. So, I agreed to the party.

I dyed my roots, struck by my resemblance to my mother in the mirror. I had her almond-shaped brown eyes, determined jaw, and ageing hands as I put on my mascara. Then I scrunched mousse into my curly hair like the eighties chick I was and poured my curves into a too-tight dress.

"Are you ready?" Ezra walked into the room. He wore jeans and a light-up reindeer jumper that Mirabel had bought for him despite complaining that it ruined his street cred. Calloused thumbs brushed my back as he zipped me up.

A frisson of pleasure ran up my spine as I turned to face him. "Do you think Lavinia will cause trouble?" There'd been an uneasy truce with his aunt since we'd found out about her newly acquired teleportation skills. Our questions had been brushed aside or unsatisfactorily answered. "You should prod her more. Maybe she'll open up to you without me th—"

My words died on my lips as the doorbell rang.

"Everything's going to be fine, I promise," said Ezra, as though mere biology erased his aunt's hard edges, the ones that made her prize power over family. "There won't be a fang, cauldron or rogue god in sight. Just a room full of loved ones, a bit of tree decoration and some party games. You'll see. Take your time finishing up. I'll get the door."

Mirabel dashed into the room, auburn ringlets wild about her head, and plopped on the bed. She wore a leather miniskirt and Nirvana T-shirt. "Can I wear this?"

I grinned at her. "The guests are here. I'm not exactly going to ask you to change now. Ezra's going to have something to say about that hemline, though."

"A shifter can't complain about exposed flesh," said our daughter tartly.

"Just try him. You raided my makeup drawer again."

"The stuff in there is about a century old."

"The cheek of you. Guess you know what to buy me for Christmas then." I pulled her in for a hug. "Come on. It's time we host our first party as a family."

Two hours later, my shapewear rolled down as I collected dirty dishes from amongst the party guests. "Santa Baby" spilt out of the speakers from Ezra's festive playlist. By the bay window, Gaia rummaged in a box of Christmas tree decorations with Lavinia and Ezra's packmate, Maximillian. Orpheus, ever the solitary figure even in a crowd, sat stiff-backed in our armchair, reading a volume of W. B. Yeats in the firelight. Echo dozed at the vampire's feet, enjoying the kneading he received from Flinar's knobbly fingers. At one end of the dining table, Dad, Great-Uncle Rajiv and Marina watched as Mirabel pulled a block from a teetering tower.

I paused to smile at Sahil and Rob, hunched over a chessboard at the other end of the table.

The detective collected Sahil's bishop. "Your brother's head is elsewhere tonight."

"A werepigeon's head is always in the clouds." Sahil knocked over his own king. "It's a lovely party, sis, made all the better for Marina wearing that leather corset—"

Marina winked at my brother and then blew Rob a kiss.

Sahil pretended to stab his own heart. "But is nobody going to talk about the elephant in the room? Death wants to stick her scythe in us, and here we are playing happy families."

Gaia dropped a turquoise bauble back into the box. She dazzled in a crimson raw silk sari with a gold border. On her forehead, she wore a *maang tikka* that reminded me of a third eye. "Deepening connections with loved ones is never wasted time, werepigeon. There is nothing quite so irksome to Death as a life well lived. She would have us choose despair in this moment, whereas we are choosing joy."

The detective sighed. "With all humility, goddess, there's only so long I can brief the Shadow Squad about impending danger without something actually happening. I'm a laughingstock in the department."

Marina came over to sit on his knee. "Poor thing. You'll prove them right in the end."

Alma shook her head sadly. "I've been doing flour ritual after flour ritual and am none the wiser as to the path forward."

The Earth goddess fussed with the folds of her sari. "I do wish you'd stop those, dear. I'm finding the residue in all my bodily creases, and at my age, it's quite the acrobatic feat to get under the flaps. I've told you before there is no point rushing Death. We will just have to be patient."

"Patience is easier for the undead and immortals," said Orpheus. "Mortals view time through a different lens. Isn't it about time the prophecy comes to fruition so Alisha can unshackle herself from the worry and constant looking over her shoulder?"

Cataracts made Great-Uncle Rajiv's eyes eerily pale. "Rushing into battle is a fool's errand. It got Rajika killed. My great-niece should avoid making the same mistake."

"Why is it a given that Alisha should fight at all?" Dad ran a hand through sparse, scarecrow hair. "Maybe she should be a decoy and leave the real fight to others with more experience or less to lose. She has a family now."

Mirabel's moss-green eyes filled with tears. Her voice trembled as if she wasn't sure she should speak. As if she was still finding her place amongst us. "My birth parents didn't fight, and they still died."

Flinar, newly appointed as Defence Minister, went to her side. "There, there, little one. The Prime Sorceress and I have plans up our sleeves. Alisha won't be fighting alone."

My chest grew leaden as I listened to them squabble. I'd just wanted one night. One night to be a normal family. My head pounded with the call of the book. The Prime Sorceress had yet to utter a word on the matter. Her skin was too thick to have been pierced by the daggered looks I'd sent her all evening. No, she was waiting for my take on the matter. Because, as the eternal girl, I rivalled her power.

Ezra walked to my side and relieved me of the stack of dishes. "Alisha? What do you want?"

I gave him a grateful look. "I am tired of waiting for the attack. I want to draw Death out. We have all the tools to defeat her, don't we? Then why have her attack hanging over us like an executioner's axe? We need to gather our troops. We need to contain the rogue gods while we can."

Gaia skewered some cheddar from the cheese board, grumbling. "Gods won't be rushed. How many times must I teach mortals that lesson?"

The foxes pursed their bow lips and exchanged glances. Quiet voices piped up in unison. "Actually, we might have something to help with that."

"We noticed a dark omen in the tea leaves. It's been centuries since the old monsters rose, but we thought opening a portal to the realm of the dead might help us prepare for what lies ahead." Faeza reached underneath the sofa for a small, flat parcel wrapped in brown paper and tied with the ribbon. "It's just a little something from Shanghai Moon."

Heart thudding in its cage, I knelt beside the sofa to untie the ribbon. A waxy, weathered box slid from the wrapping paper. The lettering adorning it looked as though it stemmed from the 1920s or 1930s.

I turned it over in my hands and discerned its purpose with a jolt.

Some things were so terrifying that you avoided all contact with them or even thinking about them, in case by doing so, you let the devil into your life. Like certain horror films. The woman with a crystal ball at rundown funfairs. Occult games. Chain letters.

Running my fingers over the smooth wooden board inside, I looked up at Fei Yen and Faeza. "A Ouija board. I've never seen one in real life. How thoughtful of you. Thank you."

I closed the box firmly, wondering how soon we could toss it on a bonfire. There was no way I wanted to introduce Mirabel to something like this.

Lavinia clapped excitedly. Tonight, her silver curls had been teased into a beehive befitting a queen. "Oh, it's been an age since I've played. My sisters are going to be even more envious that they couldn't make it tonight. Can we have a little go? It's making me all nostalgic just looking at the thing. We used to play it as children…unless you're too scared, Alisha? Humdrums have a bizarre fear of Ouija, and you did, after all, grow up ordinary."

I stiffened. "Of course not. I'm not scared of it. Ouija boards are parlour tricks."

"Well, if that's your opinion, then it's simply a bit of harmless fun. Who else is in?" said Lavinia.

"We are," said Fei Yen and Faeza.

"And me," said Marina, a big believer in both ghosts and science. "I've always wanted to test out the involuntary movement theory."

"I'll play," I said. "But, Bel, I'm afraid you can't watch."

Echo opened one emerald eye, where he lay by the fire. "Come on, little one." He shepherded a bristling Mirabel out. "We can watch *Friends* in the bedroom."

"I'll play too," said Sahil. "Maybe Mum will reach out to us."

"I'll get a pen and paper and be the secretary," said Alma brightly.

"Don't say I didn't warn you," muttered Gaia darkly.

My heartbeat sped up. No one else heeded her warnings.

"Ezra, turn off the music. My mother always used to say that a séance requires undivided attention," said Dad. "And bring out the whisky. Come, goddess, sit by me. We'll get piddled together while watching the commotion."

Gaia fumbled beneath her sari blouse and pulled out a silver coin with crooked fingers. She handed it to me. "Put this on the board. It will repel malevolent spirits. You still may not get the answers you desire."

We laid the Ouija board and the heart-shaped planchette with its viewfinder window on the coffee table. I placed the silver coin on top. Lavinia, the foxes, Marina, Sahil and I made up the inner circle around the board, surrounded by another layer of onlookers. Intricate carvings of the moon, sun and skulls decorated the edges of the board. The alphabet arced across its centre. I noticed a row of numbers, together with a *yes, no* and *goodbye*, presumably so that the spirits could take their leave if we offended them.

Lavinia whispered a spell to light a pillar candle. "Welcome all to tonight's séance. I am your medium. I'd like everyone to clear their minds, write down their questions and pass them to me. We all agree that the questions should focus on the coming darkness, yes? Excellent. Let's see what clues we can unearth."

The Book of Names clawed at my thoughts, muddying my clarity. I took a deep breath. "One question each. Then Bel and Echo can come back, and I'll bring out the pudding."

We scrawled out our questions and passed them to the Prime Sorceress. Behind us, the rest of the room craned their necks to get a closer look.

The Prime Sorceress revelled in the power she wielded. "Place your index and middle fingers on the planchette and close your eyes while I ask the question. When the planchette moves, you may follow its progress. Then, let us begin. How many spirits are here tonight?"

My mouth went dry as the planchette slid towards the number 3.

"Very good. Then let us begin." Lavinia read from a slip of paper. "How will Death attack?"

The air around us felt denser, heavier somehow. My spine tingled as the planchette jerked under our fingers, moving at pace.

E-V-E-R-Y-W-H-E-R-E.

Alma frowned as she scribbled down the answer.

I whipped my gaze around the circle, feeling stupid. "Who did that? This isn't funny."

Lavinia gave me a sombre look. "Hush, Alisha, calm

yourself, lest you turn the spirits against us. We're just looking for answers. Next question. Can we win?"

Marina giggled nervously, outing herself as the originator of the question.

A sway in the curtains as though Echo had clawed the heavy fabric. I flicked my gaze back to the pointer with its circular viewfinder. The air in my lungs thinned as it darted across the board, tracing its supernatural path.

T-H-E-P-A-T-H-I-S-S-M-A-L-L.

Ezra's voice was a growl. "This was a terrible idea, Auntie. Put the board away."

"Nonsense, nephew. Just because you don't have the stomach for it doesn't mean it's the wrong thing to do. And please, maintain quiet, or we risk losing our connection to the other realm. Not all spirits are this communicative, you know." Lavinia centred herself before unpeeling another question. "Is everyone in this room an ally?"

My blood froze as the planchette slid over the *no*.

Lavinia gave a tinkling laugh. "What fun this is! Now, now, Alisha, no playing with your wind powers."

"I didn't do anything," I said.

Not everyone in the room was an ally, the spirits had said. My mind circled through the possibilities of a betrayer within our midst, and it could only be her.

The Prime Sorceress swiftly moved on. "Spirits, who will die?"

Gaia's irises blazed with volcanic anger. "Nothing good comes of knowing that, witch."

Lavinia gave a delighted laugh as the planchette juddered into action.

Sahil's eyes bulged as it spelt out our family name.

Did it mean me, him or Dad? Or perhaps Echo or Great-Uncle Rajiv? Or Mirabel? Was the board always right? No wonder Gaia had told us not to mess with this.

My stomach clenched. Maybe the spirits we communed

with were real, or the Prime Sorceress just wanted to get under my skin. Worse, a shuffle in the shadows of the hallway told me Mirabel and Echo eavesdropped there.

"That's enough." I jerked my hand off the planchette. I should have burned this godforsaken present. "No more. This could all be hogwash, yet we'll think about it for days. The goddess was right. Leave the unknown where it belongs. The future will unfold in its own time."

The candle illuminated hollows in the Prime Sorceress's face. "I will have the last answer, druid. A witch is not afraid of the dark. Where is the Book of Names?"

The book drove a torrent of noise into my head.

This had been the unspoken question all evening. The one that buzzed in everyone's minds—whether from curiosity, concern or lust for power—and I didn't like it one bit that Lavinia had manoeuvred to wrestle the answer from us. The power to command the gods was not something to be taken lightly. Only Ezra and I knew the whereabouts of the Book of Names.

The hair on the back of my neck stood up as the planchette started its passage slowly, then with bullet-like speed, over the letters I most feared.

G-A-R-D-E-N.

Cursing, Ezra held his hand to the moon charm on his necklace.

The fairy lights and candle fizzled out and our guests— the brave and the strong amongst them—screamed.

2

G asps and cries found my ears as panic bubbled. Our guests thought the spirits had turned against them.

I knew better than that. Ezra had extinguished the light with his charm to cloak the final answer on the Ouija board. I made a mental note to jump his bones later in gratitude for his quick thinking, but first, we needed to calm everyone down.

Even with all the power and experience of the supernatural in this room, something about the dark sent our imaginations into overdrive and made us more jumpy and less rational. I could help with that. I grounded myself to the earth beneath me, calling on my druid nature. In my mind's eye, I conjured up a host of fireflies. A heartbeat later, I wrenched them from my head, illuminating our living room in their soft glow.

Alma and Dad had wrapped their arms around Sahil. Mirabel sought to light a fireball with trembling fingers. A pair of checkered boxers hung from the Christmas tree, where Maximillian had strewn them in his haste to transform into his wolf. Rob and Marina wrestled over a pair of handcuffs. The foxes huddled by the fire with Flinar on their laps between them, and Lavinia wielded her umbrella like a hockey stick.

Only Orpheus, Echo and Gaia remained calm. The vampire was a creature of the night who welcomed the dark. The leopard was a formidable nocturnal hunter, unshaken by a mere lighting outage. Gaia was accustomed to the blackest nights and the voids of time. Malevolent spirits were child's play to her. She took the opportunity to devour the cheese board while no one looked.

"For goodness sake, pull yourselves together. Ezra turned the lights off for a joke." The lie tripped off my tongue. "Time to pack away the Ouija board."

Fei Yen extricated herself from her wife's embrace and made her way over to the Ouija board. "The ritual is not yet finished." With a deft movement, she slid the heart-shaped planchette over the *goodbye*. "To close the portal between realms."

Lavinia's face clouded. "But we didn't decipher the last answer."

"The location of the Book of Names is not your concern, Prime Sorceress." My voice was the quiet before a storm. Maybe I'd lucked out, and she hadn't seen it. I sure as hell didn't have her in my circle of trust. "Ezra, let's get the music back on, shall we? I'm going to fetch the puddings."

The musky scent of Ezra's beta wolf caught my nose. He skulked at the back of the group, a muscular, medium-sized wolf, silver-white with piercing blue eyes. "Maximillian, maybe you want to change back into human form and remove your boxers from the tree?" I turned on my heel towards the kitchen, in desperate need of a breather, as the sounds of Wham's "Last Christmas" flowed behind me.

Ezra caught my waist at the dishwasher as I bent to stack dishes. "Hey, hey, it's okay. Come here."

I straightened up and wiped my hands on the dishtowel. "It's chaos."

"It's not all bad," said Ezra, his handsomeness multiplied by how ridiculous he was prepared to look in the reindeer jumper. "Mirabel looks happy. We're giving her a sense of family."

I grimaced. "She crept back in with Echo. I didn't want her exposed to all that."

He raised an eyebrow. "All what? The danger? The forbidden knowledge? Alisha, Bel's exposed to it just by being part of this family. We both know what it's like being children of parents who kept secrets from us. Maybe we should share more with her, not less."

My instinct was to protect her. That couldn't ever be wrong, could it?

"Thank goodness you got the lights. That was inspired." I didn't tell him my worry that we hadn't been quick enough. I couldn't know for sure.

Grey eyes sparked with copper. "Disaster averted."

"Your aunt was fishing. I think she made herself medium so she could ask anything she wanted."

Exasperation flooded his face. "She's a troublemaker, all right."

I stiffened. "You're cross with her but never furious enough to put your foot down. Teleporting was your skill alone. She coveted it, and now she has it. She took it by stealth. Even then, you won't challenge her properly about it."

We had teleported after her, zigzagging between the folds of the world, hoping that she had a decent explanation. We'd finally caught up with her at Ezra's parents' grave. Weathered stone. Damp moss. Buried bones. A storm-baked sky. It was as if his aunt had chosen that sacred spot, knowing that Ezra wouldn't unleash his fury there, whatever she had done. He would never desecrate his parents' memory in that way.

A vein throbbed in his jaw. "What do you want me to do,

Alisha? She's the Prime Sorceress. She's family. And we already have plenty of powerful enemies without making another one."

I couldn't stop my runaway words, even though this wasn't the time or the place. Even though anyone could overhear. "Tell me you think her explanation was bullshit. You toss and turn in your sleep. I know you're processing the same things I am. Death's scorched cigarette butts in Lavinia's office at Wildwoods. How she betrayed you. What else she might be capable of."

Even before I finished, I hated myself for putting us at odds with each other. Ignoring the buzz of the book in my mind, I delved into the fridge for tiny bowls of tiramisu topped with berries.

"Don't be angry." Ezra helped, his arm brushing against mine. "Let's just get through the rest of the evening. We can talk about this later. I shouldn't have pushed you into hosting."

Blinking away tears of frustration, I fetched teaspoons for the pudding. I wanted so much for us to be a united front. "My idea of the perfect Christmas is you, me, Mirabel and Echo nestled up on the sofa with mugs of cocoa, *Home Alone* on the telly, and you asking me whether I'd like a hot water bottle and a foot rub."

His grey eyes smouldered as he caught my hands. "I can arrange a rub, Alisha," he murmured as he dipped his lips to mine.

The tension in my shoulders melted away at his touch. My need for him hadn't diminished, but there were so few opportunities to have time to ourselves these days. How could we swing from chandeliers when there was always a problem to solve or counsel to give? I sank into his kiss, thirsting for him. He tasted of roll-ups and raspberries he'd plucked from the pudding.

Lavinia's tinkling laugh punctured the moment.

I pulled away, stiffening. Great, just great.

Ezra wiped a smear of lipstick from under my lip. His voice artificially brightened as the Prime Sorceress shimmied into the kitchen. "Auntie, can I get you a refill?"

Glittering in her pink onesie, Lavinia held out her glass for a top-up of fizz. "Pour away, dear nephew." Her discerning hazel eyes latched onto my brown ones. "I have to say, my ears were burning just then. I hope you didn't mind our little Ouija game in there. Either way, I sense there are still some hard feelings between us, Alisha. For *everyone's* sake, we really should lay them to rest."

Clearly, I'd done a poor job of hiding my simmering resentment.

Ezra's tone was stilted, but his words belonged to a diplomat. "It's kind of you to reach out an olive branch, auntie. You'll be a better leader than Phinnaeous Shine." His gaze held a plea for me to let it slide.

I fought the urge to give him a sharp elbow in the ribs. "Phinnaeous Shine hardly set the bar high."

Lavinia ignored my temper. "Covens are good training for consensus leadership."

Ezra might be ready to believe a comfortable lie, but I wouldn't be fooled twice. All those years, I'd bitten my tongue in a mistaken sense of womanly decorum. Sometimes, you had to rock the boat. Hell, sometimes you had to jump into the ocean and swim for the shore. "Prime Sorceress, what leadership did you show when Rayna died? I assume Wildwoods alerted you to the intruder? Informed you that Death lurked? Why didn't you mobilise Wildwoods' defences or set loose the sphinxes? Why didn't you teleport in to help us? Where were you with all your military precision acrobatics, your potions and your umbrella-swinging coven when Rayna bled out on the floor of the infirmary?"

Lavinia's voice was steely, but her eyes flickered. "I had to make a choice."

I lifted my chin. Still, the book buried in our garden whispered to me. I blinked and blocked it out. "She was your friend."

Why had Lavinia decided to lay down her arms when Death walked within the walls of Wildwoods? Why had she forsaken a friend in her moment of need?

Our greatest fight lay ahead of us—an inevitable encounter with Death that made the bile rise in my throat—yet I couldn't be sure that the Prime Sorceress was an ally.

Ezra's bone-white knuckles gripped the worktop. "Alisha—"

Lavinia was unfazed. "There are three things in this world I admire: Women who aren't defined by their wombs. Women who have the courage to go braless despite the onset of gravity. And women who speak their minds. You believe me to be untrustworthy, Alisha?"

I nodded. "Ezra might be ready to put the matter to bed, but I'm not."

Ezra groaned and grabbed a beer from the fridge.

I recalled the feeble excuses that had tumbled from Lavinia's frosted lips at his parents' grave. *Forgive me for keeping secrets from you, nephew. Forgive me for taking what was yours. But families should share their bounty. Now we can both teleport. We can make the city safe again.* When Ezra, his face warped with shock, asked how she had achieved teleportation, Lavinia beamed with pride, not remorse. *The coven runs the slickest security operation in the city. There is more to us than rat spies, well-honed battle skills and the ability to fly over London traffic in an umbrella formation. Who do you think drives the Otherworld taxis? Who devised the payment of a single strand of hair? Who holds a vault of DNA from almost every peculiar in this city? It's me. I planned it all. All those rides in the Otherworld cab with me since I've been Prime Sorceress, nephew, and the hairs you paid as the fare, finally came to something. But you won't let this small thing come between us. You'll have to trust that I'm acting in our best interests.*

Ezra trusted her, but I did not.

Lavinia's lips twitched. "The Prime Sorceress and the eternal girl must find a way to work together. We already have a firm foundation."

"We do?" Incredulity filled me. Even the Prime Sorceress's smile made me suspicious. Smiles were funny like that. They could be kind or malicious, signs of friendship or self-interest.

"We both love Ezra." She set down her champagne flute and screwed up her nose. "All this bad air between us will be a thing of the past once we join forces to defeat Death. You will join the senate meeting this week to hash out our plan?"

It would have been churlish of me to say no. "It's in my diary."

"Excellent. Now, enough of the solemn faces." The Prime Sorceress hooked her arm through her nephew's as the sound of The Pogue's "Fairytale of New York" drifted into the kitchen. "We have a tree to decorate. And don't worry, my dear. If you don't want to share the burden of the book with me, it's your cross to bear."

Smarting at her high-handedness, I followed them towards the hubbub, sorely tempted to dump the tray of puddings on her head. She rallied everyone to decorate the tree like butter wouldn't melt in her mouth.

Orpheus sidled over to my side. "Christmas tree clutter is my idea of hell."

I shuddered. As my family and friends picked out bright baubles and age-worn heirlooms, I couldn't help feeling the tree was a metaphor for the chaos ahead. "Me too. I like to control the placement of ornaments. I should have weeded out all the garish colours."

His voice was sandpaper dry. "Indeed. Now we are

doomed to witness the creation of a monstrosity." The vampire's dark eyes found mine. "But then, you've had a lot on your mind."

Marina flung some tinsel on the tree and then came to join us. "I can read you from across the room. Your hackles are up, Alisha. But there's something else. Like there are two channels in your head. Shall we leave them to it and sneak off for a Baileys together?"

I shook my head. "I'm okay. I just need some air."

I didn't tell her that the Book of Names, buried in the grove in our garden, called to me. I didn't tell her that its whisper buzzed relentlessly in my head. I didn't tell her I needed the senate to be incorruptible because I feared the book—with its ability to name and control the gods—would corrupt me. I had worked so hard to become who I was, but when all was said and done, I knew in my bones that I would be changed.

"I'll accompany her," said Orpheus.

"If you're sure?" Marina made her way back to Rob.

I willed myself to hold it together, there on the sidelines of our party, as our guests loaded ornaments onto the tree. The foxes clinked glasses and found some mistletoe to kiss under. Flinar used Echo as a stepladder to adjust the fairy lights. Ezra wrapped an arm around Mirabel as they admired their handiwork. He gave me a rueful smile as Lavinia rose on her umbrella to place the star on the top of our Christmas tree.

I returned his smile, though the Book of Names turned my mind to grey noise. Then I followed the whispers out into the night with a vampire on my heels.

3

______

Above me, the inky sky glittered with stars. I closed my eyes and bathed in the moonlight. Plain old humdrum me had been afraid of the night and strangers lurking in bushes. It wasn't so long ago that I'd jammed my keys into my fists in defence against a flickering shadow. That was before I had an inkling about my dormant capabilities. It was easy to feel powerless before you understood your true strengths.

Now, I was comfortable with the night. And I wondered how I could have feared it when it had always been filled with an ocean of stars.

The Book of Names called to me. I rocked on the balls of my feet, tempted to give in. Tempted to claw at the damp soil, driving my fingers into the filth to retrieve the book and drink of its power. Or maybe I should thwart it and its demands for my full attention. For the first time in my life, I considered shredding the written word. I'd arc it into the Thames until it became a sodden mess on the riverbed or pour gasoline onto it, topped by the flare of a match. Watch flames engulf it with glee. Just for a moment's peace.

I didn't want to be special. At times like these, I would have given anything to be mind-numbingly, invisibly ordinary. To let all my worries for the world float away like helium balloons until I kept only my fair share. A few ordinary concerns that I could carry easily, like whether I'd miss the bus or the milk had curdled, or I should pluck the chin hair I sprouted.

To hell with all the rest.

Except, my obstinate sense of duty made that impossible. How could I give up the one tome that redressed the power balance between gods and the rest of us? The prophecy—if I believed in these things—had spelt it out. *When Death opens the door, only the eternal girl may stop the coming Dusk, together with a disintegrating tome lost to the world.*

With a shuddering breath, I resisted the magnetism of the book and veered to sit on a bench mere yards away. Goosebumps chased up my arms. The whispers of the book ebbed as though it accepted I had won this round. As if it bided its time, secure in the knowledge that it already had my attention.

Dark vampire eyes scrutinised my face.

I sighed and lowered my mental defences. He already suspected something. Besides, he was the perfect sounding board. I didn't need to use words when I was exhausted. I didn't need to worry about my dark impulses because he had them himself. Neither did I have to worry that he'd freak out. Orpheus Might was as stoic as they come.

Orpheus raked through my thoughts and cursed. "This is what you have been going through? No wonder your heartbeat is so leaden. A lesser mortal's mind would have fractured by now."

The bench creaked as he lowered himself onto it. Silk lining brushed my skin as he slipped his dinner jacket around my shoulders. His beard oil, scented with dark chocolate and cherries, reached my nostrils.

Flakes of snow drifted from the sky, and I pulled his jacket tighter around me and gave a bitter laugh. "That bloody thing has been draining me since the moment we found it."

His quiet fortitude was balm compared to the chaos inside. "I'm glad you don't need to pretend with me. Maybe you shouldn't have buried it here. I can take it for you. Tombstones and coffins are perfect hiding places. You can trust me to keep it safe."

Meandering footprints in the snow deviated from the path Ezra had shovelled that afternoon. Human footprints that led to neither our front door nor the parked cars. Dismissing them, I turned to Orpheus. "I can't let you do that. My grandmother meant for me to protect it. She had her reasons."

"Her mistake was to fight alone, Alisha. You have me," he said harshly.

I sighed. "You're a good friend. When I need you, I promise you'll know. Did anything come of your research?"

He stretched out his spidery legs. "Calypso and I have read through every account of the Death goddess written in the languages of men. We have turned to scholars to decipher hieroglyphics, scoured the work of renowned and lesser poets, subjected ourselves to tedious and miraculous works from all continents."

A shiver ran up my spine. "What did you find?"

Dark eyebrows knitted together against alabaster skin. "That it's impossible to differentiate myth from truth. The texts didn't give us any clue as to when Death would strike because she's always present, working diligently across all cultures. The other rogue gods were weakened by the decline of religion on these isles, pushed to the periphery of their believers' minds or forgotten altogether. But our preoccupation with Death is woven into the fabric of life. Her prevalence in our minds makes her strong. It's not just goths in biker boots, heavy eyeliner and terrible postures who think of death. It's tourists to the pyramids. It's dead bodies in detective shows. It's the middle-aged man with an existential crisis. It's rising cancer and dementia rates. It's the endless talk of viruses and war. It's the death of the planet." He raised a wry eyebrow. "It's the vampire searching for meaning. Alisha, going up against Death might be an unwinnable fight. But the lemming wing of the vampires and I will nevertheless fight by your side."

I guffawed. "The lemming wing?"

He grinned. "A term of endearment for those of my kind tired of life."

I cast him a worried look. "Have your depressive thoughts returned? Are you tired of life?"

"Not since you walked into Wildwoods." His eyes held a warmth that thawed my cold bones, but there was disquiet there, too. "The night is coming, Alisha. We must be ready."

"We will be." I turned at a rustle behind us, my heart speeding.

The Earth goddess circled the boundary of the cottage, taking her sweet time. When she was done, she headed our way, her sari dusting the white ground. "Alisha. Vampire."

My breath clouded the air. I adopted a merry tone. "Goddess, we were just coming back inside."

"Humour an old lady. Would you like to see a magic trick? It has delighted the latch-key children on the estate this week. Mirabel wasn't impressed, but a little magic brightens even the weariest heart. Would you like to see?" Unfolding her palm, she revealed a tulip bulb. When she closed it and opened it again, the bulb had become a jagged rock. The goddess's wind-chapped lips curved into a sad smile. "I know you carry the weight of the world on your shoulders, druid. I know you feel it is unfair. Life isn't very good at being fair. But tonight, when I assessed the unity of your family, I sensed you might all hold together despite the fault lines. That is if you remember that kindness wins the war."

It was silly of me to think I could hide my emotions from a goddess. Especially this one, with her experience of the highs and lows on the blue marble we called home and her knowledge of the pain and joys of the smallest to the most complex creatures.

Gaia's soft face creased into a thousand folds, wrinkling with centuries of experience. She played with the thick, oiled plait on her shoulder. "The vampire is wise not to underestimate the coming days. It won't be easy, but nothing worthwhile ever is. You are my champion, druid, and you must succeed. You have all the tools and allies you need. The only thing that remains is the fight. You will know when it begins. There will be signs all around you. And when the Wild Hunt sounds its horn, that fateful day will have arrived."

My palms grew clammy despite the frost, her words thundering in my mind.

You are my champion.

What made a champion? Was it skill, fate or sheer dumb courage?

Orpheus's nostrils flared. "The Wild Hunt?"

"It is as it always was. Kali has a vast battalion at her fingertips, so Alisha must have hers."

A battalion. She wanted me to command a battalion and go up against Death.

Incredulous laughter bubbled up from my throat.

But Gaia didn't notice. Her eyes—often windows to crumbling mountains, renewed rainforests and burning stars —shuttered. Crooked fingers strummed the air, a harpist strumming on the threads of the universe itself. "I knew the book was close, even before the Ouija board spelt it out. I can feel it in the earth. Ancient pages wrapped in your mother's scarf, enclosed in a tin box, with worms and beetles all around."

It was true. I'd wrapped the book in my mother's paisley scarf, the one she had knotted around her neck in spring. Still scented with traces of her perfume despite her being gone.

Gaia's head turned to the exact spot where the book lay buried. Her eyes snapped open, her once cherubic face clothed in malice, clenched fists where only seconds ago there had been open palms. She stepped towards the book.

"Gaia?" I held my breath as shadows crawled over her.

Foreboding washed over me. I had come to rely on the Earth goddess, making her the antithesis of the rogue gods. But how well could a mortal know an immortal? My life spanned a mere fraction of hers. Gaia's motives were as complex as a kaleidoscope, layered and multi-dimensional: metaphysical, ecological, spiritual, celestial and humanistic. How many promises had she broken? How many lies had she told? How many lives had she taken?

Darkness stormed in her face. Even the best of us have dark impulses.

Gaia had asked Rajika to hide the Book of Names once.

Was that because she wanted it for herself?

I flung aside Orpheus's jacket. I hoped beyond hope that I wouldn't have to fight her. But if there were no other way, I would stand firm. "Goddess?"

The Earth goddess paused mid-step. She turned towards us, and in the moonlight, her weathered skin was a map of endless possibilities: trapdoors and triumphs. "You must ready yourself, druid. There will be parts of this journey when your allies seem far. When the bleakest night comes, all will seem hopeless. Still, you must believe."

My gut clenched. I reached out to her like a lost child. "You will be close?"

Gaia's lips tightened. "No, but I have left a fresh batch of laddus in your freezer in case you miss me. It is in your gift to influence the path of the lost gods. Make your ancestors proud, though the soil will run scarlet."

Orpheus interjected, his tone clipped. "It is too much for her to carry."

"Then you will help her carry it, vampire." Gaia's flicker of irritation at Orpheus softened when she looked at me. The wave of darkness in her subsided, and she was almost herself once more, doling out laddus and fortune cookie advice. "An ant carries more than a donkey relative to its weight. We don't know our strength until the night comes."

To my astonishment, the goddess bowed.

Not a deep bow—a blink and I would have missed it—but a bow all the same.

It terrified me. This wasn't the Gaia that I thought would accompany me as the prophecy neared fruition. I had seen many faces of the Earth goddess: mother, crone, creator, mentor, schemer, lover, madwoman. I had never seen this. The Earth goddess was jittery, more bride than warrior.

The heavy air oscillated around us, and her crimson sari fluttered.

I wasn't ready for her to leave. "No."

She paid me no heed. Trees in our vicinity showered us with decaying foliage as the goddess took her leave, returning to her Tooting flat or her favourite café for chai or her earthly duties.

Her words rang in my head, running parallel to the whispers of the book.

You are my champion.

I was her champion, though I had no experience leading an army. Though I preferred compassion to my obsidian blade. Though I was an atheist pulled into a war between the gods. Though half the time, I had no idea what I was doing.

A bitter laugh escaped me. At forty, I knew there were never any perfect answers. There was never any end to learning. At each moment in our lives, we freewheeled into the dark, clinging to the hope that we were doing the right thing. Even when crippled by fear of the unknown.

I swivelled in the snow to Orpheus, pragmatism taking over. "The Wild Hunt? Can we know what shape it will take? Can we know who they are hunting?"

Dark eyes in moonlit skin. He shrugged, his shoulders taut. "There are many and varied legends. Some depict King Arthur, Odin, Cain or Fionn Mac Cumhaill leading a group of hunters made up of souls of the dead or ghostly creatures or a band of craven elves. As for their target...I presume it is you, Alisha. We will need to get you behind walls."

"No, you heard what Gaia said. We need a battalion. To meet attack with attack." I gave a weak smile and darted a glance at the house. "No one needs to know of this tonight. We'll bring this to the senate at the next meeting."

"As you wish." He pressed the bridge of his nose. "The Earth goddess's demeanour changed when she sensed the Book of Names."

My stomach knotted. "I noticed."

His voice was a quiet ripple in the sea of the night. "Then you know what we have to do."

"I know just where to take it. Tonight, the book won't leave my side. Echo and I will guard it through the night." I raised my hands to call the winds. They curled towards me, with the ease of breath filling my lungs. With a flick of my hands, I directed them at the grove, stepping towards it as I did, tunnelling the earth to retrieve the book.

There it was, three metres deep, the tin box that determined the fate of the rogue gods and the mortals who lived alongside them. I lifted it in a cradle of wind, enveloping it against my chest when it reached me. My fingers involuntarily opened the box and unwrapped it from its paisley scarf as if I had no control over them. As if my body betrayed me. As if it craved the book's power. A robot. A servant of the ancient words within it.

The vampire's eyes gleamed in the dark. For the first time, I considered whether absolute power would corrupt friendship as it did everything else.

With great deliberation, I slammed the book shut.

I couldn't wait to be rid of the damn thing.

4

———————

Streatham Cemetery was a desolate place in winter. Across the other seasons, yellow-headed crocuses, soaring leafy trees and ripening of the earth contrasted with the gloom of the headstones and the buried bones beneath. But the russets, fawns and mustards of autumn had long deserted this place. Now, the graveyard was lonely, abandoned by colour and visitors, with supermarket flowers decaying in their plastic wrapping.

After the gathering at the cottage, I'd felt a gravitational pull towards Mum's grave. A pilgrimage to show her that she hadn't been forgotten. Once, she had been the centre of our family get-togethers. In the movie reel of my mind, I could still see her holding the fort, baking up a storm, whizzing the food blender, and artfully filling serving dishes with pastries.

I took the familiar path past the weeping angels, lingering to read the names and dates of the dead, imagining their stories from the epitaphs. When I reached Mum's grave, I dusted the headstone lightly with my sleeve and knelt at her grave. A smattering of bright pansies grew amongst the moss that must have self-seeded. I couldn't visit empty-handed. I laid a single white rose at the base of the stone. Then, with a faint sense of ridiculousness, I placed a chunk of carrot cake and decanted leftover mulled wine on the mound. Mulled wine and iced carrot cake had been her favourite winter treats.

The Jericho stone lay heavy at my neck as I talked. "Hey, Mum. We had a party yesterday, and it wasn't the same without you. I miss your warmth and counsel and how effortlessly you knitted us together. I'd give anything for you to fill my plate with the taste of home. So much has changed since you died." Tears clogged my throat. "I wish you could meet Bel. She's more than I ever could have hoped for. Stubborn as hell but brilliant with it. I'd love to be able to call you for advice. For you to tell me how you knew your decisions were the right ones. Now, Death is coming for us. I have no idea how things are going to pan out. Whether we'll win. Whether I'll be able to protect everyone."

I paused, listening hard.

She didn't answer.

I reached for Transcender's hilt, tucked underneath my jacket, desperate to hear Mum's voice. A whisper of wisdom from beyond the grave. Something to guide me. Something more than old voicemails or birthday cards.

But nothing came. All I had was the echo of past conversations in my head. What I wouldn't give to rewind the clock. To have her whole, breathing and vibrant at my side.

I whipped around at a hand on my shoulder, heart thumping.

Dad stood there in a tatty jumper and paint-splashed trainers. "You should have said you were coming, love."

I rose to kiss his papery cheek. "Hi, Dad. I missed her yesterday."

His voice vibrated with emotion. "I did, too. Rosalie was

my wife for forty-seven years. You're not your own person after all that time. You're two intertwined halves."

"But you're happy with Alma?"

His eyes glistened. "So happy. But that doesn't mean I've forgotten your mother. It's just my track went off in a different direction to hers."

He moved away to trace his fingers over the engraving of her name on the headstone, his chapped lips murmuring a silent prayer.

At his feet, the white rose on the grave disintegrated into dust.

Mum's headstone cracked down the middle.

"Dad!" Heart pumping, I lunged for his hand.

The ground reverberated beneath our feet, awakening. The sky darkened, though the clock hadn't yet struck eleven in the morning. Trees curled and blackened. Dad stumbled towards me, his face twisted in horror at a strange rummaging in the soil. A hand pushed out from a nearby grave, clicking like a beetle. The hand became a forearm as the reanimated corpse clawed its way out of its resting place, rotting flesh drooping from its skeleton.

One thought overrode all others. As much as I wanted to see Mum again, not like this.

Dad yelped in disbelief. He was as white as a sheet. "Is this it? Is this the end of times?"

"Not if I can bloody help it." I hadn't fought the dead before. Gulping, my mind flooded with horror movies in which cemeteries came to life in the most gruesome manner or the march of ghastly zombies in apocalypse shows.

I steeled myself, but Mum's grave remained still.

Thank heavens.

They came, burrowing up from dense graves, an army of the undead. Each wore new shoes, a type of lace-up brogues in different shades of leather. Hair hung in matted wisps from the corpses' heads, and hollows languished where their eyes had once been. They swung in our direction with precision as if they had been commanded to make us their target. As if they answered to a greater power.

But they were slow, and my confidence surged that I could overcome them.

Jaw clenched with determination, I drew Transcender. Usually, Otherworld battles took place under cover of darkness when I could avoid CCTV, the Metropolitan Police and oblivious humdrums—or at least arrange for Jameson and Orpheus to wipe cameras and minds for me—but the situation left me little choice. Dad was seventy-one years old and not the fastest.

"Stay out of the way." I manoeuvred him behind me and raised my sword aloft.

Two corpses rushed towards me. By the looks of the elongated dangly bit, one male, one female.

I ran at the male, aiming a horizontal cut at its neck that went clean though. The corpse dropped to the ground in two pieces, jerking and bloodless. Next, I propelled off the ground and sliced through the female corpse's torso.

Her legs kept running towards us as Dad spouted garbled terror in my ear. I shuddered, slamming it away from us with a blast of wind.

More graves opened up, releasing decaying reanimated bodies as if a channel had slithered open from hell itself. They weren't just in front of us now. They surrounded us, repulsive and dripping in flesh. My gut churned. Dad, no longer frozen with horror, found his mojo. To my bewilderment, he attacked the corpses with open-handed slaps and plucky pushes back into the graves, hollering like a yob in a car park fight all the while.

"What are you doing? I've got this under control." I panted, twisting Transcender in the gut of a reanimated old lady. I tunnelled him a path through the corpses with a gust of wind. "There's your way out. Get out of here, Dad. I'll be right behind you."

He picked up a stick from the ground and pounced on a corpse, straddling it like he was in a rodeo. "I'm too old to run. Let me fight off these goons for you. I have lived a good life. It might be goodbye, Alma, but it will be hello, Rosalie."

I eyed Mum's grave, praying she wouldn't emerge. Neither of us could take that.

"All right, Romeo. Not sure you're thinking straight right now." Had he been smoking something again? At least he wasn't falling to pieces.

Dad moved on to the next assailant, picking up a thigh bone and a shin bone. The corpse opened its jaw wide, but Dad drummed its skull almost nonchalantly. With every success, he grew in confidence, whooping, mired in a sort of ecstasy that would lead to collapse once the adrenalin faded.

I had to up my game in case he got hurt. Raising my palm, I sent a whirlwind across the north side of the cemetery, causing the skeletons to rip apart. Charging to Dad's side, I chopped and slashed at the remaining corpses, my breath coming fast and ragged, my T-shirt drenched with perspiration.

When the last corpse fell, Dad turned to me in glee. "I'm feeling a new lease of life after that. Maybe there's a second innings in me as a hero just when I thought I was on my last legs. This is going to be a bit of a surprise for the council, isn't it, love? I wonder if they'll blame the foxes or graverobbers. Your Great-Uncle isn't going to be best pleased. He still has his second job here." He dropped the shin bone. "There's going to be a lot of cleaning up to do."

His nattering went over my head. He was focused on the wrong thing. The aftermath didn't matter as much as the *why* and the *who*.

A shiver ran up my spine. This was Death's doing.

I knew it in my bones before she appeared.

Before she emerged under the darkened skies, the blue, leering, four-armed woman holding the twin of my sword. The sword she had named Surrender. At seven feet tall, she towered above us, feral in her beauty, with her naked torso and an ornate necklace of decapitated heads.

Dad averted his gaze from her breasts. "That's quite a costume, young lady. Mind you don't catch a chill, though. A bit late in the year for Halloween dress up, though, isn't it?"

A voice, unmistakably Mum's, pulsed with love and urgency, channelled through Transcender straight into my head.

Run!

My feet wouldn't move. They were rooted to the spot. "Dad, meet Death."

"What? Oh no. Alma didn't predict this." All the puff went out of him. He tried in vain to move, his moustache twitching in horror. It was a cruel blow after his heroic attempts against the corpses.

Death smiled and lit a cigarette. "Don't run away, little mice. We have so much to talk about. I like this preamble to a battle. Don't you? There's no time for words in the heat of battle. All the focus is on cracking bones, spilling blood, decapitations and chasing down cowards."

Dad lifted his chin. "My daughter is going to beat you just like the other gods. We saw off your corpse attack without breaking a sweat."

Technically untrue, but I admired his fighting spirit.

"Oh, that? That was just a little fun. I was just getting warmed up." Death stubbed out the cigarette and neared us. Her hips swayed, and the heads on her necklace thudded like a pendulum wave toy as she approached. Her eyes were of coal, her dark hair twisted in snaking braids down her back. She smelled of sweat and decay. "Haven't you realised yet, old man? I will be the last god standing because Death is always present at the end of it all."

She swept her gaze around the cemetery, still shrouded in pools of darkness.

My heart thrummed like a hummingbird in my chest. I knew the sword in my hand could cut down a god and finish this all right here and now, but I couldn't get close enough. Instead, I played for time. "Why? Why go to these lengths to shape the world in your image?"

The blue goddess's tongue lolled, and her eyes rolled like she'd had this conversation a thousand times before. "Did you know nobody prays to Death? It's a little thing, but it makes me an outsider amongst the gods. They pray *for* the dead, but never to the goddess of Death." Her full lips curled into a snarl. "That was one of His little jokes, I think. He always had more time for life. Gaia was an obvious favourite, of course. When humans stand in awe of the cut of mountains, the swell of the ocean or the changing landscape of the sky, *Gaia* gets a little boost of energy. And they wonder why my resentment grew with every passing century." She shrugged, and her array of arms windmilled towards us.

Dad recoiled.

I channelled a sly breeze at my feet, desperate to free us. The soil that had needed a spade now needed a chisel.

Death's dark eyes gleamed. "But I am resourceful. I found other ways to harness power. Grief is a monstrous thing. It is never small. It takes you by surprise, and you are never quite the same again. It grows hour by hour, pressing down on you. It changes the way you process the world. It steals your peace. It resurfaces, time and again, mingled with bitter regret. My favourite type of mourning is the steadfast widow. The grief that hollows out a face, strips a body of fat, and locks up emotions even between friends. That is the type of grief I can feed on."

"Then do it," I spat. "Why do you want more when death pervades everything?"

Disgust filled her face. "This modern world ruins

everything. I want the world to return to how it used to grieve. No one reacts anymore with genuine grief. They are deadened to the pain. Or focused on their inheritance. Or grand gestures. Or too busy documenting their emotions or mental health advice for social media. I hate performative grief. Real grief isolates you. It eviscerates your soul, leaving you unable to think of anything else, unable to function. Personal hygiene goes out the window. So does feeding your children. It all shrinks to nothing in comparison to the dark window of your pain. I want that world back."

I clenched my fists. Grief was personal. How dare she judge how we expressed it? The cheek of it, throwing accusations about acceptable modes of grief, here, in Mum's last resting place. Did she know how many times a day Mum's face loomed in my mind? How I worried that I'd forget the exact constellation of her features or the things she found funny or sad. Did Death know how many times I'd cried into my pillow or in the shower and then pulled myself together so I didn't make the world uncomfortable? "You're angry because people aren't suffering the way you want them to? How utterly egotistical. You don't get to decide how we express ourselves."

Black pits in a blue face. "I am a goddess."

I met Death's eyes and angled my sword at her neck. "Free us."

Death gave a sultry laugh, refusing to take me seriously.

My rage surged like a river breaking its banks. I flung Transcender at her neck, pushing it hard and fast through the air with a burst of wind.

The goddess reached up lazily to catch the hilt with one of her many arms.

"No!" called out Dad.

Understanding my error, I lassoed the sword in the nick of time, arcing it up and over and back into my hands. How stupid of me to almost lose my weapon in a fit of pique.

The goddess regarded me as though I were a gnat. "It won't be easy to kill me, Alisha Verma. Give me the Book of Names, and you can have everything you desire. You can have your freedom. You can have your life back, a life unconcerned with immortals. You can have your mother back."

Next to me, Dad whimpered, a lament of sorrow. "You can bring Rosalie back?"

Death clicked her blue fingers. "Oh yes. I can do that and so much more."

Dad implored me. "We could have your mother back, Alisha. We could be a family and live normal lives again. We could have it all back the way it was."

I was tempted, so very tempted. To be able to turn back time and recoup all those lost moments. To have Mum meet Mirabel. To tell her about our escapades. To watch her grow into old age instead of having her cruelly taken from us from one day to another. Tears pricked behind my eyes as I snagged on my moral compass. Deep down, I knew whatever Death promised, we couldn't trust her.

"At what expense, Dad?" I couldn't look at Mum's grave. "Who has to die, who has to suffer, for it to be that way?"

Death's cold eyes rested on my face. "You won't give me the book?"

I bit my lip, drawing blood. "No."

She raised an eyebrow. "No matter. My minions are searching for it as we speak."

Panic raced through me. Ezra had left early for a seeker mission with his pack. Echo and Mirabel were alone at the cottage. Taking Transcender, I hacked at the ground, eroding it with wind funnels. My heart hammered in my throat as I dragged out one foot, then another, leaving gashes on my skin where the ground had clamped me tight at Death's command. Then I turned my attention to Dad.

He shook me. "Don't turn your back on her."

"You think she couldn't have killed us already?" I hissed, yanking his foot.

An ominous smile danced on Death's lips. "The end times are here. Be ready, Alisha Verma. The Wild Hunt shows no mercy."

Death strode away under the darkened skies, leaving us quaking in her wake.

I broke Dad free as a horn sounded in the distance. A chilling, funereal timbre, with the note held longer than humanly possible. Its vibrations hit me straight in the chest. I gasped at the impact.

The Wild Hunt had begun, and I was its prey.

5

With jittering hands, I called Ezra. "Bel and Echo might be in danger."

His voice was harsh and menacing. "Where are you?"

A double-decker bus pulled up, and I urged Dad onto it. He was in no fit state to fight another battle today. "Outside the Streatham Cemetery."

Ezra arrived as the bus pulled away as if stepping out of a tear in the fabric of the world. His eyes narrowed at the overcast sky, then recoiled at the wasteland the cemetery had become. "Christ, what happened here?"

The whispers of the book pulsed in my head, faint but ever-present.

"I'll explain on the way," I said. "Take us home."

We ripped through the undercurrents of the world, zigzagging to avoid projectiles. The pathways had been choppy since Morpheus's nightmares had disrupted the balance of the world. Ezra cocooned me with his body, taking the brunt of the risk.

At the cottage, I left the circle of his arms, nausea rising.

A tornado had hit our garden. Or worse.

Wordlessly, we surveyed the damage. Our once idyllic

garden, with its neat lawn blanketed in snow, had been upended. Rubbish from our wheelie bins had spilt out: festering food waste, smashed Prosecco bottles and the ouija board I had dumped. Deep holes and chunks of turf marred the terrain. Roots and buried bulbs had been exposed with wanton abandon, desecrating our little oasis. Worst of all, the grove was a muddy pit.

A pit which, until yesterday, had hidden the book.

We took off at a run towards the house, a plaintive cry on repeat in my head. *Let Mirabel and Echo be okay. Let them be okay.*

I drew my sword before we crossed the threshold, senses on high alert. Inside, the curtains were still drawn. So far, so unusual. Mirabel had been asleep when we left.

The house was deathly quiet. That was the worrying thing.

"I can't smell anything out of place," said Ezra by my ear. He skirted the boundary of the living room and then the kitchen, checking for trouble.

I headed straight for the back of the house, opened Mirabel's bedroom door and swung my sword directly at Echo's nose. Behind him, Mirabel lay tangled in her duvet, still fast asleep.

I slumped with relief. "Oh, thank goodness."

Emerald eyes twinkled. "You almost took my eye with that metal."

Ezra sprinted up the hallway. His voice dropped a notch at the sight of Mirabel. "All clear back there. Are you both okay? I can't believe she slept through it."

The leopard tilted his majestic head towards his charge. "Don't worry. I performed my duty admirably. You were like this as a teenager, Alisha. Almost nothing could rouse you from your slumber. It's a shame, really. I prefer sleep-shy toddlers. I can sing to sleep with my dulcet tones."

"The book?" Its whispers addled my brain.

"Right here." He padded over to the bed and nosed out the tin box that housed the Book of Names. "I was going to make this room my last stand, but curiously, they never attempted to come in here."

"You did well." I sheathed my sword, taking care not to wake Mirabel, knelt and buried my head in the leopard's neck. Slowly, my heartbeat returned to normal. I'd second-guessed my decision to move the book, but following my gut had been the right thing to do. I did a double-take. "They?"

A roar rumbled in the leopard's throat. "My hearing alerted me to the kerfuffle outside. At first, I thought it was moles or a rabid fox. When I remembered England doesn't have rabies, I grew suspicious and hungry. I went to the window. That's when I saw the dead. They saw me but didn't enter. My formidable warrior aesthetic quite clearly made them reconsider their chances."

Ezra's eyebrow lifted a fraction. "Another plundered cemetery?"

I held my finger to my lips as Mirabel shifted position. "Most likely. We need someone to round up the dead and wipe the minds of the living. It's dangerous when humdrums panic."

"I'll call Orpheus," said Ezra. "He and his vampires can deal with the mind wiping."

"Can you ask him if Bel can hang out there today? She shouldn't be alone." Since the *Buffy* DVD marathon, Mirabel had felt at home at Orpheus's gentleman's club. Security had been improved to fortress levels since the dream god's attack, and Orpheus had an understanding with his clan—any harm to Mirabel, and he'd turn them to dust. "I'll call Flinar to mobilise the defence ministry against the dead. I think we're going to need him more than once today."

Ezra nodded and dipped out of the room.

I collected the book from the floor. Then I perched on the bed and stroked back frizzy auburn hair from my daughter's face. "Bel? Wakey, wakey, darling. You've been asleep for more than half the day. I need you to pack your things and hang out at Orpheus's club today."

Mirabel groaned and opened one eye. "Oh, brutal. Do I have to?"

"I'm sorry. Things are getting dangerous around here. We need to keep you safe."

She propped herself up on her elbows. Her voice was groggy, but there was no mistaking her determined spirit. "I'm a fire fairy trained at a world-renowned magical school, and my best friend is a leopard sworn to protect the Verma family line. I think I'll be okay."

The duvet rolled down to reveal her boyband T-shirt. She was so young yet thought she could conquer the world despite her past experiences.

It made me proud and infuriated me at the same time.

Echo purred with pride. "She has a point."

"No, she doesn't." The whispers of the book overwhelmed me, a constant irritation, a constant reminder of what lay ahead. "Echo is going with you to the club. Now, please, just do as you're told."

Mirabel folded her arms across her chest, thirteen and defiance personified. At times like these, I wondered what she'd been like as a toddler and mourned those moments when she hadn't been ours. "There's training at Wildwoods this afternoon. I told my friends I'd go. It's not fair."

I filed away that piece of information to the back of my head. By all accounts, learning at Wildwoods had taken a more physical turn under Isadora. "You can train another day, Bel."

She jumped out of bed, moss-green eyes flaring with rebellion. "You sent me out yesterday as well. When you used the Ouija board. What is wrong with adults? You try and protect me, but all you do is hide the truth. It sucks."

I frowned. "Mirabel, this isn't about your parents. It's

about keeping you safe in the here and now. You're going to Orpheus's. End of story." I didn't mean to butt heads with her, but there was no time.

Ezra returned, eyes darting from me to our sullen teenager. "Alisha's right. Orpheus has a visitor, but he said Bel is welcome anytime. Pack your things, Bel."

She glared at us both, then stomped to a corner of her room to get her rucksack.

I closed the door quietly behind us, knowing she'd vent her exasperation to Echo and find comfort in tangling her fingers in his glorious fur. I had been there often enough as a child. I just hated being the bad guy in this scenario.

Ezra squeezed my hand. "She'll come round."

I sighed. "Who's the visitor at the club?"

"Seskel's cousin from Ireland, here to pay her respects to his remains."

I winced. Seskel was Orpheus's predatory clan member I had killed. "Let me put in that call to Flinar. Then we'll take our stubborn girl and travel-sick leopard to the club."

Troubled grey eyes found mine. "How could Death have known the book was here, Alisha?"

"It wasn't Orpheus, if that's what you're thinking. I trust him with my life." My thoughts whirled. "How was Death able to trap me and Dad at the cemetery?"

Ezra shrugged. "We're just finding out the extent of her powers."

I beckoned him to the kitchen, my voice hushed to prevent Mirabel from overhearing. "But the earth is Gaia's domain. Nothing is buried in it or crawls from it without her knowledge, whether animate or inanimate."

His brow furrowed as he filled two glasses of water and pushed one my way. "Don't say it, Alisha. She's a valuable ally. We wouldn't have survived these past months without her."

"Is she *still* an ally, though?" Dread crawled inside me. It

"You need the freewheeling freedom of teleporting as much as you need to run as a wolf." I adjusted the strap of my baldric and secured the contents of my bag. Whispers raged in my head as I scanned the terrain. "Come on."

The meat he carried slopped in its carrier bag. "Are you sure about this plan?"

"I can't think of a better way." We set off across the frosted ground, both burdened by worry. Unspoken words rankled between us. "Maybe it's not Gaia at all. Maybe Lavinia is in cahoots with Death. She could have read the answer on the Ouija board before the lights went out."

He harrumphed. "We're back onto my aunt again? Put a sock in it, hellfire."

"You know what I don't get? You forgive her even when she doesn't show any remorse. I mean, she obviously sleeps wonderfully. Have you seen her glowing skin?"

He flushed with anger. "That's not fair. Have you ever really given her a chance?"

I pedalled back. I'd grown so reliant on us being on the same page. This fracture pained me. "Ignacio told Marina that the rats have a night-time rota to apply potions to her skin because of all the extra media attention."

"That's plain old gossip. Don't make light of this." He raked his hand through his hair. "We need to hash this out once and for all. You don't trust my aunt. She's important to me."

"Do you even know what she's capable of?"

Ezra's eyes flashed. "At this point, you're just flinging about wild accusations. Listen to me, Alisha. My aunt has no reason to ally with Death. She just wouldn't do it."

"You can't know that. Who would stop her if she did? No one stands up to her. Lavinia Drach rules the roost at the coven. And she has filled all the key positions in the senate with allies or people who owe her or navel-gazers who are there to serve anyone but themselves. And Margola has been running endless puff pieces in *The Otherworld News* since she took office."

He whipped around, irate. "*I* stand up to her time and again. I found a safe haven for the elves. I helped you hide Tielbu from her clutches. I spurned the coupling with Rashida. Because *you* are the love of my life. We didn't listen when she tried to convince us that Bel was lost in the dream god's grip. I make decisions that are right for me, just as my aunt makes decisions that are right for her. That's life."

The wind swirled around us. I couldn't be sure whether nature or my passions had unleashed it. "You let her get away with her omissions and half-truths. You give her more than she gives you." It wasn't like I expected reciprocal benefits in my relationships. But life was too short to keep forgiving those who consistently let me down. I respected myself too much to let that keep happening.

Ezra bristled. "Not everyone gives in the same way."

"Her compass is power. Not love. Power. That's what she'll always follow. Don't you ever want to show her the door? I know you can't do it professionally—not while you're both on the senate—but you could personally. Just shut the door on her toxicity. She's just so *dysfunctional*, and you're so bloody forgiving. I mean, forgive her if you want, but why continue to give her access if she hasn't truly changed?"

His eyes glinted dangerously. "You might have reached your limit with her, but I haven't. Maybe my limits stretch with her. We have a past full of good *and* bad. Like you do with Sahil. I mean, all the things he has done, and you still forgive him." His voice dipped with grief. "Just like I forgave Gunnolf. Because family and love are complex. They aren't a tally sheet."

I gulped. It was easy for me to forget how I had always been surrounded by love and how Ezra had fought for scraps. "I'm sorry. You're right. I'll let it go. I just don't want you to get hurt again. It's just… She's hiding something, Ezra."

Grey eyes locked onto mine. "I don't doubt it. But she's a link to my mother that I don't want to give up. She may not have proved it yet, but I have to believe that she would never truly hurt me. That she'll come through for us when it really matters."

"I hope you're right." I interlaced my fingers with his to smooth the prickles of our disagreement.

He returned the pressure of my fingers, rubbing his calloused thumb over the back of my hand.

If the witch shattered his heart, I'd make her pay.

6

The answer to how to hide the book had come to me in a rush.

Others overlooked the elves. But not me.

Ezra and I strode through the bare oaks and birch trees under a sky dense with blue-grey altostratus clouds. The sound of the Wild Hunt's horn haunted me. Every now and then, I glanced over my shoulder in case the promised Wild Hunt emerged like a fairy-tale monster at my heels.

Our destination lay only a little farther. It would have been rude to teleport directly into the settlement. It was unwise to go directly there, in case we had been followed. Nobody could know we had been here today. The fate of humdrums and peculiars depended on it.

To casual onlookers, elvish fortunes were on the up. The Prime Sorceress had named Flinar the new Defence Minister. Meriel Naehorn had been knocked from her perch as the most spurned criminal in London's Otherworld; that label now belonged to Phinnaeous Shine.

While elven standing had changed on paper, they failed to recognise that not everyone wanted them to succeed. Elves faced jibes and sneers, the defacing of their homes and slammed doors. Little wonder that a sizeable community remained in the woods, where Ezra had once hidden them from nefarious elements of the senate. Including his aunt, who—along with Phinnaeous Shine—had scapegoated them for Pan's earthquakes.

"Every visit, I'm gobsmacked at what they've created here." Ezra's eyes widened at the settlement.

He ran with the pack here and knew the trails well, accustomed to the changes wrought by the seasons. But the elves' arrival had changed the story of the woods. The woodland elves hadn't colonised the place so much as slotted into the natural environment and thrived here, where they felt safe.

Flinar excused himself from his conversation with a deputy and rushed to meet us, beaming from ear to ear. "Welcome, Alisha and Ezra. I see you like the improvements we are making."

"You've worked wonders here, my friend. The elves are lucky to have you as a leader." I hugged him hello and cast my eye around the dwellings made from oak, pine and thatch, situated deep in the woods. Dwellings camouflaged behind rows of daffodils in the spring, sprigs of bay trees and summer blooms in the summer, desiccated leaves in autumn and heavy banks of snow and dirt in winter.

"It's impressive indeed. You don't miss living in the city?" said Ezra.

Flinar sighed. "Most of my people continue to spurn the city. Do you blame them for being unwilling to integrate? For decades, we have been vilified by the magical community. Why would we want to live amongst them?"

I liked to paint Flinar as happy-go-lucky. It took me aback to see his bitterness surface, but I understood it. The elves had been barred from Wildwoods School of the Wondrous, preventing a rounded education. They had been made outsiders because of their former queen. They had been forced to take on lowly positions in magical society as street cleaners, wayfinders or odd-jobs men on twilight contracts. Other peculiar communities became richer while their own opportunities fizzled out.

"You know we don't feel that way, Flinar," I said.

He blew out his grey cheeks. "You have never made me feel like an outsider. You've helped the elves. You didn't think badly of our queen, though she overstepped the line. You improved her conditions at the Ritz. You invite me into your home. We are friends."

I nodded. The story of the elves convinced me that the Otherworld would have been a different place if power had been shared more equally. The roads of our lives curved and forked. Perhaps with different choices, Meriel Naehorn might have been my grandmother's friend instead of her murderer.

"What I am asking of you is immense," I said. "I need you to know that I would not put you in this position if I did not admire you. I have seen your courage, loyalty and resilience. I've witnessed how generously you and your kind have cared for my dragon in this woodland home since his return from Bulgaria. I am in awe of your black hole magic."

Flinar's muscular chest puffed out with pride. His full lips spread into a smile that revealed his poor dental work. "You do not need to blow smoke up my bottom, Alisha, although it feels good. I could not say no to you."

My chest tightened. "Things could get dangerous. I'm putting my faith in you and my dragon. The book will be yours to guard."

Only time would tell if I'd live to regret it.

The elf's large, milky eyes flicked to the satchel I carried, hungry with curiosity. "Is that it?"

My heart was in my mouth. "Yes."

He wrung his four-fingered hands together, betraying his nervousness. "I have briefed my best elves, and the dragon, too, stands ready. Our black hole magic is growing day by day, hastened by Rayna's renewed attention on us before she died. Living together in a community has given our magic a boost. I used to be able to create a small pocket. Now, a group of elves working together can hide a whole row of dwellings. With the dragon's help, we can and will protect the book."

"Where *is* the dragon? I can smell him. He must be close," said Ezra.

Flinar gave a throaty chuckle. "He is right under your nose, wolf."

The elf stuck two knobbly fingers in his mouth and whistled.

Reality distorted as if a sheet had been peeled back from the canvas of the woods before us. Tielbu dozed in a clearing, circled by half a dozen sweat-drenched elves in winter onesies. The dragon summoned to life from childhood stories and the turquoise blues of Dad's painting. The dragon that had unlocked my ability to animate before I could pull winged creatures directly from my mind.

I was so very glad to have him close as the final battle loomed.

Flinar dismissed the small band of elves.

Running to the dragon, I laid a hand against his scaly flank. "Tielbu."

Opening a deep-set amber eye, he snorted a hello that propelled rancid smoke from his nostrils. "I've been waiting for you, Alisha. The elven black holes are a strange place."

I scolded him. "You make it seem like I don't visit. You know we have to be careful about your whereabouts and being followed. For some, owning you would be their greatest conquest, Tielbu."

"You created me, druid. I am part of you. Any parting from you leaves me feeling less than whole." The dragon swung around to focus his unblinking eyes on Ezra. "You come bearing gifts, wolf."

Ezra emptied the carrier bag of roadkill Marina had

sourced from her supplier. "We have brought you some flesh to dine on."

"How kind. Seasoned well, I hope?" Tielbu devoured the meat and gave a hideous burp that made my toes curl. "Please, send my compliments to the chef."

With juddering effort, the dragon heaved himself up so that he towered above us. The four horns protruding from his head reached the height of the tallest oak encircling the clearing. His wings looked bonier than usual, but he was otherwise in perfect health, his black talons sharp as ever and his long tail threatening to topple anyone who got too close to his rear end.

I craned my neck to look up at him, then lowered the satchel to the ground. "We have brought you and Flinar something to look after."

Flinar nodded with grave solemnity. "We will achieve this feat with a combination of secrecy and strength. I will hide the book in a black hole with the dragon. Who would dare go up against his fiery breath?"

A swell of whispers in my head. I blocked them out. "If the book is in jeopardy, you must destroy it rather than letting it fall into faithless hands."

Flinar hesitated. "Why didn't you choose the Wildwoods vault for safekeeping? The Prime Sorceress's bread and butter is security. Surely, she could have helped?"

Alarm bells rang in my head. Flinar was indebted to Lavinia for bringing the elves back into the fold, but he wouldn't betray me. I had to believe that. "Wildwoods has been breached before, Flinar. Not all who venture through those halls can be trusted. Death herself infiltrated the school. Somehow or another, this will all be over soon. For now, let's keep it between us."

The elf sighed. "If you think that is necessary, then let it be done. After all we have suffered, elves have become a pragmatic people. But please understand, Alisha, if I have to choose between my people and the Book of Names, I will always act in the interests of my people."

Ezra's jaw tightened. "Then let us hope, Defence Minister, that those interests align."

Flinar squared up to him, though we were friends. "Indeed, Justice Minister."

I frowned, disconcerted. "We will see you at the senate meeting, Flinar. We won't speak a word of this, but you have my gratitude."

"It is an honour, Alisha. Please excuse me. I'll breathe easier once the dragon and book are hidden." He hurried away to issue instructions to six of his most trusted elves.

We lingered as they created the black hole, faces tight with concentration, their movements in sync. The book seethed at my abandonment of it. Then the dragon and book vanished, no longer accessible to me without the elves' intervention. As the black hole closed, the whispers abruptly stopped, as if the book had been sealed away in a soundproof room. I sagged with relief at the break in our connection.

Ezra's grey eyes sparked with copper. "I'd say that's a slam dunk for the good guys."

In the distance, Flinar searched my face, his milky eyes like probes, his expression closed.

I quashed the niggling feeling that new alliances were already being drawn.

7

As the clock struck midnight, a crescent moon hung in the inky sky. I preferred to be tucked under my duvet with Ezra by this time of night, but it was in the Prime Sorceress's gift to determine meeting times. So I stepped into Ezra's arms, and he whisked me to Crystal Palace Park, a jewel amongst the city's concrete landscape and smoking chimney stacks, where magic lurked. When we reached the sphinxes on the Italian terrace, their stone heads turned to impossible angles to fix us in their sights.

Rhokon's terracotta lips curved upwards. "Good evening to the both of you."

I startled. "Rhokon, I'm not sure I've ever seen you so cheerful."

He harrumphed. "My arthritis, compounded by my stone form, is much improved. The new Prime Sorceress allows us to stretch our legs more frequently than her predecessor."

Mammatas chuckled. "He has been a more pleasant companion under this administration."

Rhokon's sandpaper voice clawed from his throat. "You laugh at me, brother, but a boss who takes care of the staff is a fine thing. All our centuries of labour have finally been rewarded with a little more freedom. It is enough to make me weep in gratitude, were my tear ducts not compromised in this form."

"The Prime Sorceress is a friend only to herself. You would do well not to have your head so easily turned," said Mammatas. "I wish you luck tonight, druid. There are those who would wrestle power from those delicate hands of yours."

I suppressed a shiver, my mind cartwheeling through possible outcomes for the evening.

The warmth of Ezra's hand at the small of my back urged me onwards.

"Excuse us, sphinxes," I said.

At the yew tree, Ezra stood back as I pressed my palm to the rune. Wildwoods emerged from behind its curtain. Mirabel had alluded to changes at the school, brief hints when she gossiped about her school day—decorative elements that felt like a fortressing, a move away from bookish learning to physical activity and a rule never to roam the grounds alone—but she didn't seem overly worried.

The Prime Sorceress had shaped the school in her image.

There was a femininity and strength to the new Wildwoods. It was, of course, a school that weathered change. A school with the ability to camouflage and transform. A seat both of learning and political plotting. A place shaped by the evolution of its leaders.

I looked at Ezra in astonishment. "It's utterly transformed."

A multitude of Lavinia's beloved umbrellas hung open and inverted from wires stretched between the cabins, a canopy of colour that blocked out the sky. The cable cars had been repainted in a striped beach-hut look in her signature fuchsia and stone white—the equivalent of a dog lifting its leg to claim territory. Lavinia had never been shy about staking her claim.

But it was the presence of students at this late hour that truly surprised us, together with the activities they were engaged with. A barrage of sounds and sights met us, not only from the arena where pupils traditionally practised their skills but on rope bridges, in the reading nook and on the roofs of the cabins and the obelisk.

Wildwoods had been turned into a training ground.

Some fought under floodlights, others in pools of shadow so dark I squinted to discern them. Wolves faced off against each other, teeth bared. Fallen angels left me breathless as they swept past, flying low and hard. Elemental fairies created pockets of peril for witches to overcome. Vampires of different weight classes squared up to spar in a makeshift boxing ring. A group of young leprechauns tried in vain to control a magical warthog, and students appeared to have commandeered some of the witches' umbrellas to conduct a form of death-defying acrobatic racing around the obelisk.

I winced at the ramifications for student care. "They shouldn't be out here at this time."

Ezra's daddy instincts had been honed by our care of Mirabel. "This is a failure to enact the Educator's Law. New users of magic must be supervised until they pass the trial."

Deep down, I admired her for being her undiluted self. Lavinia Drach didn't care a jot about proving herself to others. She didn't concern herself with what they thought. She didn't cower before anyone or silence her own voice for fear of offending. She didn't deviate from the pursuit of her goals. Or hide her bits in a changing room. She was unapologetically herself.

But this wasn't any old change of direction. The Prime Sorceress and her headmistress sister had rewritten the norms of Wildwoods overnight. Gone were the days when peculiars pored over academic texts, learned the histories of the Otherworld or watched teacher demonstrations before venturing into the arena for careful practice sessions under the watchful eyes of their mentors.

"This isn't just practical study time. It's war gaming. Your aunt means to get the kids involved in the coming battle." Nausea rose in me like a wave. I hoped I was wrong.

Ezra stared at me, aghast. Then he placed his thumb and forefinger in his mouth and whistled.

I raised a palm, sending the whistle around Wildwoods on a sliver of wind.

Inch by inch, metre by metre, bone-weary pupils disengaged from their activities, swooping earthwards on their umbrellas or dropping the scruff of another pupil's neck to face us. A flurry of excitement swept through them at the sight of us. We might as well have been celebrities, the way their eyes lit up and how the tittering started. The attention embarrassed me. I blamed Margola Silver for fuelling the legend of the eternal girl.

Ezra's deep timbre travelled far and wide. "That's enough for today. Go home."

A bold, muscular wolf stepped forward amidst the crescendo of grumbles. "We want to prove ourselves, Minister."

"We will fight side by side with the eternal girl," said a vampire in goth boots and blood-red lipstick.

Ezra's tone brooked no room for argument. "When it is your time, you will. Tonight, you all go home to your parents. Tomorrow is a new dawn."

The throngs disbanded, albeit reluctantly. We pushed through them to the cable cars in Lavinia's signature colours. Upwards, we lurched towards the vaulted cabin for the senate meeting. I stepped through the arched door behind Ezra, heart thudding, the memory of Mirabel's parents' screams echoing in my ears as they perished here at the hands of Cardea.

The new Education Minister and headmistress

approached first, mouth pursed in disapproval under her red elfin haircut. "It is not your role to dismiss my students, nephew."

Ezra hitched an eyebrow at me and gave her a cursory kiss on the cheek. "I apologise, Aunt Isadora. I thought you must have lost track of the time."

"Hardly, Ezra. I've planned every second of their education from now until the end of the school year. They really were very behind in their studies. There has been far too great an emphasis on books. We all know magic is more than books. It isn't theory. It is action. More a storm than a meandering river. These children had it too easy under the former headmistress."

I had never missed Rayna Willowsun's gentle kindness so much. "As long as we remember they *are* children."

Isadora's look would have withered a lesser woman. She strode ahead through the shadows of the vaulted cabin to the table, which glowed in the light of a tight circle of pillar candles on four-foot-tall metallic candelabras.

I ducked past them to take my seat next to Ezra at the stone table, wincing as I nearly set my ponytail aflame. I scanned the attendees. Isadora, Flinar, Orpheus, Margola, Calypso, Helio, Cillian, Erelim and—to my surprise—Rob Jameson had already taken their seats.

It was unusual to see a humdrum invited into this space, but this was a new era under new leadership, and fraught times called for extraordinary measures.

One empty chair remained.

"Where's Lavinia?" I whispered to Ezra.

No sooner had I spoken did she teleport into the meeting with the energy of an actor arriving for an awards ceremony. The narcissist.

I rolled my eyes while Ezra stared pointedly ahead.

The Prime Sorceress made her way to the remaining chair and waved her umbrella above her head. A scroll and feathered quill appeared there. She didn't bother with hello. "This is our first full meeting of the senate under my leadership." The quill sprang into action, scratching the scroll above her head. "We live in a world where shadows vie with the light. Where those in power, in the halls of Westminster and the palaces of this country, even those in Wildwoods, sometimes have feet of clay. But Phinnaeous Shine has gone, and it is a new day."

She paused to gather her breath, and not a pin drop could be heard, such was her power with Phinnaeous gone.

I was tempted to throw karaoke-singing Echo into the mix to puncture her ego.

The Prime Sorceress twirled her trusty umbrella at her side, never one to resist a dramatic flourish. "I want you never to forget the privilege of your seat. We are here to build advantages for peculiars in an uncertain world without destroying the humdrum communities we live alongside. That is the clearest way I can distinguish this administration from the fallen one under my predecessor. Under my leadership, those who serve on the senate do not do so for their own advancement."

She stared at each of us in turn in what can only be described as a supremely uncomfortable few minutes.

I prayed no one was having trouble with their sphincter muscles.

Satisfied with her game of Who-Blinks-First, Lavinia continued. "To that end, item one on the agenda is the renaming of the Sorcerer's Senate. From this day forth, it will be called the Peculiars' Senate. To approve the new name, raise your hands. Alisha and Rob, you are not senators and, as such, have no vote."

I lowered the mental defences that I could now effortlessly erect and met Orpheus's eyes across the table. *Another rebranding exercise.*

Your cynicism is quite delicious, Alisha. The vampire

smirked. *Of course, the Prime Sorceress's Senate would have been quite a mouthful.*

The senate raised their hands in a unanimous yes. Even kick-arse Calypso was reduced to a meek schoolgirl in this incarnation of the senate.

"Eleven ayes." Isadora, who seemed now to be deputy, motioned to the quill to record the vote.

Her opening gambit over, the Prime Sorceress sat, but her tart voice still carried effortlessly around the vaulted cabin. "The next item on the agenda deserves lengthier consideration. Never has the Otherworld, indeed the world, faced such menace as the coming of the rogue gods. Centuries ago, the great Chameleon Tale was written for this very moment. This past year, this very senate recognised the existential threat faced by all living creatures, peculiar or humdrum, when we voted to adopt the New Pragmatist's Law, allowing us to thwart the will of the gods when there is a significant threat to peculiar or humdrum lives. We are here to discuss our strategy. However strong the enemy, a good strategy can turn the game in our favour. Perhaps you may summarise where we stand, Alisha."

I steadied my nerves.

Maybe I should have played dress-up. Maybe I should have come here in a knight's armour or wearing my grandmother's chainmail to show them I meant business. I crossed my fingers, hoping I had enough credibility and buy-in to sway the senate towards giving me a battalion of my own.

Under the table, I balled my fists, making indents of crescent moons in my palms. "Two days ago, Death attacked me and my father at my mother's grave. She seeks the Book of Names and offered to resurrect my mother in exchange for the book. She had the power to turn the dead into her army."

The candlelight flickered as stifled gasps sounded around the stone table.

8

Margola chewed on her pencil. "That's quite a story. Did you manage to snap any pictures?"

"We were too busy fending off the dead," I said. "My elderly father played his part, too. They were slow and lumbering and easy to kill. What I'm worried about is what happens if humdrums stumble across the dead. I'm all but certain that what we saw isn't the full extent of the goddess's powers."

"Hell hath no fury like a woman scorned, apparently. I take it rumours of Death and Gaia being former lovers are true?" said the Minister for Information, who appeared to be dressed in a nightie.

I sighed. Often, titbits from senate meetings would end up in *The Otherworld News*, but according to the rumour mill, the final editorial say now resided with Lavinia. I picked my words carefully. "They once had a relationship, yes. It's why Gaia has insight into Death's tactics. Just as the Earth goddess said, the Wild Hunt sounded its horn. A further attack is imminent."

Margola arched a shapely eyebrow. "The Wild Hunt is a myth, Alisha."

Calypso's midnight blue suit contrasted with the selkie's satin nightdress. "It's foolish to discount myths. Often kernels of truth hide within them, Margola."

I nodded. "I didn't imagine the horn. The Wild Hunt will show its face."

"Neither did we imagine the excavation of our garden," said Ezra next to me.

"Someone or some *things* tried to unearth the Book of Names." I studied the Prime Sorceress's unlined face. "Only a handful of people around this table and the Earth goddess knew of the location of the book. We were betrayed."

Lavinia's hazel eyes glimmered. "I hope you are not accusing the Earth goddess of treachery."

I met her gaze. "She would not be my first choice, no."

"Thank you for your report, Alisha." Lavinia thrust out her Lycra-clad chest. "We must be vigilant. My rats have reported footsteps trailing in the snow where no man has walked. A lingering of the night when it should be day. Unexpected migrations of birds clouding the London sky. This is only the beginning. We must assume the gods are acting as one to change the course of humanity. With this in mind, I invited Detective Robert Jameson of the Shadow Squad here today to brief us on what support we may rely on from the government."

Rob coughed to clear his throat. His usual relaxed baritone faltered as he spoke, revealing his discomfort in presenting to the full contingent of the senate. "Since the crimes committed by Ra, the Home Office has slowly but surely been investing more money in the Shadow Squad. Once, our files on immortal beings were wafer-thin. The gods took care to blend into society and surfaced once in a generation. That is no longer the case. Over the past year, there has been a surge in immortal activity that spills over into ordinary people's lives. The Prime Minister was particularly concerned about the harm to national structures during Pan's earthquakes and the dream god's flair for tampering with the nation's sanity." He gave a wry smile. "Of course, imprisoning a god is not something the government wishes to involve itself in. It already has its hands full with domestic and foreign difficulties. Nevertheless, we have a vested interest in this matter, and as such, the Prime Minister sanctioned a doubling of manpower to gather intelligence on the gods through a mixture of CCTV evaluation and old-fashioned sleuthing. I've had my guys working overtime on this."

I bit my lip. *It sounds impressive, but I know the Shadow Squad to be only five men strong.*

Orpheus waggled his eyebrows. *Men are always exaggerating the size of their appendages. You know that.*

Lavinia propped her bony elbows on the stone table. "Do share, Detective."

"The rogue gods all have dwellings close to places of religious worship—churches, mosques, synagogues, temples, gurdwaras. We have knowledge of their vices. Alcoholism, gluttony, gambling, sheep sex, you name it. We have knowledge of their pastimes and a limited understanding of their powers. Death, aka Kali, for example, is the de facto leader of the gods. Her past professions tell the story of her dwindling fortunes. She used to work as an arms dealer, then in BP Public Affairs and then in pharmaceuticals. Over the past three decades, she has been a Lucky Strike door-to-door saleswoman, a short seller, a technician in a funeral parlour and, now, a shoemaker. We think that's why you noticed the leather wares on the dead, Alisha. She made brogues for the dead to walk the earth. We can even pinpoint the location of the gods' homes. The problem is we don't have the personnel or arsenal to be effective. The government's defence capabilities against immortals are woeful. Plainly speaking, we are powerless to take on these dickheads ourselves."

Next to me, Ezra stifled a chuckle.

Isadora frowned. "Is that language really necessary?"

I've always found a good curse word eases my stress, I said.

I admire a man who can curse inventively. English offers such delightful extremes of language. Orpheus's mouth twitched before settling into a semblance of seriousness. "It is time then to launch a full offensive, given we know at last where the gods reside."

"I'm not convinced we should fight at all. Perhaps the reason the gods have become destructive is because the eternal girl constantly threatens them with annihilation," said Cillian, the short and rotund Minister for Finance with a peach fuzz beard. "As impressive as you are, Alisha, you have started a war that can't be won. I am sorry to voice what the rest of you dare not say out loud. Alisha Verma should be banished to appease the gods. Then return to the status quo."

Ezra flushed with anger. "How dare you blame the eternal girl for the actions of the gods when she has learned our ways and put herself on the line to help us every step of the way? What would you have us do? Send her to outer Mongolia because you are too chicken shit to deal with difficult problems?"

The leprechaun gave a lascivious chuckle. "The wolf is too focused on bedroom gymnastics to see sense."

Under the table, I reached out for Ezra's thigh. Then, I skewered the leprechaun with a look of utter disdain. "I'm taken aback that you put the blame at my door, Minister. I didn't ask to be anointed as your chosen one. I am not responsible for the actions of immortal beings. I could leave this city, this country, but are you so sure that you can handle the threats without me? Be careful, lest the senate follow your advice and your feet are held to the coals." *Is he on crack? How many peculiars think the same way?*

Cillian has always been a fool, said Orpheus. *Little wonder the real power in the senate lies with only a few individuals. Most men have cotton wool for their brains. If they lived as long as I and had access to the best libraries in the land, it would not improve their intelligence.*

Calypso looked at Cillian as if he'd lost his marbles. "Once an enemy has stepped over the line, do they ever retreat without being pushed back? The most celebrated peculiar in the Otherworld, the great Rajika Verma, laid down her life to prepare us for this day, and you would punish her kin for showing courage? How very cowardly of you."

"Mind your tone, Custodian," said the leprechaun. "I have weighed our odds. Luck doesn't affect the gods."

The Prime Sorceress assessed the fireworks, eager to gauge how factions emerged and who would come out on top before putting her own stake in the ground.

Flinar's sail-like ears billowed in distress. "Please, colleagues. Traditionally, the elves have been reluctant to fight for the Otherworld. Too often, we have been pawns and not active shapers of our fate. But there will be no world left if we do not lift our heads above the parapet. Even the elves cannot live in isolation in our black holes. Think of the Otherworld as a knitted blanket, one stitch dependent on the other. We are all part of this fight."

"You are a glutton for punishment, elf. They will crush us like beetles under their boots," said Erelim, the Minister for Diplomacy.

"Not if the eternal girl stops selfishly hoarding the Book of Names and the weapon she carries. Instruments that can deal a blow to immortals should be communal resources," said Isadora.

The Prime Sorceress and Flinar exchanged glances.

My chest tightened, wondering if the elf had given away my secret.

Helio, the Bestiary Minister, steepled his fingers under his pointed chin. His fat lizard ducked out from beneath a lock of hair, side-eyeing the senate as his master spoke. "She has been equally selfish hoarding the dragon. I'm afraid you rather act like a rogue agent, my dear."

Ezra lurched forward, ready to defend me.

I gave a slight shake of my head. This was my battle. I didn't need to prove myself. I already had. "The agenda says we are here to strategise how to defeat Death, not weigh up my character."

It wasn't the first time a finger had been pointed at a woman who dared to take her own path. A man would be admiringly called a maverick. A woman, a witch. You'd think, after Salem, the world would have learned to live and let live.

The Prime Sorceress's pearly whites gleamed, but her tone was dangerous. "Maligning the eternal girl comes within a hair's breadth of doubting the Chameleon Tale, Helio. That's not your intention, is it, dear boy? For some, that would be tantamount to blasphemy."

How many times had I all but written Lavinia off before she came out swinging on my side? Being her ally was like being friends with a Russian doll. You never knew quite who would show up.

Helio's golden glow paled to the colour of the cliffs of Dover. "Of course not, Prime Sorceress."

Lavinia's pink frosted lips curled upwards. "Well, that's a relief. Nevertheless, we are a democracy. There might be some amongst us who don't wish to sit on the sidelines in the coming fight. There will be no judgement. Well, not openly." She exchanged an amused glance with her sister. "We will put this to the second vote of the evening. Senators, should London's Otherworld join the battle against the rogue gods? First, the ayes."

Lavinia raised her hand like a flag. Isadora, Ezra,

Orpheus, Calypso, Flinar, Margola and poor cowed Helio followed suit.

Lavinia frowned at Cillian and Erelim. "Gentlemen, you abstain?"

"With great sorrow, Prime Sorceress," said the leprechaun. "I abstain. Luck is a fickle thing. I fear it is not with us."

Erelim shifted in his seat, his dirty blond hair and ashen wings against the stained-glass windows of the vaulted cabin, making him worthy of a portrait in the National Gallery. "I, too, must abstain. History has not looked kindly on those who have pitted themselves against the gods. Just ask Lucifer."

Orpheus rolled his eyes. *At least Lucifer wasn't a fence sitter. The only reason to keep Erelim around is as eye candy for those whose tastes veer that way.*

"Eight ayes and two abstentions," said Isadora to the scribbling quill. "Let it be noted on the record."

"Excellent," said Lavinia. "The majority agrees, and the motion is carried."

That was it then. War it would be. A fate decided by a handful of peculiars who happened to have clawed and stumbled their way into positions of power.

I'd stayed up late for a tarot reading with the foxes, hoping for a clear sign forward. My gut told me this was the right thing to do. Here in the room where the gods had slaughtered Mirabel's parents. Yet still, I'd hoped for a signal that the universe would reward my little family for bravely stepping onto this path. Would I regret puncturing the peace of our domestic bliss? Were we rushing into an unwinnable war?

Life never gave us any guarantees.

The urge to look at Ezra was magnetic. His copper-grey eyes bloomed with pain and resolve.

I took a deep breath. "It's probably a good time to tell

you. Gaia told me that Death would have a battalion. And I should have mine."

Lavinia threw back her head and laughed like a drain.

The vampire's eyes gleamed. *Now you've done it.*

9

———————

"What nonsense is this? *You* want to command a battalion?" said Lavinia. "But, my darling girl, impressive as you are, you have limited battle experience. And what, pray tell, is your strategy?"

I'd known she would resist, and it was true—many around the stone table had more battle experience than me. But I was over-doubting myself. Battles weren't only won with might. They were won with strategy, courage and intuition.

I might not trust Lavinia, but by now, I sure as hell trusted myself.

I uncrossed my legs, bouncing one foot against the floor, but above the table, I projected calm. "The detective has the individual whereabouts of the gods. That's all well and good, but killing on the battlefield is a different prospect to murdering someone in their own home."

"If you ask me, gods aren't necessary, and violence is a natural endpoint to all they have wrought. I have no problem with it," deadpanned Orpheus.

Flinar piped up, his triangular head only just visible above the height of the table. Next time, I'd bring him a cushion. "Alisha is right to be cautious. On home territory, one or more of the gods would be likely to escape. Moreover, the gods are embedded in their neighbourhoods and would likely cause an uncontainable ruckus. *If* we walk this path, then targeting the gods all at once is the only option."

Ezra nodded. "The battalion makes sense. We have to ambush the gods simultaneously, rounding them up and giving Alisha a chance to contain them. Or kill them."

"You speak of killing gods," said the fallen angel Erelim. "There will be a price to pay."

Calypso's midnight skin glittered with the dust of distant planets. "There is a price for killing gods but also for allowing them to run riot. Both lead to imbalance."

"You're right. We can't do this lightly." I recalled my search for the Book of Names in the Celestial Library and how the words held within it unleashed searing power when I spoke them out loud. I relived the moment I plunged Transcender into the dream god's stomach and twisted it, how he writhed in pain and vanished from sight. How the planets swirled around us, and anything seemed possible. My story was still being written. "I don't know if immortals can truly die, but my gut says we need to gather the gods in one place and surround them with a battalion. I will have the book, the sword and the Jericho necklace. All the pieces will be in place. And we might have a chance of holding back the dark."

Lavinia raked an assessing look over my face. "Very well, Alisha. You will have your battalion."

Next to me, Ezra slumped in relief.

Atta, girl, said Orpheus. *It is not often I see the witch give ground.*

With one win under my belt, I reached for more. "The pupils won't fight."

Isadora flushed. "That is not your decision, druid."

"You are mistaken, auntie. Training the children in self-defence is one thing, but making them an active part of the fight is a dereliction of duty," said Ezra.

"They will be reservists, nephew," soothed Lavinia. "We will not call on the children unless we have to. This will be a three-pronged fight. We have the meagre might of the UK government, the remarkable resources of Wildwoods and the prophesied eternal girl."

"Certain specimens in the bestiary might be helpful in herding the gods in one place," said Helio. "Magical moose, perhaps. Or a platoon of platypuses to entice and distract before they are surrounded."

"As tempting as that sounds, we have a plan, don't we, Detective?" said the Prime Sorceress. "Spin classes are a great place to think. All that sweat and churn is like a clear-out for the brain. This plan will, however, require agreement and a helping hand from our Justice Minister."

Ezra stiffened. "I'm listening."

Rob pressed his lips together. "We want to allow Phinnaeous Shine to escape from prison."

Helio, Cillian and Erelim laughed out loud.

Quite frankly, it sounded absurd to me, too.

Orpheus's eyebrows disappeared into his hairline. "You can't be serious. That man is a threat."

"It's not a joke." Rob reddened. "Phinnaeous had a deal with Death. He dragged his feet on action against the rogue gods in exchange for peculiars being able to use magic openly in the remade city."

Orpheus grunted. "Yes, yes, we suspected it was something of that sort. All the more reason to keep him locked up. If the shapeshifter had an issue with having to shift shapes all his life, he should have booked a therapist, not betrayed the very peculiars who depended on him."

Cillian spun a gold coin on the table and then caught it. His blue eyes twinkled. "Ah, but you are missing the point, vampire. Phinnaeous is too arrogant to use the chance of escape to build a humble life for himself."

Ezra nodded slowly. "I think you're right. He'll head straight into the arms of the rogue gods as a shortcut to rebuild his fortunes. But with his shapeshifting ability, he's hard to track."

Lavinia clapped her hands excitedly. "Not if we use a tracking spell on him. It's an easy enough spell if the coven works together." She giggled. "I already have a strand of his hair. Then we wait for the gods to gather in one place."

Thoughts ping-ponged around my head. The perils. The audacity. The hope. "It's a good plan."

"It's a dangerous plan." Orpheus looked to Ezra for support. "Neuhoff, surely you are with me on this? Phinnaeous was not an easy man to capture the first time. Putting him in the vicinity of the gods is an explosive risk."

"Sometimes risks are necessary." A vein throbbed in Ezra's jaw. "This could be it, Orpheus. This could give us the upper hand."

Calypso nodded. "Books only take us so far. Sometimes, we have to act. To nudge the future in the right direction."

"The plan requires surveillance. The assumption is that Phinnaeous will lead us to the gathered gods, but it's too dangerous for my men to be involved," said the detective.

Ezra's shoulders curled forward. "So you'll need my seekers? Or the coven's rat spies?"

"Actually, the werepigeon has volunteered. It'll be a much easier job if airborne." Rob gave me an apologetic look.

I sucked in a sharp breath. "But his shielding powers fizzled out after he betrayed Hermes. He can't even reliably hold his spider form anymore. Werepigeon is all he has."

"He just has to fly and stay out of harm's way. Look, Alisha, he wanted to play his part." Rob grimaced. "I would have run it by you, but the Prime Minister told me to liaise with the top of the organisation and get all the pieces in play first."

His words hung in the air as I turned the plan over in my mind.

There was still a piece missing, but I couldn't see what yet. I needed to insulate myself from Lavinia's control of the game. Helio had been right. What made me strong was choosing what worked for me. I wasn't bound by the constraints of being a senator. I hadn't grown up a peculiar. I trusted my friendships more than the Otherworld structures.

Orpheus's dark eyes glimmered as his voice delved inside my head. *Suspicion swirls in your head. You're still not sure who around this table is an ally.*

There's so much I can't see, I said.

Lavinia wordlessly rose to her feet. She muttered a spell under her breath, and silhouettes slipped from the end of her dull brown umbrella and into the rafters of the vaulted cabins. The figures grew large and monstrous, and I understood them to be the gods. With a jerk of the Prime Sorcerer's umbrella, in one fell swoop, an approaching battalion encircled them. The battalion parted like the Red Sea, and in walked a woman with a book and a sword.

My stomach churned. The woman looked so alone.

Under the table, Ezra's thumb drew circles on my hand.

How easily I could get myself killed. At least I'd be going out with a bang rather than a wheeze.

Lavinia turned to us in triumph. "It is decided. Our plan has been hatched, and we have declared war on the gods. May history be kind to us." One by one, the pillar candles extinguished themselves. "This meeting is closed."

Ezra's lips at my ear. "Let's go home, hellfire. It's been a long night."

Only at the cottage did I find a parcel in my bag with a note from Orpheus.

Alisha,

In my experience, it never hurts to keep a few cards close to your chest. The way to ensure a win is the element of surprise. At least, that has always worked for vampires.

The enclosed diary belonged to Rayna Willowsun. She left it in my care for you. I think the moment might have come for you to make use of it.

Meet me at the Shanghai Moon. Bring the empath. I have cleared it with the Custodian. The final lesson of your studies awaits amongst the stars.

Yours,

O.

My stomach churned. Orpheus was accompanying Marina and me back to the Celestial Library. What was more, in my hands, I held a dead druid's innermost thoughts.

10

The veterinary surgery reeked of disinfectant and cat piss. Marina was elbow-deep in the cage of a family of guinea pigs, which, as far as I could tell, suffered from a balding affliction. She was a nurse down and had only Echo as her extra pair of hands, but of course, a leopard couldn't clear out cages, take a dog around the block or mop the floors. That left my rainbow-haired bestie looking frazzled and uncharacteristically frizzy for someone addicted to her hair straighteners.

Bum in the air while she toiled, Marina's voice was thin with exhaustion. "I called your dad this morning to say hi. I've been worried about his state of mind since what happened at the graveyard. You know, for someone who put the Otherworld off limits for his children for aeons, he's adapted remarkably well to all these peculiar goings-on at this late stage in life out of love for you. I mean, his son is a werepigeon, his granddaughter is a fairy, and he has to fight the dead alongside his saviour daughter. Joshi has a heart of gold."

"Hardly. He put netting on the koi pond," said Echo.

"That's hardly the action of a man with a heart of gold. Those fish miss fighting for their lives as much as I miss terrorising them."

He lazily licked blood off his paw. Acting as a consultant on Marina's magical cases meant that she sometimes let him gorge on remnants as a perk of the job. Pretty disgusting, but according to Marina, he showed a very caring, restrained side in the surgery and didn't care for other benefits she could offer, like bank holidays or pension top-ups.

"It makes his day when you check on him. Funnily enough, the graveyard fight gave him a new lease of life," I said. "It really made him believe in himself."

Marina applied some topical cream to the fattest guinea pig. "So I gathered. Alma said his boost in confidence really shows in the bedroom. Apparently, they are nearing Sting and Trudie levels of sexual prowess."

I gagged. "That's a thought that will scar me for life."

I traced the soft flesh of my left inner arm, where I had once had a circular scar of nine dots, white and raised as if they were braille. I missed it sometimes. Nothing remained there now. The map to the Book of Names had disappeared once I held the hidden tome in my hands.

"I know you're busy," I said. "I wasn't dropping by just to get under your feet. I wanted to persuade you to travel to the stars with me. Orpheus has offered to give us our last lesson. I think we should take him up on it."

Marina stripped off and pulled on a fresh pair of scrubs, exposing glorious buxom curves, 1950s purple lace underwear and her array of tattoos. "Look, babe. Between you and Rob, I'm pretty clued up on what we're up against, including the batshit plan to release Phinnaeous Shine. But I can't leave today. I'm too busy to be jaunting off to the Celestial Library in the middle of the working week."

I sank onto a stool, frowning. I was desperate for Marina to be able to defend herself.

"I have fond memories of training together." Echo honked with laughter. "Like the time I forgot my oath of protection, fell prey to my animal instincts and chased you two down at Wildwoods like you were fresh off a barbecue."

"I remember all too well." My mouth twisted. "This time, Calypso has a whole weapons room to show us, Marina. Crossbows, bejewelled daggers, spears, pistols and thigh holsters." That last one was bound to sway her. She loved a bit of kink.

Marina dumped a sodden mess of newspaper and sawdust in the bin and peeled off her medical gloves. "I burst with pride when you two go into warrior mode. I dig killer kitty. And your wind and animation thing is wild, Alisha, but it's just not me. Even as humdrums, you were into kickboxing, and I was into leather catsuits and pole-dancing. If I get into a tangle with a god, it'll be like when any other arsehole gets out of line. I'll go straight for their eyes. In a city like this, you can't go wrong with a key in your fist and a spray bottle of deodorant in your bag. Until then, I'll just do what I always do. And don't you worry, my empath skills are deepening all the time. I use them here every day to treat my patients."

A purr from her emerald-eyed kitty admirer. "Marina Ambrose does indeed practice her skills and not just on the animals. She spent her toilet break this morning talking to the baby rose bush in the back garden. It might be winter, but it's in full bloom."

Marina grinned. "I can't wait to compare notes with Gaia."

I hesitated. "The thing is, I'm not sure she's still on our side."

Echo hissed. "Take that back. The Earth goddess is nothing short of a saint. The ground at her feet is a bed of clouds. The slightest touch of her hands is like a week at the spa of a posh London hotel. Her wisdom is greater than the combined knowledge of the books in the lost library of Alexandria and the Buddhist monks of Nepal. I wouldn't be surprised if the ABBA medley had been written in her honour. And she is scented with heavenly oils."

I'd always found her Indian head oil fairly pungent, but to each their own.

"The night of the party, she gave me advice, but there was something about her body language. A warning that she wasn't herself. Expressions I didn't recognise. It was as if the book was corrupting her. Or maybe the thought of controlling the other gods." I shook my head. "All I know is that she knew the secret of where it was hidden, and then someone tried to dig it up. And she was in love with our enemy. You know how it is. We share characteristics with the people we fall in love with."

Marina stared at me. "Alisha, there's no way the Earth goddess would choose to betray you. As for that bollocks about mirroring people we fall in love with, you couldn't have been more different from Alex. Sometimes, we fall into relationships on the rebound or as rebellion or just because they'd be good in the sack. Romance doesn't have to be meaningful or forever. It can simply be fun, an exploration of ourselves or a fuck-up. Maybe Gaia messed up. Maybe her romantic life is as complicated as everyone else's." Her words contrasted with the superstitious rubbing of the cross at her neck.

I pressed home my advantage. "There's a war coming, Marina. We can't afford to give anyone the benefit of the doubt. Not even the Earth goddess. The only thing we can do is prepare ourselves. Come with me. I need you. Please."

Pensive cornflower blue eyes met mine. Then she picked up the phone and dialled. "Laura, how do you fancy some overtime to top up that holiday fund of yours?" A pause. "Today, yes. How soon can you get here?" She replaced the receiver in its cradle and straightened her shoulders. "When do we leave?"

During late afternoon, the sun dipped in the sky, leaving wintery London awash in grey. I stood in Balham beneath a lamppost on a pavement speckled with chewing gum.

"See you inside." Marina followed Echo into Shanghai Moon, pausing to joke with an elderly couple about how her Bengal cat followed her everywhere.

Gulping, I listened to the beautiful banality of their exchange, taking in the doddery old couple beaming at the passing words. The cyclist impatiently waiting for the traffic light to change. The woman lovingly tweaking the Christmas display in the charity shop window. None of them aware that all their worldly preoccupations might be turned upside down if Death had her way.

Taking my phone, I sent Ezra a text. *Off to CL now Echo with me. Lasagne in the freezer for you & Bel.*

Barely a second passed before my phone pinged. *Shine released. Sahil in play. Be careful, my love.*

Anxiety and warmth swirled in my belly. The plan was in motion. He loved me. Then I heaved myself off the lamppost, tugged at the sports bra that had flattened my boobs into pancakes and slipped into Shanghai Moon.

Incense sticks burned inside the tea and occult shop, dispersing smoky coils of jasmine and sandalwood through the shop. The foxes had closed to customers for the day. I hugged the foxes hello, then stood aside as they worked in practised synchronicity to prepare for the tarot reading that would propel us to the Celestial Library.

Orpheus lurked, silent and brooding, next to the sequinned, midnight blue curtain that would soon be pulled around the tarot table. "You'll get nothing. I'll have you know that the leopard spent the past five minutes singing Aretha Franklin's 'Natural Woman' at me. It was quite unsettling."

Echo's tail flicked. "You loved it, really. I was right on the beat."

Marina smirked like that was up for debate.

"I'll have you know that seeing the Queen of Soul live at the Royal Albert Hall in 1970 was an almost holy experience. Your rendition was a disaster." Orpheus's heavy brows gathered together. "Did you read the diary? I must say, for a mild, taciturn woman, she wielded her pen as a scalpel. Her entries are not more than a couple of lines a day but filled with candour and wisdom."

I pulled it from my pocket and thumbed the pages of the unostentatious notebook with its slim, velvety, green cover and unlined pages. Inside, Rayna's writing looped in fountain pen. "I should have given her more time. There was more to her than kindness. Now I realise she just held her tongue." I ran my finger across the page. "Margola as 'a megaphone wrapped in a pout.' Helio described as 'too self-absorbed to look after animals.' Lavinia described as 'impressively flexible but devoured by ambition.' You as 'the last well-read man in the city' with both 'fangs and a marshmallow centre.'"

Orpheus snorted with disdain. "And what, Alisha Verma, did she say about you?"

With a puff of annoyance, I turned to the second to last entry in the diary. "Apparently, I'm too afraid to find out where my limits are."

The vampire's inky eyes glimmered dangerously. "That's why we're here."

We clustered around the tarot table. An antique hand-painted lamp topped a sateen tablecloth in the deepest sunset. Faeza pulled the curtain around the table.

Fei Yen frowned. "As you know, bridging the gap to the

Celestial Library very much depends on energy. Yours is depleted, Marina." On impulse, she darted behind the curtain and brought back a wicker basket filled with gemstones. She pressed two into Marina's palm, one glossy black, the other heavenly blue with golden internal flecks. "The ebony signifies protection and knowledge, intuition and defence. Blue lapis, beloved of the Pharaohs in Egypt. It brings wisdom, confidence and vision."

Marina's eyes widened. "I love them. I've been meaning to expand my collection." She patted her scrubs. "But I don't have a bag, and they will fall out of my pocket. Keep them safe for me."

"Pop them in your bra," said the foxes in unison, as if they'd used the phrase a thousand times before to convince dithering customers. "Carrying crystals close to your body attracts good energy."

Echo perched on a chair. "I don't carry a bag or wear a bra. Do I not receive a gift?"

Rolling my eyes at him, I secured my possessions for the journey ahead. Rayna's diary, check. The Jericho necklace, check. My sword, check. Then I took a seat.

Faeza shuffled a deck of art nouveau tarot cards in the style of Alphonse Mucha, romantic and full of deep golds and intricate flowered designs. At her nod, I tapped the cards, infusing my energy into them. Faeza dealt the cards, her mouth pursed in concentration.

After a moment of indecision, I chose two cards. The Chariot card: depicting a woman in a flowing autumnal-coloured dress. The world card: showing a woman in a headdress looking to her left. I stared at them, tingling with premonition.

Faeza flipped the cards and sucked in her breath. "Oh yes, of course."

The door to Shanghai Moon jangled.

Fei Yen peeked around the curtained table. "We locked that. I wonder who—"

Her eyes widened.

Faeza absorbed her wife's terror. "What is it?"

Fei Yen's mouth opened and shut like a goldfish. She scooped up a handful of crystals from the wicker basket and pelted them at an unknown foe, her disability no brake on her courage.

Faeza's chair toppled in her hurry to help. "Is it the teenagers again?"

Fei Yen wheezed, lobbing crystals all the while. "Afraid not. The gates of hell have opened."

A roar from Echo as he pelted around the curtain. Crashes ensued.

My heart rattled like a runaway train. I exchanged a grim look with Marina, then ripped back the curtain. Orpheus rushed past me before my eyes decoded what unfolded.

A dozen creatures, maybe more, striking my friends, gnawing, clawing.

Even after all I had seen, my mind struggled to process what transpired.

The Wild Hunt. Did it always appear in this monstrous configuration, comprising creatures that slithered from the underworld itself? Shanghai Moon had been overrun. Delicate displays of teas overturned. Jars of Chinese herbs smashed. Candles, incense sticks and altar items littered the floor. All secondary to the creatures.

Curved horns. Fiery symbols. Bulging nodules on bony bodies. Blubbery limbs armed with prehistoric weapons. Gnarled ears. Dangling chains. A putrid, retch-inducing stink. Skin as thick as leather. Some on two feet, others on four. Reptilian intent in pupilless obsidian eyes. Trails of dirt. Laboured breathing. Crawling maggots. Deafening wails. An unholy clamour.

They had no singular look, though they did have a united purpose.

Given that their cruel eyes were trained on me.

My lungs constricted. They had found their prey.

I froze as the foxes battled a group of demons side by side. Magma oozed from one demon's nostrils. Another flicked his withered scythe-like wings, a malevolent smirk on his lips. Undaunted, Fei Yen and Faeza used the self-defence skills they had learned in my night class. Punches and kicks and, with the stash of gemstones depleted, the gutsy use of anything within reach: iron teapots swung like clubs, frisbees of K-Pop CDs, qigong balls and an avalanche of takeaway boxes intended for recycling.

But the demons were difficult to subdue. Quick and devious, their jagged bones as dangerous as the rusted weapons they held.

With a look of love at each other, the foxes shifted into their soul-devouring *hu hsien* selves, leaving their pharmacist's coats and Marks and Spencer underwear on the floor and emerging wild, magnificent and vengeful. Fei Yen was three-limbed and russet-coated, Faeza with snowy white patches since her wife's injury. Both had six tails, quicker, more vicious in their *hu hsien* forms, freed of their polite kindness.

At the other side of the shop, Orpheus and Echo fought side by side. Orpheus was all vampire strength, fangs and raised fists pummelling swollen, veiny heads. Echo tore a chunk of thick flesh from a demon with runes embedded in its spiked skull. The leopard was enjoying himself, throwing himself entirely into the hunt, a whir of golden fur, tombstone teeth and roaring delight. I retched as maggots flew my way, my eyes drawn magnetically to the shop window.

In the dim light on the street outside, Death, cloaked and smiling, straddled a monstrous stallion.

Panic swelled at my core.

Who would complete the plan if I died? Was I special or simply a fool? For a moment, my mind blanked to static.

"Alisha." Marina reached out to touch me. "Do something."

A jolt of resolve snaked up my spine. I reached behind my neck to draw Transcender from its baldric. "Stay there."

With a flare of anger, I ran into the fray.

11

Determined to take the brunt of the attack, I sprinted towards danger, fog-horning my fury to draw the attention. In my mind's eye, I conjured up a swarm of hornets. I pulled them from my thoughts and into reality, three centimetres long, with striped bodies and reddish wings. They surged, their given purpose to blind the demons.

The Wild Hunt turned my way as if I were the sun. Their gaping mouths swallowed my swarm of hornets like fresh popcorn. One escaped the foxes and jolted towards me, square-jawed and covered in scars, the smell of death coming from its serrated mouth.

I almost released the contents of my bladder there and then.

Would I ever unsee these things?

I lunged and twisted my sword into its middle, exposing warped organs within, then moved onto the next creature and the next until my breath came in short bursts.

Marina appeared next to me, wielding a chair. A shout of disgust. "You've ruined my favourite colours for me. Take that." She whacked the chair around the head of a purplish demon with thick, pink snot dripping from its beak-like nose.

"What the hell are you doing?" I jammed my fist into a decaying mouth that gaped to an abyss.

Her face was flushed. "I have crystals in my bra. Like a conical Madonna. I'm your wingwoman."

"Christ, Marina, get to safety." I lifted my palm nonchalantly to drive a forked-tail demon into the counter, then brought down the ceiling light on him.

"We're the same age, and you're in a lower weight class. *You* get to safety." She abandoned the chair and roly-polyed out of the clutches of a salivating monstrosity, clearly chuffed at her repertoire of skills. Not everyone our age could do a roly-poly.

Orpheus grunted as a demon with a burning rope looped around its torso dug its jagged bone into his side. He ripped off the demon's head in retaliation.

I gritted my teeth. A shout ripped from my throat as I lifted my palm. "Stand back."

Enough was enough.

Marina, the foxes, Echo and the injured Orpheus flattened themselves to the shop walls.

Wind curled out of my palm, a tingle that whipped into a tornado, sweeping the demons up, tearing them limb from limb in a whirl of flesh and gore and skulls and tongues. I dropped my hand, and the body parts thumped to the ground.

But it wasn't enough.

They replenished themselves, body parts crawling across the floor. Severed limbs found others to reattach to that had not been theirs minutes before. Frankensteins incarnate.

A revolting, nauseating, never-ending dance of death.

On the street outside, an infuriating smile played on the blue goddess's lips. Then she turned her stallion and cantered down the street, safe in the knowledge that the Wild Hunt would finish us off and bring her the remains.

The arrogant cow.

We fought to keep the demons from reforming. It became a game of sport, skewering demon flesh on Transcender and tossing it into different squares of the room, added by the foxes and Echo. Meanwhile, Orpheus tried to find a way to destroy them for good. Matches and flame. Bucket and water. Ripping them into the smallest possible masses.

Marina frowned. "Look at them, writhing around on the floor. They're like slugs, aren't they? The foxes must have some salt around here."

She rummaged through the jars, fingers clumsy.

Snowy Faeza cocked her head and shrieked at Fei Yen in the fox lament common across South London. They shifted back into human form, their bodies pale and shaking with the physical exertion of the past few minutes. With grim bleakness on her face, Faeza picked her way across the danger-ridden, scorch-marked floor to make a beeline for a jar that had rolled into the corner. She prised it open.

"This will do. Salt and pepper seasoning for use in Chinese crispy chicken, prawns and spring roll recipes. But will it work on demons?" She flicked a pinch at the nearest writhing flesh.

It sizzled and squirmed until, finally, all movement and striving stopped.

Marina whooped in delight.

"Go!" said Fei Yen. "Pick the portal card. We will finish the job and guard the portal card so you may return." Even as she spoke, demons reformed.

I shook my head. "We can't leave you."

Faeza liberally sprinkled a chunk of demon intestines with salt. "Remember, time passes differently in the Celestial Library. You'll be back before we know it."

Emerald eyes met mine. "I will stay and protect our friends. Go! Get to the Celestial Library."

I exchanged glances with Marina and Orpheus, who held his bleeding side.

The art of war is about strategy, Alisha, said the vampire. *Death keeps on surprising us. We need to surprise her. You need a safe place to learn. Away from Wildwoods. Away from here. Why do you think your grandmother kept a sanctuary in the library amongst the stars?*

Anxiety swirled in my stomach. "Let's go."

With a last look at the foxes and Echo, I sprinted to the tarot table with Marina and Orpheus on my heels. There, two tarot cards—the Chariot and the World—waited. This time, I didn't hesitate. I lunged for the Chariot, and when the portal gaped open, Marina and Orpheus dove in. I launched myself after them, with no time to consider what type of journey awaited.

A painful gasp as something clawed at my feet. A retraction of wings and a demon forced its way into the portal alongside us.

I spun, determined, cursing like a sailor and acting on sheer impulse. I was grateful for all the training: the hours in kickboxing classes, pounding the streets of London in yoga gear that crept up my crack, duelling with Calypso and pushing my limits with Ezra.

A slash with Transcender severed a gaunt head from its sinewy body.

Sickly smoke and the chopped-off head followed me into the portal, making me gag.

I'd really earned a holiday or a granny nap, but my day wasn't over yet.

Every journey to the Celestial Library was different. Adventures borne of the Celestial Library's complex imagination, adventures decanted from the pages of the books it held. As the three of us tumbled, ricocheting through the universe, across snowy wildernesses and forlorn rocks of gargantuan size, I forced my eyes open and swam desperately towards Marina and Orpheus, knowing that if we didn't make it, at least I wouldn't die alone. At least we tried. At least we had love and friendship.

I gripped their hands—first Marina's, then at an inhuman stretch, Orpheus's—as we rocketed past mammoth herds and through swarms of bats, under dying stars and cooling planets. The vampire's cheekbones were prominent under chalky white skin that flaked with the force of the propulsion. Blood oozed from the gash in his side. Marina's blue eyes glazed over with terror. She clung to me as if I were her buoy in the ocean, her parachute in the sky.

Breathless fear and undying hope as we landed in the library amongst the stars.

A welcoming whinny brought tears to my eyes.

I reached up to touch Nightfall's muzzle.

The Custodian slid off his back in a flash of metal and silver dreadlocks. She towered over us, hands on her hips, dressed exquisitely in a dark blue tailored suit. "What the hell took you so long?"

To compensate for the perilous journey, the Celestial Library transformed the great hall into a space to soothe an injured vampire. In the blink of an eye, the paintings of angels and cherubs customarily on its ceiling faded from view to be replaced by a night sky of the deepest black. The armchairs lost their chintzy grandma feel and became instead high-backed elegant affairs in cherry-leather. Three glasses of whisky on ice stood to one side.

I took a swig, winced, and then sank into one armchair to wipe the gore from my sword.

Orpheus, seated next to me, grew still as Marina mopped

his brow. His hair was slicked back with sweat. His lips curved in a wry smile as he leaned his head back and listened to the roar of the fire. "I could get used to being fussed over by a trio of worthy ladies."

Calypso rolled up his shirt, exposing the wound. It wrapped around his side, seeping with blood. Pustules had formed at its centre, and a purplish tone coloured the taut, chalky skin around it. "He needs to feed to replenish the blood he has lost."

"I have supplies at my club," said Orpheus, wincing as she applied antiseptic to his skin.

"I'll patch you up, but then you're going home." She worked deftly, with a non-existent bedside manner. "This is the worst place for a vampire frenzy. Three bodies and a horse to choose from, plus the potential to ruin large quantities of books with careless blood-spurting."

Nightfall whinnied in dismay.

I didn't blame them for wanting to protect the books. I refused to lend mine to anyone who dog-eared pages or left a smear of chocolate on beloved novels. Neanderthals.

His brow furrowed. "I'm not leaving. Not until we achieve what we came here for."

Calypso's face hardened. "I am the Custodian. You do as I say when you are within these walls, Orpheus."

The vampire's voice thinned with pain in the strangely dark hall. "If I read this room correctly, the Celestial Library has warped itself to reflect a vampire's needs because it fully supports my intentions in bringing Alisha and Marina here."

"You are insufferably arrogant." Calypso's melodious voice muted the sting.

"But almost always right." Orpheus reached into his jacket, wincing with unease. "A first edition of Virginia Woolf's *Orlando*. As per tradition, when I visit. And as a gift to compensate for any mess I might make."

Calypso took a sneaky look as she taped gauze to his side.

Her eyes widened. "You know just how to press a woman's buttons, Orpheus." She accepted the gift. "Very well. You may stay. For now. A younger vampire wouldn't be able to hold out, but your strength means we can wait a little longer. But if your condition worsens, you'll return to your club on my say so. Do I have your word?"

The vampire nodded. "You do."

"We must be quick," said Calypso.

You're putting me first, I said.

Be quiet and listen. "This is the safest place in the universe to keep a secret when we don't know who to trust. A place that, through its connection to her grandmother, favours Alisha. It's why she was able to animate the dragon here after a score of fruitless attempts. A place that values learning. It's where we will find if the eternal girl and her friend can break through their limits." He staggered up and held out his hand. "The diary, Alisha."

I handed it to him, prickles of anticipation on my nape.

"I admired Rayna without limit," said the vampire. "Someday, I will raise a fitting memorial for her. But for now, let me say that of all her qualities—her ability to help others without judgement, her mild manner, her skill with healing and her keen sense of the internal world of her pupils—there was one that always stood out. Rayna Willowsun could see potential. And she mourned even the slightest trickle of waste." He flicked to the back page of the diary to an indecipherable list of abbreviations and symbols that I hadn't long dwelled on. "All these initials are crossed out apart from two."

Calypso peered over his shoulder. "A.V. and M.A."

Orpheus smiled. "That's right. The rest are all crossed out. Only A.V. and M.A. remain. Each school year, Rayna would write a list of pupils who needed her help. Don't you see? She had managed to work her way through her gigantic workload, and only two names remained on her list. Alisha

Verma, paired with wings, and Marina Ambrose, paired with a third eye."

My heart raced, having seen those symbols before on a syllabus Rayna had shown me when Ezra first took me to Wildwoods.

Black eyes gleamed. "The teacher you deserved may be dead, but I am willing to try. The question is, ladies, are you ready to throw caution to the wind?"

The library didn't wait for an answer. The inner sanctum opened onto the endless bookshelves, multiplying in depth and height. Doors appeared between the aisles, in different places than I remembered: a bronze one where there had been a steel one, an impossibly slim one painted with Monet's water lilies where there had once been a matt black one. The Custodian had once told me that the library was a living organism, its components moving like blood cells around its body in a never-ending but random cycle of renewal.

The library wanted us to enter.

And I had never been one to refuse the wisdom of a library.

Nightfall tossed his dark mane and trotted through the towering shelves.

Marina's cornflower blue eyes twinkled, all tiredness forgotten. "Now we're here. It would be rude not to."

I clasped her hand, and together, we went in search of our limits.

At our backs, the flames leapt in the hearth, primaeval and true.

12

The planets swirled above us, flashes of clouded, pitted brilliance, and first editions of the greats of world literature spanned the shelves beside us. Yet I knew that this time, the knowledge I sought had to come from within. What piece of my internal puzzle remained to be discovered? The symbols etched in Rayna's handwriting left me dizzy with anticipation.

Wings for me. A third eye for Marina.

Calypso's blade-runner prostheses flew across the floor. "Keep up. Time is short."

"I've worked on my look for decades," said Marina. "A third eye isn't my thing. Can you imagine me riding Rob and then a third eye opening? It'd send him screaming from the bedroom."

Orpheus rolled his eyes. "Try for a less literal interpretation."

"No need to be salty," said Marina. "Injuries don't excuse impoliteness unless you're a chinchilla or platypus. I can forgive them anything."

Scents caught my nose: musty books, horse dung, freshly cut grass and blue-veined cheese—mysteries sealed in the library amongst the stars. I could spend a lifetime here and never be bored.

Calypso veered left after Nightfall, pulling up short next to a stumpy doorway with an oak carved into its gnarled surface. The horse tossed his head and snorted, nosing the door.

"All right, all right. Hold your horses." Glowing eyes framed with a deep sweep of metallic eyeshadow turned to us. "This room is one of my personal favourites. When up here amongst the stars, it is not unheard of amongst Custodians to long for a verdant earth brimming with life. Many druids have become Custodians across history, not just your grandmother. The twenty-sixth Custodian, Rodric Grainow, created this particular room. Perhaps it can be a conduit to your inner selves. Welcome to the Grove of Tomorrows."

She twisted the doorknob and ducked into the room.

Nightfall's rump blocked our view, and then a new world opened up to us.

It was larger inside than I'd anticipated. Hexagonal. A veritable TARDIS. However, the size of the room came secondary to its composition. It brimmed with life. Every surface had been used. Every sense tingled. Living walls soared heavenwards, planted with herbs, grasses, and climbers. Insects flitted through thyme and heuchera, chirping and trilling. Vines laden with fruit gifted flashes of colour. A great oak took centre stage, with a picnic table, fairy rings of mushrooms, stones and acorns at its feet. Patches of wildflowers—springy clover, purple monkshood and rosettes of pink primrose—dotted the ground. My trainers couldn't dampen the sense of life thriving underfoot: worms, dung beetles, fat moles and parades of ants. The air thrummed with clouds of butterflies. Above us, the planets and stars turned.

Dimples flashed in Calypso's midnight skin.

"Magnificent, isn't it?"

Marina rotated 360 degrees. "Like paradise."

"Well, don't get too comfortable." Orpheus headed for the picnic table, his movements leaden, his speech strained. "We have work to do. We'll start with you, empath."

We slid onto the benches, awaiting instruction. The Grove of Tomorrows called to my senses. I took off my jacket and sword and kicked off my shoes to stretch my toes in the springy grass beneath the picnic table. Marina followed suit while Orpheus flicked the pages of Rayna's velvety, green diary with his piano-player's fingers. He seemed to use it less as a reference point than as a talisman.

"Orpheus?" prompted Calypso. "I loved Rayna too. Her mode of teaching involved trial and error. Finding magic in ordinary things. A quiet bravery. That saying of hers... 'A pond is stagnant. A river flows. It is in moving forward that we thrive.'"

Sweat lined his brow. "There are many means of foretelling the future scattered through history. Humans have always been a bit twitchy about uncertainty. There is aeromancy, that is, watching for clouds or rain. A subtle linguistic change gives us aleuromancy—"

I perked up. "Ooh, I know that one. That's what Alma does. Throwing around flour or discovering messages after baking. It's a bit hit and miss."

The vampire held his side. "Astragalomancy is an option. Throwing small bones. Or perhaps anthropomancy, divination using the entrails of humans. Allegedly a pastime of Jack the Ripper."

Marina grimaced. "Not keen on that one. I have healing hands, not murderous ones."

Calypso interjected. "We're in a rush. They don't need to know all the technical terms. You could consider predicting the future by throwing an axe on a post and watching how it falls. That one's better than going to a therapist. What,

Orpheus? Surprised you're not the only bookish one here willing to show off your knowledge?"

Orpheus lifted a heavy brow. "There is bibliomancy. Divination by books." He shuddered. "Particularly the bible. That is, letting a book fall open and foretelling the future based on whatever your eyes fall on first."

"Ha! We used to do that with a Collins dictionary when we were bored at school. Oh, and at temple, some Indian ladies suspend a ring on a strand of their hair to divine how many children a person is destined to have and what gender. By now, I should have a five-a-side football team," I deadpanned.

"There's ceromancy, foresight based on shapes formed by melted wax in water. In my opinion, it is faintly ridiculous, but a beloved pastime of a number of altar boys." Calypso shrugged. "Better that than them playing with their peepees in mass, I suppose."

"Let's not forget foretelling the future by watching the flight of birds. Or necromancy. Divination by the dead." His eyes were vacant. "Alas, that one's forbidden. I'd love to convene with my dead friends."

Calypso leaned over to check his bandage. Blood seeped through. She cast me a warning glance but kept her tone light. "Why so morbid, Orpheus? You forget divination by dreams. And divination by cards. Dealing cards to foretell who one might marry."

Marina giggled. "Maybe this won't be as hard as I thought. I've been carrying out some of these without even realising it. I remember doing that to kill time during Latin lessons at school."

Calypso stood. "This is taking too long. We need to split up. Marina, you come with me to your old stomping ground in the lab. We can use the oven there to rustle up all the items we need. It's been temperamental recently. Only yesterday, it spat up incontinence pads instead of tampons."

"Maybe it can tell the future," said my best friend.

A flinty gaze. Orpheus thumbed through the book. "We're missing something. Yes, there it is. A tiny clue."

In a flash, he grabbed a handful of acorns from the bottom of the oak tree and handed them to the Custodian before collapsing onto the bench.

Her eyes narrowed in concern, but she pocketed the acorns. "Good luck, both of you."

Nightfall gave a plaintive whinny.

The Custodian startled. "Of course. If you insist. You can stay here."

She left, taking Marina with her.

With a weak smile, Orpheus staggered off the picnic table. He sank onto the grass, his suit now marred by both blood and grass stains. *And now you.*

You really need to discover a love of casual clothing. I sat beside him, hit by a sudden realisation. *You're not speaking out loud because of the blood loss. We need to get you to your club to replenish you.*

The blue goddess's demons really did a number on me. Quite unexpected. A shaky sigh. *Rayna and I used to go to the pub after a long evening teaching at Wildwoods. Whisky on the rocks at a pub in Crystal Palace. Sharing our perspectives on life. Her full-throated celebration of druidry. Her knowledge of plants and their healing properties. Her sense that every living organism has its place in the circle of life. I wished I could access that profound belief.*

I frowned. Had he ever been this pale before? His sentences were staccato, disjointed, as if his wound had disrupted his ability to string thoughts together. He had held himself together while Calypso and Marina had been there, but now he seemed to unravel faster than before. As if, with me, he didn't need a stiff upper lip. As if he could be vulnerable.

Dark lashes against chalky skin. *How foolish it feels for a vampire, a manifestation of death, to be talking to a druid of nature. Do you remember long ago, the Earth goddess chided you for trusting me? I wonder if her dislike of vampires is because she can't forgive herself for becoming embroiled with Death herself.*

You're not well, I said as a kaleidoscope of swallowtail butterflies darted past us.

A pulse of anger. *Listen. I'm trying to help you. The symbol of wings in the diary. Your affinity to winged creatures. Rayna thought you have the potential for wilding. That you can shift into another creature.*

My heartbeat raced. *That's ridiculous.*

I couldn't think of many things more galling than the public nudity poor shifters had to endure. My arse cheeks clenched together just thinking about it.

Not ridiculous at all. Think about it. The bandage no longer impeded the spread of his blood across his shirt. *Shifting has already been proven to be genetically possible for Vermas. Your brother is a werepigeon.*

A snatched memory of Sahil's pink-clawed toes and orange beak. I cringed.

I've witnessed a myriad of awakenings in you, he continued. *Your physical connection to druidry, your wind powers. Your deep sense of humanity. Generosity to the elves, Kraglek and Meriel Naehorn. Your responsibility towards your creations.*

Now wasn't a good time to mention how creepy some visitors to London Zoo were finding the shoebill storks.

Orpheus's mouth twitched. *Rayna spoke of the Welsh word 'awen.' Divine inspiration. Is that what your father does with his painting? What you do when you animate creatures? But you've been moving so fast, reacting to the chaos around you, that you haven't fully extended yourself. Your druid nature has become an afterthought. That's what's holding you back. That's the lesson Rayna wanted to encourage in you. We're not in the city now. There are no bus timetables or diary entries or doorbells ringing. Time has a limited impact here. Let me close my eyes for a brief moment while you bathe your druid nature in what it craves.* His eyelids fluttered shut. *Use the Grove of Tomorrows to ground yourself. Look around.*

"Orpheus." My voice sounded desperate. I shook him.

A shuddering of his chest. *I'm fine. Get to work. Discover the herbs. Forage the fruit. Meditate. Feel the vibrations of the ecosystem. Inhale, exhale. The zipping insects on the living wall breathing the same air. Tap into a deeper consciousness and hear the song of everything within this grove that thrums with life. Commit to your druidry. Dance in the rain instead of putting up an umbrella. Find joy rather than fear in the deepening twilight. No more dying bouquets on the table when they could thrive in nature. No more crushing of spiders seeking warmth in your home during the winter. Connect to the web of life. Build an altar.* A crescendo of intent. *Now, Alisha. Now.*

I sprang up, struggling to fathom what he wanted from me. His instructions reverberated in my head as he lay corpse-like on the lawn. The sooner I managed this, the sooner he'd let me take him home, the stubborn fool.

My bare feet against the lawn, I inhaled and exhaled, finding the scents and sounds around the Grove of Tomorrows again with a sense of wonder. The berries and oranges. The sturdy oak. Nightfall chomped the grass, his ears turned towards me. The planets above and the insects beneath.

Closing my eyes, I tapped into my own heartbeat and the heartbeat of the universe, feeling a oneness—a deep sense of gratitude. Thoughts slowed, one bobbing to the surface of my mind.

An altar. Orpheus wanted me to build an altar.

I could do that. I searched for materials, gathering fallen leaves, fruit, pebbles from beneath the central oak, and some mistletoe and acorns. I piled them into a beautiful sculpture.

Gazing at it, I wondered what I could do next. Honouring my druid self left me with no clues as to how to wild. Was it a deepening of my true self or an othering? I didn't know if I really wanted to find out. Did I have to really want it, or would it come to me regardless?

Sahil had achieved it by falling from the obelisk, surrendering to freewheeling terror. How could I possibly recreate that in a place of such peace? What would be my trigger?

As my thoughts meandered in the Grove of Tomorrows, Nightfall shrieked a warning.

I spun in a circle, palms raised, a shadow falling over me.

Vampire fangs bore down on my neck.

13

───────────

My body acted on instinct. A fight for survival.

At a kick to his stomach, Orpheus sprawled backwards. He wasn't himself. His eyes were dangerous with intent, veins straining against his skin, fangs protruding. His injury had clearly worsened to the extent that it had addled his brain, but feeding on me wasn't an option, however deep our friendship was.

Blood pounded in my ears, my throat dry with rushed breathing.

I should have gotten him proper help before. A vampire was strong and fast. In this depleted state, his blood lust was insatiable. I'd need help.

When he rushed at me again, I raised my palms and let him feel the force of the winds I could summon. A gust of wind, too, to throw open the door to the main library, allowing Nightfall to gallop to safety.

The winds didn't stop Orpheus for long. His vampire agility enabled him to leap over the current. He knew my tricks. He could anticipate my every move.

I have been waiting to do this for so long. His voice in my head taunted. *What a conquest it will be to feed on the eternal girl.*

I shuttered my mind from him, not wanting to hear the violent lust in his voice, desperate not to pollute my memories of him. With a flash of inspiration and a lasso of wind, I reached for my sword, cushioned on my folded jacket on the picnic table. The length of Transcender's obsidian blade allowed me to maintain a distance from the vampire's sharp fangs. I slashed at his shoulder, holding back from a deeper cut. I worried that if my sword could kill an immortal, it could do the same to him. Our friendship was a barrier to me truly hurting him.

The vampire cracked his neck to one side, recognising my weakness.

If only I could trap him.

A shudder as the Grove of Tomorrows joined forces with me. Roots crawled from the ground to ensnare the vampire's feet. Pebbles from my altar pelted his way. Honeybees carried leaves brimming with liquid—a sleeping draught?— to tip into his mouth.

This wasn't my doing. It was the library defending me.

I doubled down, this time roping a vortex of wind around Orpheus.

He gave a guttural shout of frustration, bending at the knee, launching himself upwards and out of the wind tunnel, ripping the roots that bound him with the ping of a rubber band snapping.

As the vampire surged towards me—savage, dishevelled and animalistic in his bloodlust—I braced myself. Holding out Transcender, I readied myself to impale my friend, my heart a thudding, fragile organ in my chest. I thought of Ezra and Mirabel, Dad and Marina, Echo and the foxes fighting another battle far away. And Sahil, tracking Phinnaeous Shine so I could carry out the rest of the plan. So I could stop the chaos of the rogue gods.

Vampire speed. Roman nose flaring, neck corded.

He came from the back, fangs ready for their reward.

I spun to meet him, every cell alert, every cell dreading what I had to do. Then I lifted my blade, a diagonal sweep, top right to bottom left.

But as I executed the move, Transcender slipped from my grip.

My skin and muscles grew elastic. My clothes dropped to the floor. The metamorphosis was strange, painless, and primal. There was a bending, a distorting, a thrusting out, my thoughts peaceful, with a sublime consciousness of a gentle shrinking and feathering of my body. A hop and a bounce as I leapt into the air.

A glimpse of Orpheus's face, mottled with fury, as I evaded his grip.

My feet claws. My arms wings. My eyesight sharper than ever before. I was different, but still me. My concerns existed, my great loves remained mine, but I found a new perspective. Boundaries expanding, like being locked onto a jazz station when all my life I had listened to rock. The universe was vast and full of wonder—a new richness. Molecules danced. Planets hummed. Leaves in the grove rustled. Ancestors whispered. Fear paled in comparison to the joy of flight. The exhilaration of soaring, sailing, climbing higher and higher. My intuition as well tuned as a concert piano.

This was why Sahil spent so much time in werepigeon form.

I flew to the topmost branch of the oak tree, admiring my reflection in the glass ceiling of the Grove of Tomorrows, my inner landscape unruffled and tranquil.

I wasn't a werepigeon.

I cocked my head to one side. I recognised myself from a series of Dad's paintings. My blue-grey body measured half a metre in length, my wingspan twice that. The Jericho necklace adorned my neck still. My short beak curved, and yellow ringed my chocolate brown irises. Black feathers lined my head, and I had a black moustache—ironic, given how Indian women threaded their moustaches with religious fervour—that contrasted with my white face. I had long, broad wings and a white chest dusted with black dots.

I was a peregrine falcon.

A burst of gratitude ebbed from me into the universe. *Thank you, Rayna. Thank you, Orpheus. Thank you, ancestors.*

I would have liked more time to absorb my new layered identity, but Orpheus sprang up the tree in ever-larger increments until he landed on the same branch with a look of ravenous hunger.

He launched himself at me.

I moved again. A merry game of not-quite-tag while I tested out my wings. He was angry, fists clenched. I was centred, wings extended. He tired quickly, drained by his loss of blood. My breast swelled with compassion for him. He would be himself again. I would see to that.

When Nightfall returned with Calypso and Marina, the vampire stood at the base of the oak tree, glittering eyes assessing whether to take the three of us on. Plus, the winged horse, who had been clever enough to bring help.

The Custodian didn't need an explanation. The Celestial Library had told her of my fate. With a half smile of acknowledgement, she found me on the living wall, pecking a ripe plum. She whispered a sonorous word in an unfamiliar language—the library conversed in endless tongues—and channelled the library's defences at the vampire, binding his wrists and ankles like a book. A stacking. A gloop of hot-melt adhesive. A threading. An end to this chapter of his story.

Marina's cotton-blue eyes scanned the room, her face ashen. She picked up my sword from the altar and then scooped up my jeans, sweater, granny pants and tatty bra with a stifled cry.

Unable to endure her despair, I dove to ground level. I was damn fast, an effortless plummeting and neat landing, needing no brain power, no mathematical calculations, simply presence and instinct. I became human before my bare feet touched the lawn, stark naked, with the exception of the Jericho necklace in the hollow at the base of my neck. With no hint of shame at my nakedness—how can shame be attached to such a cosmic gift?—I hugged my best friend before tugging on my clothes.

Her mouth gaped. "You did it. You wilded."

She danced a jig right there and then, always the first to celebrate my successes. Always the first to offer her shoulder for me to cry on.

Marina tucked in the clothing label that stuck out at my nape, then signalled towards Orpheus. "He turned all murderous, though, huh?"

"I don't want to lose him." My throat constricted. I knew what I had to do. My stomach quivered as I turned over my wrist, translucent skin over blue veins, and offered it to him. "He needs blood."

A cry of dissent from Marina.

"No. You're too important. His clan will see to it that he gets the care and sustenance he needs." Calypso stormed to my side and wrenched back my hand. "I'll deliver him to his club. It will take the bending of rules and some negotiation with the library for him not to use the usual mode of return, but given how the library was predisposed to him before, it should work." She tutted at the vampire. "You came very close to falling foul of your own moral code."

She had an eighties rucksack on her back that corroded her air of authority.

Orpheus glowered and strained against his bindings. Marina took tentative steps to his side and laid a hand on his shoulder. His face relaxed, and he slept.

I stared, incredulous. Orpheus wasn't a virgin vampire; as

head of his clan, he was a formidable opponent. To send him to sleep—without a coffin at that—showed Marina's powers had grown.

"Tell her," said Marina. "Tell Alisha about the message. While we were in the lab, Calypso got one of those paper plane messages the library likes so much, built from the torn pages of a pulp romance novel. Such a shame, really. Those are my favourite go-to reads when I'm having a difficult poo. Instant escapism."

"Is my family okay?" Worry in my voice. I gulped. "What about Echo and the foxes?"

"It's time for you to go home. Your brother needs you," said Calypso.

A tightening of my chest. A balling of my fists. I knew Sahil had done the wrong thing in volunteering to track Phinnaeous. What would it take to convince my brother that he didn't need to earn my forgiveness or prove himself? My thoughts pinged to Ezra. He was right. Love was complex. I loved Sahil regardless of his past mistakes.

"You'll have company on your way home, Alisha. I believe you made Nightfall a promise. He is very interested in your welfare, no surprise, given he was your grandmother's creation." Approaching the horse, Calypso laid her forehead against his muzzle. "For a long time, you've been a prisoner of this place. Your oath to the seventy-eighth Custodian has been fulfilled. It's time for you to feast your eyes on other plains, to gallop across meadows with the wind in your mane."

The horse's jaw softened, his tail swinging freely as he pulled affectionately at her silver dreadlocks with rubbery lips.

"I will miss you, my friend." Calypso turned to us and slipped her rucksack off her shoulders. "You're going to need this. No returns required. Trust me, that doesn't happen very often here."

The rucksack was black and emblazoned with a Guns N' Roses motif. The Celestial Library was obsessed with rucksacks from the 1980s, a manifestation of its quirky humour. I accepted it and unzipped it, my heart twisting at the sight of my grandmother's chainmail.

"Thank you, Custodian, for everything," I said.

"It's an honour." Calypso swept her gaze to the sleeping vampire and Rayna's diary beside him, which would now enter the library's collection. "Now go to your brother."

Nightfall snorted and tossed his head.

I took it as an invitation to ride him. Securing my sword and rucksack, I gave Marina a leg up onto Nightfall's bare back, then used a channel of wind to manoeuvre myself behind her.

"Just think of the gateway from which you came. You have all the experience you need. Trust in the universe, and it will reward you. The empath tells me the next time we meet will be on the battlefield. Until then, my friends." The Custodian hit Nightfall's rump.

We jerked as the horse galloped out of the Grove of Tomorrows and into the central atrium of the library, charging past shelves of books that fluttered their goodbyes, serenading the horse that had been a friend to them through the decades.

Marina leaned forward and curled her fingers in Nightfall's mane. A shout of glee ripped from her throat.

I wrapped my arms around her waist, a question buzzing in my mind, knowing that any second now, the breath would be stolen from my lungs and prickles of fear would prevent all thought as we travelled back through a new incarnation of the portal.

My mouth at Marina's ear as Nightfall raced. "How did you know that we'll next see Calypso on the battlefield?"

She turned her head so her words could reach me. "We baked acorn bread in the lab. I ate a mouthful, twiddled the healing crystals in my bras, and was floored by a premonition."

I strained to hear her as Nightfall's hooves thundered across the marbled floor of the great hall. With more space, the sleek satin of his coat shuddered beneath us. Plumes of black feathers rose from his sides, caressing us as they found their rhythm. We flew past pillars.

"A premonition?" I shouted.

"Yes!" Her single, elated syllable lengthened into a scream of terror.

We tumbled, freefalling in a tangle of wings and hooves and pink hair and Guns N' Roses memorabilia. A black, magical horse on white snow. Cliff edge after cliff edge of snow. Snowflakes caked my eyes. Plugged my nostrils. Snow, earthy and bitty in my mouth. Tastes my brain couldn't decipher: honey almonds, snow cones and urine.

I gagged. Marina's body shivered against mine. Nightfall groaned as he wrapped us in his wings. Someone panted. Air whittled out of my lungs. My mind emptied until only a primordial sound remained.

I wasn't scared.

I was ready.

14

———

We plunged through the portal card into Shanghai Moon. Nightfall collapsed with a groan, wings retracted, his mane and tail matted and awry. Marina and I landed after him in quick succession, her face in his rump, my nose in her armpit. A furore of whispers reached me through the whiteout of my mind. Loved ones' voices all tangled together. I couldn't be sure what was real and what was imagined.

Faeza's exasperated voice cut through the haze. "At first, we were her students. Now, I mostly feel like her cleaner. Will she ever stop destroying our shop? First, the dragon. Now a horse."

"Maybe she plans to go through the whole Chinese zodiac," said Fei Yen.

"Then the ox and monkey are mine," said Echo. "I crave a more varied diet than South London butchers or hunting inside the M25 can provide."

Relief swelled in my chest. Complaining meant that they had coped with the residual demons. Literally. I staggered up, brushed the snow and ice from my hair and clothes, and flung off my sword and rucksack. Marina, too, stumbled up, her immediate concern Nightfall. His panic showed in his flared nostrils and rolling eyes, but the slightest touch and whispered words from her soothed him.

Swaying, I turned to greet my friends, sheepish about the damage.

"Sorry about that landing. How long have we been gone?" My voice faltered as I ended my sentence.

Ezra crossed the floor of the shop, cutting a path through my family and friends. He took me by the shoulders, grip rough as if he didn't know whether to shake or hold me. His hair dipped into his eyes. Grey eyes flashed copper like he'd been over the coals. "I've been so worried." Then his lips swooped down to crush mine, bruising, demanding, furious. "They told me what happened. That Death came here. That a demon followed you into the portal."

I placed his hand on my heart. "I'm okay. We're okay."

Breaking the intimacy of our connection, I scanned the room. Next to me, Rob stared in alarm at the bruises already springing up over Marina's tattooed skin. Dad hovered, wielding a dustpan and brush, a pained expression on his face. Great-Uncle Rajiv scraped his shoe over a scorch mark. The foxes stacked black bags of demon flesh against the wall. Mirabel skulked in a corner, moss-green eyes wide, fists clenched.

Echo looped around my legs. "I resent how the dog gets first dibs on Alisha's affection."

I stroked his majestic head, then opened my arms to Mirabel. She bolted into my arms in a blur of auburn curls.

"Were you worried?" I squeezed her tight.

My daughter shrugged her tense shoulders. "Only a little bit. It's not like you were gone for long."

Dad rushed over to throw his arms around us, rocking us in his passion. "My girls. My girls."

I let him baby us, enjoying the closeness. An expression of

fatherly affection that peters out by the time a child reaches their forties or even twenties.

Great-Uncle Rajiv's watery blue eyes narrowed on me. "Your father told us you seek to be even more powerful than your grandmother. It is a fool's errand to compete with ghosts from the past."

I wasn't trying to compete with Rajika. Not anymore. I just wanted to be my best self. But I kept my mouth shut It had taken me a long time to learn that some people were too entrenched in their ways to accept another view and that the energy expenditure wasn't worth it.

I made a non-committal noise. "How did you all come to be here anyway?"

Emerald eyes gleamed with pride. "When the demon followed you into the portal, we thought we should call for cavalry. I called Ezra, Joshi, the detective, then a disreputable waste disposal company."

My eyebrows shot up. I looked at his paws. "You made a telephone call?"

The leopard's tail swished. "No need to mock me. Faeza put me on speakerphone."

"Why the disreputable waste disposal company?" I said.

"Because I figured all the demon goo wasn't going to fit in the brown bin, and a disreputable company wouldn't check to see what they were carrying," the leopard said. "And a skip outside would block the view of all the otherworldly comings and goings."

Fei Yen nodded. "We were very grateful for all the help cleaning up."

"Until the leopard started spraying urine everywhere," said Faeza.

"To stop the demons from getting ideas again." Echo prowled as he weighed up whether Nightfall was a fair target.

I swatted him. "Nightfall is an honorary Verma, Echo. You're sworn to protect him."

Whiskers twitched. "Oh, goodie. Another one."

Nightfall whinnied like he had reconsidered his decision to leave the Celestial Library.

Dad continued. "Then your brother called. So we sent a message to the library, and then suddenly, here you are." He dug in his pocket for his phone, an old Nokia, his fingers blundering over the keyboard. "He was calling from a telephone box in central London. He didn't have his mobile phone because he's tracking Phinnaeous in werepigeon form. He would only speak to you."

"Or he just wanted a peek at the naughty calling cards in the telephone booth," said Echo.

I took a deep breath. "Something has to be up. Maybe he lost track of Phinnaeous."

"I'll get him on the phone for you. His number is right here. Hang on," said Dad.

Mirabel's eyes flashed with exasperation. She held out her hand. "You're hopeless with that, Granddad."

Heat radiated through my chest. I'd never heard her call him that.

Dad's cheeks flushed with joy. He gave it to her. "My password is…"

"Rosalie's birthday, I know." Mirabel quirked an eyebrow, as cool as a cucumber. "What? It's not like I'm going to siphon off money from your bank account. Ezra and Alisha don't let me go anywhere alone."

"Bel!" I chided her, but not too much. She was a fire fairy, after all. I could handle a little backchat now she had found her voice again since her trauma.

Ezra had backed off to give Dad some space. He lounged against the counter, lit a roll-up and took a deep drag. "I thought Orpheus accompanied you."

I'd never seen him so on edge. "He's back at his club. He needed to feed."

A frown from Rob. "Orpheus usually regulates his needs too well to be caught short."

Marina and I exchanged glances as Mirabel handed me the phone. I placed the handset to my ear. It rang and rang, a blare in my eardrum, as my blood pressure rose. Finally, there was a scrambling noise, and my brother's nasal werepigeon voice came down the line, panicked and squawking.

I put him on speakerphone.

"You have to come, sis." A triumphant grunt. "I found them. I mean, I followed Phinnaeous, and the stupid old man led me straight to them. The gods. All gathered in a courtyard in Soho. I've been eavesdropping on their conversation, and after catch-up on their favourite television shows—a mix between fans of *The Witcher* and *Bake Off*—they've started getting down to the nitty-gritty. I'm going to return to my perch and listen in. Maybe you can bring the cavalry. Maybe you can nuke them all now."

The line went dead.

Dad hung his head in his hands. "It's so dangerous."

Echo roared. "This is our chance."

Rob shook his head. "No, it's not. We'd need the lie of the land. We can't just target them in the middle of Soho. There are civilians there. Who knows how it would play out. And we'd need the Prime Sorcerer on board."

My mind whirred. "Rob's right. It'll be a massacre if we mobilise Wildwoods forces in the middle of London. We're dealing with Death. She doesn't care about collateral damage. Besides, I'd need the Book of Names, and we have no time to pussy foot around right now. I have to get to Sahil."

Dad moaned.

"Alisha," murmured Ezra. "Do you trust your brother?"

I bit my lip. "Yes."

"Okay. Let's go after him." Grey eyes on mine. "We'll stake the joint, see what we're up against."

I shook my head, wanting to tell him everything, every tiny detail of my experience. An outpouring of my day to the man who loved me. But there was no time. "I think we might stand less chance of detection if I go alone. There's something you should know."

I whispered in his ear.

His head jerked back, and then he whistled low and long. "You did it." He cupped my face in his hands. "I'm so proud of you."

"I know. Want to watch?" A glance in the round, lingering on Mirabel and Dad. "I'll be back with Sahil before you know it." Then, I led the way into the night, pausing out of sight next to the enormous yellow skip.

Ezra kissed the top of my head. "You're sure about this?"

I nodded and rubbed my hands on my trousers. "Here goes nothing."

I didn't have to undress. My falcon mass was much smaller than my regular mass. When I shifted, the clothes just fell off. Recalling the rituals I had carried out in the Grove of Tomorrows, I grounded myself in the environment. Not the honking cars and smoky exhaust pipes. Not the neighbour cursing at a stray football or the smashed pint glass on the sidewalk. I focused on natural elements. The cloud of vapour from my mouth in the cold air. The stars dotted in the sky. The boughs shedding their last leaves. The withered council planters. The tiny triangle of lawn in the driveway across the road. The sharpened sight of my falcon form and how it had felt to soar.

My skin stretched and twisted. The sensation wasn't painful, more strange. I leaned into the strangeness as my form changed—the claws, the beak, the feathers—eager to claim the freedom and clarity again.

Suddenly, I was airborne.

Ezra's whoop of joy followed me skywards. He stood riveted, watching my progression.

My gaze turned towards my destination as I raced over chimney stacks and outer London parks. I'd read somewhere that the peregrine falcon was the fastest bird in the world. I put that theory to the test in my urgency to reach my brother, zipping through the sky. I sliced through the darkness, bird bones melding with aerodynamic forces. Minutes later, I soared over Leicester Square, over a red-carpet movie premiere, comedy clubs and theatres towards Soho with its free-spirited nightclubs, massage parlours, restaurants and sex shops.

I scanned the area, my falcon eyesight keen enough for me to note the gay couple tongue-fencing underneath a lamppost. The Dorothy of Oz living statue peeved at passersby who took a photo but left no coin. The vacant-faced woman who touted for business dressed in patent leather and wedge shoes. The old Chinese man drinking bubble tea with his granddaughter on an iron bench underneath swinging lanterns.

Soho was the perfect place for a meeting of the gods.

Even in their true forms, who would blink an eye at strangeness here? Where so many shed their skin to reveal their true selves, where everyone basked in a red glow and dipped into the shadows, where flamboyant costumes were the norm and risqué choices were preferable to staid normality?

A jolt of recognition as I spotted Sahil, with his werepigeon bearing, his muscly grey chest oddly upright for a bird, his feathers too bedraggled to be beautiful. He perched on a rooftop overlooking a pub courtyard strung with fairy lights. I landed next to him clumsily, still not fully accustomed to my new form.

A small group sat in the courtyard, which was otherwise

empty. It was winter, after all. Most customers preferred to down their brews inside, cherishing the sticky charm of British pubs.

This group had good reason to seek privacy.

It was a queen's court, with Death at its centre. Matted hair sat atop her black-blue naked torso. Instead of a skirt of rotting human arms, she wore an oddly romantic straw skirt that she could have picked up on the beach in Honolulu. Perhaps even Soho wasn't the place for her true self. The necklace of severed heads adorned her neck, but tonight, it seemed like a Halloween prop. Ornate bracelets clanged on her wrists, and her nails were filed to a point.

She wasn't alone. Courtiers hung on her every word: Ra, Hermes, Mami Wata, Cardea and Phinnaeous, cowering with fear but determined to have a seat at the table. Five gods all in one place, plus a weasel. Not that they made space for him.

Gods didn't rub shoulders with mortals.

Not without an agenda.

Sahil pecked at me, fiery eyes in a green-tinged head flashing me a warning. "This roof is mine."

I spun around, slightly smaller than him. "It's me, you buffoon."

A shrill *kree-kree-kree* came from my mouth before I realised I couldn't speak in my peregrine falcon form, at least, not like he could. Damn it.

The werepigeon flattened himself to the roof to avoid detection.

Oops. I racked my brain, wondering how to reveal my identity, but it was probably best to wait until the fireworks were over. He probably thought I'd left him in the lurch. Never mind, explanations would have to wait.

Sahil gave me a side-eye while I moved some distance away but still close enough to hear the action.

Ignoring him, I tilted my head, allowing the wind to carry the voices across the courtyard.

Elevated above the action, my heartbeat was calm. My falcon form seemed removed from my human one. My hatred for the actions of the rogue gods was present but muted, my thinking clearer, my perspective broader, like it had been in the Grove of Tomorrows, less prone to seesawing emotion.

We were spectators here. That was all.

There was nothing to worry about.

"So much for your dream of peculiars living out in the open, shapeshifter," Death raged, blue arms flailing, threatening the spread of wine glasses and pints of beer. "We had a deal, and you failed me. You come crawling back, having delivered the grand sum of *nothing*. The Book of Names is in the wind. The eternal girl is still a thorn in my side. Her talents and confidence grow by the day. It was your job to make her small. To disarm her. Tell me why I shouldn't take you to hell?"

She made it all his fault when I had bested each and every one of the gods sitting around her table.

Phinnaeous Shine trembled. He'd thinned out and needed a barber.

"I have much to offer you still. A knowledge of the school and the players involved. The senate's likely strategies. The girl's weaknesses." This wasn't the professor I remembered heading the senate or enthralling classes with his haughty knowledge. It was a man without a shred of dignity who had pissed away all his privileges. He could have learned from his errors, but instead, he doubled down.

Lavinia and Rob had concocted a brilliant plan.

Death lunged towards him, her hair a black cloud about her. "And what do you want in return?"

Phinnaeous flinched from her breath in his face. "The death of my enemies. A return to the seat of power. For immortals and peculiars to walk the earth. Never to have to hide our powers again."

Ra, dressed in his customary boiler suit, rescued his beer and took a sip. Froth lined his upper lip, and yet all I could think of was the blood he had on his hands. "You are a dreamer, old man. Yet you act like a thug."

Death toyed with her necklace of severed heads. "Like us, he forces his imprint on the world." A sly smile and promise in her coal-black eyes. "He is our thug."

Phinnaeous bowed his head, quivering like he needed a lie-down.

Not that I cared. I was hoping he might get his comeuppance. More's the shame.

"We know what is coming," said Death. "The Creator is gone, so we will create in His stead. When we are finished, unrestrained lust will be socially acceptable. Sin will rule over virtue. Ideologies will become entrenched, leaving only division." She pointed to Cardea's blackened fingers. "Ancient and new diseases will spread, riddling the world with sickness. Addictions will become the norm. The climate will degrade, bringing sulphur storms and ice ages. Wars will break out. Governments will rise and fall like waves. Conceits will run rampant. Humans will crown themselves gods and gurus. We won't need prayers to survive. We will have chaos." She banged her bare breast. "We will have it all. And it all begins with my visits tonight."

Cardea and Mami Wata threw back their heads and laughed. They clinked wine glasses and poured the alcohol down their throats as if immune to its impact.

Mami Wata poured the remainder of the wine into spluttering Phinnaeous's mouth. "It's a shame *she* isn't here yet to join in the fun."

Death twisted her hair onto one shoulder, where it lay like a serpent. "She will come. Her nightly ritual at that café is a holy act for her."

Hermes, dressed all in black with a raven on his shoulder, turned to Death. "What of the traitor?"

I reeled with a flashback to how I had ripped him apart, conducting a symphony of crows. My heartbeat sped up, wondering which traitor would emerge into the courtyard. Was it Pan he meant for telling us about the Rejuvenation Pool at Shakespeare's Globe?

The blue goddess smiled. "Go wild. Crush his pigeon bones."

I froze in horror as the gods looked up at my brother.

Hermes opened his jacket, and a treachery of ravens flew towards us.

15

———————

Three ravens, so dark, their plumage could have been slicked in oil. Their croaking call filled the air and my head. Shaggy throat feathers gave them the look of the damned. Beady eyes fixated on their target. Birds that feasted on the decaying flesh of dead animals. Carrion eaters but also skilled predators who killed baby birds in their nests. Birds associated with loss and ill omens.

They landed on the rooftop, dwarfing him—and me—in size.

Fly away, you fool.

But he didn't. He twitched with fright, forlorn and alone. My brother would die. Worse, he would die thinking that I had left him in his hour of need.

The god's laughter carried on the wind. They'd always enjoyed blood sport.

The trio of ravens closed in on Sahil, making a deep quorking sound. He shifted to his spider form, hairy and bulbous, scuttling away from their thick bills as they pecked at him. He didn't even have his shield anymore.

I had to do something.

Instinct took over. I launched myself out of the shadows,

climbing high above the Soho rooftops, smoking chimneys and red-glow drinking holes.

Beneath me, Sahil shifted from spider to werepigeon to human form, red welts on his body. His voice switched like gears from squeaky to nasal to bewildered mortal fear. "Get off me, you rotters!"

With a wail of terror, Sahil, in his human body, took the noisiest raven in his hands. He flung it against a satellite dish with the force of a professional cricket player. The raven slithered to the floor, concussed, while Hermes glowered and Death led the others in taking bets on the outcome.

He shifted into his werepigeon form, finally cottoning on that Hitchcock had long ago proven that birds—especially en masse—had the advantage when attacking humans. At least as a werepigeon, he could dip and dive and fly out of the way. At least as a werepigeon, he had teeth hiding in his beak. He used his teeth to defend against the fury of the ravens at the fate of their friends.

This pair fought well together. Caw-caws interspersed with pecks and talons. Working in tandem as if they were lifetime mates.

High above my brother's ordeal, I pivoted, hovering in the air for a brief moment before diving at blistering speed, slicing through the air, talons ready. No one knew I was coming. No one expected a peregrine falcon to intervene in a fight between ravens and a muscly-chested pigeon.

More fool them.

My wings came in, and I dove, faster than a speeding bullet, to my brother's rescue.

Sahil flapped and squawked for help. He had me, even if he didn't know it.

I entered the fight, my talons ravaging the first raven, driving into its flesh, and gripping hard enough to do permanent damage. The raven's feathers glooped with blood. It stumbled, and my brother took his chance to finish it off, were-teeth flashing yellow in the night, the sound of ripping flesh puncturing the air.

Its mate came at me, fluttering up to leverage its talons.

But it wasn't as quick as me. It didn't have my speed or agility. Its talons paled in comparison to my sabres, like bringing a knife to a sword fight.

A pure sense of purpose filled me. I wasn't here to play or vocalise or prance about. While in my human form, the thought of killing animals shook me to my core. I believed in the druid concept that we all had our place in nature. Antpowder and mouse traps repulsed me. But in my peregrine falcon form, I had no such qualms about killing.

I was a bird of prey; it was in my nature.

I fought the remaining raven. A death match in the dark night under a crescent moon. We sparred on the rooftop, leaping and gaining inches before clawing each other, the Jericho necklace warm at my throat, but instinct told me to climb higher. So I soared upwards past the treeline and banks of clouds, then careened down, dive-bombing, twisting with my talons, my movements vicious poetry carved out in the sky. The last raven took a ferocious strike and ca-cawed. It struck out with a claw, desperately seeking revenge, nicking me, but its movements flurried where mine were exact.

I bled. A slashed wing, a bleeding neck.

But the raven fared worse.

It circled for advantage, but it was too slow. I hounded it onto the next rooftop and the next, out of reach of the power of the hollering, drunken gods and their wily minion Phinnaeous. There, Sahil returned to help me ravage it.

Clever birds but no match for shifters.

We felled the last bird, and I sprang back to take in our handiwork.

My brother turned his bloodied, werepigeon head towards me. Blood oozed from gashes all over his body.

"I'm not going to sleep with you, you know. I'm not into

falcons." One fiery eye assessed me, and then he gave a nasal coo. "Thanks for the save, though. I would have been toast without you."

With that, he swept off the roof, his wings beating hard.

Once an idiot, always an idiot.

I thanked my lucky stars we'd survived the encounter and cocked my head at a sudden movement in my field of vision. Every cell in my body grew alert.

The trio of mortally injured ravens reanimated across the rooftops. Their bones cracked into place, their necks straightened, and their wounds healed. But they didn't seem interested in me. They spun towards the courtyard, where their master waited.

I rose into the air for a view of the gods, breath stilling to see Gaia there.

She was glorious in an orange sari that brightened the dark and sat at Death's right hand.

A jolt of sorrow filled me before I spiralled into the air and swooped after Sahil to ensure his safety. I caught up with him over the premiere in Leicester Square, maintaining my distance as he shifted back into his human form in the shadows and ran across the red carpet, bloodied and bruised.

Security deduced him to be a threat. They brought him down hard, rugby scrum style.

The paparazzi leapt into action, snapping photos that would grace the tabloids in the morning.

My poor brother. I'm not sure this was what he envisaged for his fifteen minutes of fame. I turned into the night, secure in the knowledge of his safety.

16

———

I spiralled through the starry night under the glow of Great
Bear, Little Bear, Cassiopeia and Draco. Blood ebbed from
my wounds at a trickle rather than a gush, thanks to the Jericho
necklace. The discomfort didn't bother me. I didn't find a place
to rest. I pushed upwards, beyond the reach of human suffering.
Strong winds cleared my mind of attachments to loved ones.
The sense of freedom was heady. There was only me in the
skies. A peregrine falcon, one with nature, without any of the
debris and clutter that marred human lives. It was magical.

Yet, something tugged at me, mooring me to the earth,
gossamer threads that couldn't be snapped. Their faces came
to me in a rush—Dad, Ezra, Mirabel, Marina and Orpheus—
reels of memories unfolding in my head, jolting me with
yearning.

Death's plans echoed in my head.

My body responded. I plummeted back towards the city
lights, soaring over weary newspaper men leaving their
offices after setting the last edition, tipsy couples walking
home arm in arm and cleaners heading to offices for the
twilight shift. I flew over ordinary houses where grans baked

pies, dads helped with math homework, and mums nuzzled milky newborn heads. Where siblings fought over the last squeeze of the ketchup bottle, and dogs buried their bones under the sofa. I swooped over frosty grass, moist boughs, evergreen bushes and icy puddles.

It was a world worth saving.

With an abrupt pivot, I made a beeline across the city.

MARINA LAY outstretched on her plush purple sofa in her living room boudoir. She hadn't drawn the curtains, and the gothic chandelier illuminated the room, allowing those at street level to peek into her world. A ball python, which she'd brought up from the surgery, slithered in a large cage on her shag pile rug. The television was off, and a half-empty glass of red wine sat on the side table. A half smile flitted over her lips at a Bon Jovi tune blaring from the bathroom, where Rob showered.

I watched her from my perch in the chestnut tree outside her open window.

The blue goddess came, appearing in Marina's living room without the need to ring the doorbell or breaking and entering. Because she was Death, and Death could walk wherever the living could and had no need for invitations.

It all begins with my visits tonight, she had said tonight. And now I understood.

I jittered with panic, but she had no weapons. She merely stood, smoking her cigarette, eyeing the dance pole in the middle of the room. Rob's playlist had moved to "Losing My Religion" by R.E.M.

Marina sat up, cotton-blue eyes wary. "I knew you would come."

"I like you," said Death. "You are a sexual deviant like

me. Although you could tone down your colour palette. You're a little Acid Barbie."

Marina stuck her chin out. "Jessica Rabbit, actually. And I'm nothing like you."

Death clenched her fists. "Just imagine what this world could be. Just think of all the barriers that would be knocked down. All you have to do is bring the Book of Names to me."

We'd kept the location of the book a secret from Marina, but she gave it to Death with both barrels anyway. I never could have lived without her.

"If you knew anything about me, you'd know I won't betray my friend." She extracted the ball python from its cage and waved it at Death. "I have a whole shop of horrors downstairs if you want more of this. Balding guinea pigs, a spaniel suffering from diarrhoea, vomiting hamsters and a diabetic Labrador that will eat anything it can get its jaws into."

"Puh-lease. I swim with serpents in the underworld." Death's laugh twisted into quiet confidence. "All those creatures you've lost on the surgical table. The guilt you feel. I can resurrect them. Your dead parents, who always misunderstood you—you can have them back. Prove to them who you are."

Marina glared at her. "I said no."

In the corridor leading to the kitchen, my falcon eyes glimpsed a shifting in the shadows. Rob emerged, a damp towel riding low on his hips. The shower still ran, and the playlist still cycled through its tracks. Marina really had known Death would come. She and Rob had prepared.

Rob's towel dropped. Marina was a lucky woman. Without missing a beat, he pointed a gleaming gun at Death's forehead. "You heard the lady."

Death blew rings of cigarette smoke into his face. "It's your funeral, sweet cheeks."

She vanished, leaving the burning embers of her cigarette on the shag pile rug.

Marina's hands trembled as she placed the snake back in its cage. "I hope the other two cope as well."

Rob put the safety back on his gun. "Your warnings mean they will be prepared. The vamps say Orpheus is himself again. And your vision of us on the battlefield means they'll both survive the night."

"I hope you're right." Marina sank her head into her hands. "Where the hell is Alisha?"

My heart was a stone in my feathered breast as I disappeared into the night.

THE BILLIARDS ROOM of Orpheus's gentleman's club in Charing Cross held the last stragglers of the night slumping over dregs of whisky. I swooped alongside the Georgian building, past the shuttered and curtained windows, scanning for access, any access at all.

Orpheus's voice filled my head before I found him tucked away in the basement, towards the back of the building. *Stay out of sight, little birdie.*

I fluttered down onto a drain adjacent to cloudy glass block windows. Relief flooded me. There he was in low lamplight reading at his desk, healed but wan. He wore joggers and an overstretched grey T-shirt, his goatee unkempt.

Death is coming, I said.

She is already here, said Orpheus.

"Quite the outfit you have here." Death sidled up to him, oozing sexual prowess. "A club full of vampires and a six-handed masseur serving the Otherworld. You don't seem scared of me, vampire. Why is that?"

Hooded eyes full of pain. "I have spent half my existence craving oblivion."

"There is room for you at my side. All you have to do is bring me the Book of Names."

I shuttered my mind to him, afraid he'd draw out the secrets of where the book lay.

Orpheus closed his book with a snap. "Why would I do that?"

Her lip curled. "Because you are sick of the guilt. The demon bone in your side only brought out what was already there. You yearn to take the druid's blood. How long has it been, vampire, since you last took a fresh drink from an innocent, rather than feasting on the arseholes that the Prison Service sends your way? And I thought vampires liked to be spontaneous. It turns out you're just a self-denying heap of dry skin."

Orpheus pushed back his chair and drew himself up to full height. "You nearly drove me to kill someone dear to me. If you wanted me on your side, perhaps you should have played your cards differently."

Death's four hands gripped the desk. She leaned forward as the decapitated heads writhed on her necklace. "I can bring back all those you have lost during your long life. For one little exchange."

Orpheus didn't flinch; his voice, though thin, was dismissive. "Nothing of your offer tempts me. I might be a vampire, but meeting you has made me convinced of one thing—life is sacrosanct."

A blue-black hand snatched out to lift him as if he weighed nothing. "Then why should I keep you alive?"

Orpheus's eyes were bleak with nihilism. "You'll be doing me a favour."

She believed him and dropped him like a stone. "I can make you mortal again, vampire."

He stilled, a vein throbbing in his temple.

A slow smile spread across Death's face. She plucked a small bronze bell from her skirt of rotting arms.

"To summon me when you have it." Then she disappeared into the swell of the night.

A burst of vampire speed brought Orpheus to the window, barefoot, tousled, his eyes shadowed.

I stared at him a moment, then sprang into the air.

"Alisha, come back," said Orpheus. "Come back, dammit."

His shouts faded with the beat of my wings.

Death wasn't finished, and neither was I.

I LANDED in a bare ash tree, relying on my blue-grey feathers to camouflage me.

The blue goddess rapped her knuckles against our cottage door. With four fists, it sounded like the drum section of a jungle track. How odd that the goddess would knock rather than pierce the safety of our sanctuary like she had done with everyone else.

My tiny heart thudded, and I fought the urge to rush to my family's aid.

Death had no gleaming twin of my sword in her hands. She didn't mean to kill; she meant to corrupt. Though I had no reason to doubt Ezra or Mirabel, we had to know what we were up against.

Ezra opened the door, eyes wild with worry. "Alisha—"

The outside lantern cast a pool of light around the goddess. His face twisted into horror.

Death lifted her foot and tried to cross the threshold but met invisible resistance. Her silken voice reminded me of a snake. "You are well prepared, wolf. This is deep magic. Not many can delay my entry. There is something familiar in its signature, perhaps the witch's work." She cast her coal-black eyes around our pitted moonlit garden. "It's a shame my army of the dead didn't unearth the book, but no matter. We'll get there in the end. The end *is* coming."

Ezra was dressed in his seeker clothes—jeans, a moth-eaten T-shirt and scuffed trainers—like he'd been out with his pack. Like he'd been looking for me. He set his jaw. "Is this what gods and goddesses have been reduced to? Visiting like door-to-door salesmen as their chances dwindle? You wouldn't be here unless you were rattled."

"I am always rattled, wolf. Everything God told you was a lie. Death knows no contentment, only yearning." The blue goddess thrust out a hip, and her skirt of rotten arms swung in the wintery air. "It's not much different to the living really. I can sense those deep pockets of pain inside you, Ezra Neuhoff. The losses you have endured. I know what you want."

Grey eyes flashed. "I want you to go crawling back to the hole you came from."

"Liar." Death's voice carried on the wind. "What's a little secret in exchange for the chance to see your parents and uncle grow old? Such pitiful deaths."

His chiselled face was an open wound. "They are my past, not my future."

It pained me to look at him. What would he give to undo the hurts of the past? To have a second chance at relationships lost to time? To be able to say all the things he hadn't been able to say, to ask questions that burned a hole in his heart? And yet, I doubted him less than I doubted myself. Ezra Neuhoff was as good and honourable as they come. Capable of violence, yes, but not capable of betrayal.

But Death had a way of unearthing the core of someone's nature, like a dancer who always found the right steps to the rhythm. "Then Alisha Verma will die."

Ezra's handsome face stretched into a snarl. "Death does not control fate."

"That is true. But I've always been excellent at sensing momentum. The skidding of a car filled with joyriders. The stuttering of a plane engine before it plummets. The powdery thrust of an avalanche. The build-up of tar on a smoker's lungs. The blind courage of heroines before their eventual fall. I thank fairy tales for deceiving humans into believing that good always wins. And I have so many pieces in play." The blue goddess leaned closer. "I hope you remember that I tried to help you when you are burying your remaining family."

An animalistic growl erupted from Ezra. He reached against the inside wall of the cottage and levelled Transcender against her neck, though the doorstep separated them.

"Not before you," he said.

The blue goddess giggled, suddenly playing seductress, as though Transcender's obsidian blade at her throat was a mere flirtation. "You would kill an unarmed woman? There *is* dishonour in you, wolf. I am pleased." Throwing back her matted head of hair, she laughed with abandon. "You're incapable of besting a warrior with millennia of experience. A blink and that sword will be twisting in your stomach."

Ezra's neck corded. "I despise you."

From my perch, I willed him on. The two of us could end this now. Without Death, the other gods were easier to overcome. With Morpheus dead, that would leave only four. With the main threat gone, maybe we could target them one by one, away from humdrums.

It wouldn't be difficult to best gods we already knew how to beat.

I fluttered above the ash tree, ready to descend with haste and shift back into my druid form. To attack the blue goddess from behind as Ezra attacked from the front. Together, we could overcome her. Here, on home terrain, under the cover of night.

The blue goddess's words spiralled into the sky. "If you want that to do lasting damage to me, the sword is only half of the puzzle. Otherwise, all it takes is a dip in a Rejuvenation Pool for a new me. You see, I have more planned than just the Wild Hunt. That was just foreplay."

My mind flashed back to reading from the Book of Names, then plunging Transcender into the dream god's stomach before he faded from sight. Fear snaked up my spine. Did that mean that Morpheus could return? I filed away the nugget of information and vowed that Death's boastful nature would be her downfall.

Copper-grey eyes flashed upwards, pleading with me to stay hidden.

Death was too busy enjoying herself to notice. Spite flowed in her veins like blood. "I pity you. All that pent-up love, and you can't even protect your family. Has the fairy child broken the yoke of her parental chains yet?"

Ezra's body tensed, on the verge of springing. If he shifted into his wolf and went outside, I feared Death would put him down like a dog. His voice was a howl. "What have you done?"

"I just whispered in her ear," she purred.

Death stalked into the wintery night, lips curved in a delighted smile.

Ezra clutched Transcender's hilt, shaking with anger. Long moments passed before he breathed a shuddering sigh of relief and looked at the ash tree. "You can come out now."

17

———

I plunged downwards, shifting just before I fell to my knees on the cold ground outside the doorstep, where the blue goddess had stood moments before. In human form, the cuts and bruises inflicted by the crows stung like hell.

Ezra dropped to the ground and wrapped me in his arms. "I don't know whether to kill or kiss you right now. You've been gone for hours. I nearly went out of my mind."

A wry smile. "It's not like I could call. I don't even have a voice in falcon form." Panic flared in my belly. "What about Death's goading? Where's Bel?"

He cupped my face. "Listen to me, Alisha. She's safe at Wildwoods with Echo. I thought it was safer for her to be there when Marina said she'd had a vision about Death visiting me here. Those things Death said about the whispers. They're all lies. Lying is all she has."

"What are Bel and Echo doing at Wildwoods?"

"She's signed up for one of Aunt Isadora's combat sessions." A wry smile. "Isadora said she'd give them a lift home. It doesn't take a second now that the coven can teleport."

Tears filled my eyes. "I need to see her, Ezra. I need to see Bel."

Grey eyes raked over my body. He swore under his breath. "Let's clean you up first, okay? You look like you've been through the wars."

He helped me to my feet slowly, as if I was made of glass.

"There's so much I need to tell you." A wave of exhaustion crashed over me. I frowned, my thoughts carouselled until I couldn't keep them apart, memories tangling.

"Take a breath, Alisha. I remember the first few times I shifted. It's disorienting." He cradled me against his side, led me into the house and locked the door behind us as if such a small precaution would keep out all the ghouls and demons that hunted us. He draped a blanket around me and scooped me into his arms. "Let me look after you."

I sank against him, no longer needing to be strong.

My heartbeat galloped as my eyes fluttered open. It slowed only when I recognised the familiar mattress dipping beneath me. How long had I floated in and out of consciousness?

Snatches returned to me. Ezra mopping my body with a warm washcloth dipped in diluted antiseptic, his voice soothing. Salve applied to my wounds. A comb teasing the knots out of my hair. A duvet drawn over me that smelt of us. A rough kiss on my forehead. An uneasy sleep deepening into oblivion.

I turned my head on the pillow, and my neck twinged with stiffness. The night was still dark enough to need a lamp.

Ezra lay on top of the bedspread beside me, head

propped up in his hand. Deep blue shadows lay beneath his eyelashes. Stubble lined his cheeks. "Hey, you."

I smiled. "How long have I been asleep?"

"Barely a cat nap." His eyes glinted. "I ought to strap you to the bedposts, so you have to rest."

"I'll look forward to that. But we have to—"

"Stop." He got up on his knees and pulled me up to face him. "We've been tumbling through the past weeks and months, Alisha. All I want to do is stop just for a minute and look at your face. To learn the curve of your cheeks, the arch of your eyebrows and the laughter lines just there." He traced the crevices of my mouth with his calloused thumb.

"Ezra Neuhoff, you old romantic."

"When you flew away after your brother outside Shanghai Moon, I was so proud and so scared. And when you didn't come back straight away, I could barely function."

I reached out to him. "I'm fine, I promise."

"No, let me finish." He cleared his throat and rubbed the back of his neck. "I don't get scared for myself. I was scared for you. And tonight, when the blue goddess told me that you will die—"

My stomach clenched. "She's wrong. She's pulling out all the stops to get someone to betray us."

Anguish twisted his face. "Maybe someone will. We can't control the game of the gods. We can't control the other players on the board. Dammit, we don't even know if we can trust my aunt. But we can control what *we* do—you and me. We can hold onto every bit of beauty we have together. This family of ours. It means everything."

I locked away my worries at the back of my head. We had earned this moment together. With everything coming for us, we might not have another one. Besides, I wasn't a teenager anymore. I couldn't run on empty without replenishing myself. Maybe I didn't want to talk about all the dangers and the traps around us. Maybe I wanted to be selfish for a change. I wanted to focus on something good.

I couldn't take my eyes off him. Calm, clear eyes. Soft lips. Tousled brown hair that greyed at the temples and was a fraction too long for him to be a suit. Rough, worker's hands that I always wanted on my body. The charm necklace at his neck. The smattering of stubble across his chiselled jaw. Low-slung jeans and a concave belly. The scent of earth and roll-ups and mountain air. The way he carried me through the universe in his arms. The danger he never baulked from. The father he was. The friend he was. The lover he was. The quiet promise in his eyes that he would make me his world.

When he already had.

My scalp prickled as he reached into the pocket of his jeans. The world slowed. There was only me and him. Our bedroom and our mingled breath, the wind howling outside. Our clothes heaped on the floor. Our need and our love.

He pulled out a small, blue velvet box. "I was going to wait until after this is all over. I had it all planned out. Flowers, a moonlight serenade, a European mountaintop where the wind swept through your hair, and I went down on one knee. But this feels right." He opened it and lifted out a ring. His voice thrummed with emotion. "It was my mother's engagement ring. I never wanted to give it to anyone until I found you."

"Oh!" My stomach fluttered, my skin flushed.

The ring was exquisite: a pear-shaped diamond on a platinum band. My eyes widened as the slightest touch of his thumb and forefinger revealed three layered bands inside—representing the celestial equator, declination and the meridian—engraved with astronomical symbols. The entire universe on my finger.

I was the luckiest woman alive.

My werewolf lover, so often an outsider, had found family with me. Somehow, in between my divorce and falling foul of Death, I had found family with him. My marriage with Alex had been like trying to force two magnets together at the same charged end. It seemed like only yesterday that the thought of remarrying made me want to run for the hills with Marina. Life was hard. The people we chose to spend time with should build us up, not tear us down—straighten our crowns, not stomp on them. Being with Ezra had healed my fractured heart, but was I ready for this?

His brow furrowed. "Alisha?"

My heart pounded, and my palms grew sweaty.

I didn't want to jump into marriage this time. I wanted to come at it clear-headed, with my logic satisfied and my heart full. I wanted to be a hundred per cent sure that I wasn't being foolish. That I wasn't giving away more of myself than I wanted. That I wouldn't regret it when we were both old and haggard and could only eat soup and soggy bread for dinner. I wanted to be sure that the glow of love would remain when I brought him his tatty slippers or he helped do the zipper up on my jacket.

I couldn't take heartbreak again. Not when my love for Ezra shone brighter than the sun.

Once you'd had the sun, how could you live without it?

I paid attention to how Ezra made me feel: nourished intellectually, emotionally and physically. If I said no to him, I would regret it for the rest of my life. I didn't need a get-out clause.

My face open like a sunflower, I inched closer to him. Tingling with joy, I held my breath.

Copper danced in his eyes. "Alisha Verma, I love you, every inch of you. Indian-French you. Druid you." He chuckled. "Feathered you. I love how you throw yourself into adventures and are always ready to fight for what you believe in. I love how you nurture Mirabel. How your eyes light up when you see me and how your laughter fills me up." He lifted the ring. It gleamed in the lamplight. "They say the world is falling apart, but I won't believe it. Because my world is you." A pause punctuated by his ragged breath. "Will you marry me?"

I leaned in to kiss him. The duvet cover dropped as I melted into him. Our lips clung to each other, tinged with hope. When I pulled back, I breathed a word against his face, and I'd never been more certain of anything. Never been more sure of putting my fractured heart on the line.

"Yes."

I held out my ring finger.

Ezra's grey-copper eyes fired with intensity as he slipped it on.

It sat snugly as if it had always belonged there. I stared at it.

He gripped my hips and pushed me back onto the mattress, a growl in his throat. "You're mine now. I'm never letting you take it off again."

My dark hair fanned out behind me. I glanced down, lashes shielding my expression, suddenly shy. "I've been yours since the moment we met."

"Prove it."

My body was still tender from the ravages of the night, but the bulk of him on top of me stoked my desire. I didn't care about the soreness or exhaustion. He was the balm I craved. He was everything. I raked my hands through his hair and brought his lips to mine, tasting him, our tongues exploring, teeth nibbling, a kiss so sweet and poignant that it scared me. His hand moved to the peak of my breast, and I moaned.

I pulled at the barrier of his T-shirt, frustration mounting. "You're fully dressed. That's not fair."

He pulled it off with a throaty chuckle, enjoying the proof of my desire. A cocked eyebrow. "Does that satisfy you, madam?"

I fumbled with his belt. "And the jeans and boxers. Quick."

He undressed, but when he got back into bed, he slipped his fingers inside me, his eyes drinking their fill of me. "We'll take it slow. I want to savour every moment."

I moaned and flung my head back, losing my bearings, surrendering to him as his tongue darted around my nipples and his fingers found the softest part of me. He explored me, diving, kneading until my toes pointed like a dancer's, and I quivered at his touch. When I couldn't take any more, I straddled him, wanting him to gasp like I did.

I didn't let him enter me. Not yet. A slow, sensual smile as I lifted my palms, scooping up a pair of silken scarves from the bedroom chair that we had used during sex before. Without a word, I tied him to the bedposts. My being in charge turned us both on. I could see it in his greedy gaze like no other thought existed in his head except me. I lowered my breasts onto his chest, grazing him, teasing him, as he begged me with his ragged breath to get closer. I sent a shiver of wind down his taut stomach, over his erection and his muscular thighs. He trembled with desire, and I moved my body to cover his, sucking his earlobes, and his bottom lip, trailing kisses with excruciating slowness down to where he throbbed.

Ezra groaned, and something more carnal took over. He wrenched his hands free of their silken bondage. His hands swam up my thighs and squeezed my arse, staying there as he raised his mouth to my breasts, pulling the tight buds of my nipples with his teeth. I responded in kind, biting the contours of his shoulders, leaving bursts of kisses on his chest, my hand dropping down to cup him, the air hot between us.

I ached for him and needed desperately to be closer. I slipped him inside me, utterly ready to receive him. His grip on my buttocks tightened, and our breath came in short bursts. I rode him, rocking my pelvis and rotating my hips. He flipped me over effortlessly and took over, slow and rhythmic, then faster and deeper until he called out my name, and sweet spasms rocked us both.

We soared together like birds before plummeting down to earth.

Afterwards, he picked up the duvet from the floor and pulled it over us.

Salty tears ran down my face and into my mouth as we sank back against the pillows. The sex had been so intense that it had seemed like a farewell. Could the universe play such an awful joke on us? Gift us to each other, bring us Mirabel, only to take it all away?

I shuddered at the thought and turned my face to his. "Why now, Ezra? Why did you decide to ask me now?"

He tucked me into the nook of his arm, where I could be pliant or strong, quiet or passionate, angry or patient, reckless or calm. Any version of myself that I chose.

"Because I want you to understand the promise I am making you. I'll be here for you even when the world is darkest. Even if it falls apart." Then he folded my hand into his and kissed the ring he had given me.

Ezra would be my husband, and I would be his wife.

A promise to savour despite the coming dark.

In the glow of that promise, I told him everything, snagging on the details that hurt—Gaia's presence at the Soho pub, Death's visit to Orpheus and the little calling bell she'd left him, how I had feared Sahil would die, Death's plans for chaos—but also the good. How Orpheus's injury had unpicked his tightly controlled vampire nature, how the Grove of Tomorrows had unlocked deeper access to my druid self, my soaring flight, the headiness and freedom of being yourself but not quite yourself.

Ezra told me of the first time he had shifted when he'd been fourteen years old, how scared he had been when his bones cracked despite the pack trying to prepare him. Then we slept, tangled in each other's arms, daring to dream of the future.

In the deep of the night, I stretched out, and Ezra wasn't there. I sat bolt upright, heart pounding.

He found me in the dark, stumbling into my dressing gown.

"Echo and Bel are home. She's already sound asleep. Come back to bed, my love." He slipped the gown from my shoulders, scooped me up and tucked me back in as if I were a child.

"I could get used to this." I curled up against him.

The sound of his heartbeat lulled me to sleep.

18

The toaster pinged. I picked out thick slices of granary bread, smeared them with marmalade, cut them into triangles and laid out three plates. My engagement ring glinted in the morning light, but Echo didn't notice. Animals didn't care for jewellery, not even the lapdogs dressed in Burberry and jewel-encrusted collars.

"So you're a bird now," said Echo. "At least you're not a chicken or a duck or an emu. Or, god forbid, a pigeon. They don't have much gravitas. But we can work with a falcon."

Ezra poured coffee into two mugs and pushed one across the counter to me. He grinned, enjoying the secret that shimmered between us. "She's my bird."

The leopard continued, oblivious. "You'll be pleased to know that Marina twisted an arm to get Nightfall his own paddock near the surgery. She cleaned him up, sorted out some fresh hay and gave him some Granny Smith apples. Unfortunately, he wasn't used to being locked in at night with all the freedom at the Celestial Library and got all skittish, so she moved him to Wildwoods. The Bestiary Master said he's free to roam the grounds unless he empties his bowels all over the place. Luckily, being a clever pegasus,

Nightfall has promised to only defecate outside Helio's office. There was a standoff with the sphinxes, but I settled that by chasing Nightfall, pretending I wanted to eat his juicy rump. He ended up having the best gallop of his life."

"What an introduction to his new home." I sighed. "He's going to end up wanting to go straight back up to the stars."

"When you said you were going to face death alone, wolf, I worried you were feeling morbid because Alisha outshines you. Just like the great Rajika Verma outshone her contemporaries. I didn't think you were actually going to face the blue goddess." He licked his paws in the middle of the kitchen like a king at court while I tripped over him to get to the sink.

Ezra raised an eyebrow. "I didn't break a sweat, mate."

I washed out the empty marmalade jar and flung it in the recycling. "I was in the tree watching it all. He was brilliant."

"But did you tell her the most important thing? That we would rather exist only on legumes for the rest of our lives than betray Alisha," said Echo.

"Yes, I told her exactly that," deadpanned Ezra.

"Oh, good. Living with me has obviously rubbed off on your sensibilities. Stick with us. We will make something of you yet, wolf." He strutted around the kitchen, humming a tune.

I patted Ezra's arm in sympathy. We'd been trying to block out Echo's woeful singing since 8 a.m. "I've been thinking about forking out for some singing lessons for you, Echo, but I've changed my mind."

Emerald eyes shone with mirth. "Perhaps concentrate on forking out the salmon in that tin, Alisha. That way, I won't have to eat the neighbour's husky. Although, I might be doing her a favour. He is very vocal." With no hint of irony, he launched into his fifth rendition of "Wild Thing" by The Troggs, which he'd found amusing since finding out about my new wilding abilities.

It turned out his rock phase was even more annoying than his pop phase.

Mirabel padded out of her bedroom to the kitchen, bundled up in an oversized hoodie and joggers, her face bleary with sleep. She flopped on the leopard, and they tumbled to the floor together. "You're the best, Echo, but you're a brutal alarm clock." She turned her eyes to me. "I've missed you at home."

Home. She called the cottage home. I kept my voice steady as I set down Echo's bowl of fish and pressed a kiss to the top of her head. "I've missed you too."

A shy look at me from under thick lashes. "So, can we go out and try out our wings together at some point, just you and me? Like, maybe St. James's Park after dark?"

I nodded. "Sure. How did it go last night at Isadora's class at Wildwoods?"

Mirabel tucked into her toast. "It's pretty fun. Sometimes, she just chucks a load of weapons in the arena, and it's a free-for-all. Or she has us line up like we're at a gym class at Baba Yaga's and wants us all synchronised. Real battles aren't like that, but it's pretty fun hanging out and hitting stuff and not having to be at our desks."

"What did you think, Echo?" I said.

Echo polished off the last of the salmon. "They play at schoolyard fisticuffs. It's harmless until a broomstick ends up in someone's eye."

Mirabel wrung her hands together, marmalade smeared in the corner of her mouth. "I was wondering if I could go to the one today. The sphinxes promised a bit of rough and tumble."

I exchanged glances with Ezra, Death's words playing on our minds. "I don't know. It's Saturday. Besides, I don't know if you should be messing around with your fire fairy skills like that, Bel. It's not just fangs or claws you're dealing with. Fire is deadly."

She jutted out her chin. "I'm supposed to sit on the sidelines just because I'm powerful? That's not fair. You don't do that. And all the girls are talking about how we want to be your backup. Lots of them would have been picked for the Kraglek trial until you came along. We're valuable team members. Isadora said it herself."

I bit my lip, anger swelling in my chest. Isadora shouldn't have been feeding them all this nonsense. They weren't wind-up dolls. Just the thought of them on the battlefield made me sick to the stomach. "Bel, whatever is going on, whatever Isadora has been telling you, this isn't a kids' game. You need to leave it to the adults."

She chewed her lip. "I know that. I'm not an idiot."

Ezra folded his arms across his chest. "No one's come and whispered in your ear?"

Her cheeks burned with embarrassment. "A couple of boys, maybe. I'm kind of the cool girl now I live with you two. Can we talk about something else now?"

"Sure, kiddo." Ezra locked eyes with me. "Maybe we should let her go. Anything untoward, and I can be with her in a flash."

Echo honked with laughter. "Like extracting a sneezing toddler from a ball pit."

Mirabel cringed, her eyes darting from me to Ezra.

For so long, she had avoided her friends. They poked at her grief and made her relive it, but with all the excitement over battle skills, the little wretches finally had something else to focus on. My gut told me I should say no; the world was too dangerous right now. But of course, teenagers wanted to spend time with their friends. It was perfectly natural. The threat of Death didn't mean we should live life any less fully. It meant the precise opposite.

I wanted to keep the mood light for as long as possible. Was that so bad? "You can go, Bel, as long as Echo stays with you."

The leopard sighed. "I am the definition of a glorified babysitter."

Mirabel bounced up and down on the stool, beaming. "Thank you. You're the best."

A glint in Ezra's eye. "Now that's sorted, shall we tell them?"

Mirabel frowned. "Tell us what?"

I held up my engagement ring, laughing as she rushed at us, and the leopard broke into the falsetto of The Darkness's "I Believe in a Thing Called Love."

My mobile phone rang, puncturing our joy far too soon.

I picked up the receiver and listened, my smile falling away. "Hi Rob…The dead are where?"

The detective's voice, funereal, stunned. "All over the city. We've had to move the monarch, the corgis, the PM and the cabinet to a secure location."

Fear snaked up my spine. At my expression, Ezra hurried to the living room to turn on the telly. Scenes of horror spilt out from BBC News, seasoned correspondents struggling to process what they saw, the dead streaming through the city like a virus, gangs of men roaming the streets with makeshift weapons, emergency vehicles abandoned with their sirens still blaring.

My eyes drifted to the ring that symbolised our future. "We'll come right away."

19

The dead roamed the city of London in polished brogues made by the blue goddess; shoes designed to bring vibrancy to dead feet. Though I had experienced many forms of magic, necromancy drove dread into my very bones, causing the hair on my nape to stand on edge, a weakness in my limbs and time to skew.

I made a group chat, fingers fumbling as dread rose in my throat, including all our loved ones: Dad, Alma, Sahil, Rajiv, Alma, Marina, Orpheus, Fei Yen, Faeza and Flinar. On a whim, I added Pan, using his mobile number on the Battersea Dogs Home website, and Gaia. Not that she ever checked hers. Not that I could even be sure that she was on our side. I sent the text. *Check the BBC. It's happening. The End of the World. Come to Wildwoods. Nowhere is safer.*

Ezra pressed Transcender into my hand and touched the Jericho necklace at my throat. "This is it."

I nodded. The lump in my throat hurt. "What about Tielbu and Nightfall?"

He shook his head. "Leave them where they are until we know more."

We stood in a circle, the four of us, and hurtled between

the worlds towards Wildwoods. The winter sun stole across the park, illuminating vast expanses of frosty green.

The unthinkable had happened, not in the dead of the night, but just after breakfast, with humdrum eyes wide open. This wasn't a small, contained area of the dead like the dozen Dad and I had fought at Streatham Cemetery. It was a contagion. Every minute that passed, corpses reanimated and clawed out of the city's graveyards. My stomach churned just thinking about the kids turning up for forest school or a Saturday wood-carving course in the woodland grounds of a cemetery to be met with a reanimated grandpa. Besides, London wasn't some backwater town where this could be hushed up. Images would be broadcast to the rest of the world, shaking the foundations of reality.

It couldn't get any worse.

The sphinxes, freed from their stone forms, stalked the boundary of the school as peculiars streamed past the yew tree. Lavinia had obviously come to the same conclusion as me: the Founder's Law about maintaining the secrecy of the Otherworld no longer mattered if the gods had already shattered the illusion. Phinnaeous Shine must have been jumping for joy.

"Go find your friends," I said to Mirabel. "Keep your phone on loud. Echo, keep her in your sights."

A hint of sorrow in his emerald eyes. Was this the look he had given to my grandmother the night she died when she had asked him to look after my brother and me and not accompany her? Then, the leopard bounded off after Mirabel.

Ezra took my hand as we wove through the crowds, his face grim. The cable cars heaved with passengers. All around, faces lined with worry, seeking advice and sanctuary until the storm passed. Small children still in their pyjamas with milk moustaches from their breakfast. Some had brought their pets with them. Others, torches and weapons.

I kept my head down, not wanting to be recognised.

When we reached the top of the track, the cable car ejected us onto the main rope bridge. We surged into the vaulted cabin and joined the senate at the front of the room. Rob hovered at the outer edges, face tight with anxiety.

The Prime Sorceress acknowledged our arrival with a nod. Her skin glowed like she'd taken a 6 a.m. spin class, followed by a power smoothie.

I'm starting to think your arrival in the Otherworld hastened the apocalypse, said Orpheus. *I still haven't apologised for what happened in the Grove of Tomorrows. And afterwards at my club. What you overheard…*

I whipped my head around to find him a few spaces along. *You don't need to apologise for falling prey to your nature. You were hurt. Your turning forced me to adapt. But why did you accept Death's bell?*

He hesitated. *Being mortal means to revel in the sweetness of life because it's finite. It's no secret that I miss it. Death took my hesitation as agreement because she believes that we all have dark souls waiting to be hers. Especially vampires. You don't doubt me, do you?*

No, I said. *I don't think I do.*

Good. The intensity of his gaze burned my cheek. *I sense new joy beneath the strain.*

I slipped off my ring and put it in my pocket, not wanting to hurt him, not wanting to lie and understanding that this needed to be a quiet moment between us, not a public one.

Ezra leaned his head to mine. "She's about to begin."

Lavinia raised her arms, and the room quietened. Her tone was bright and breezy, like she was a Scout leader rather than the head of London's Otherworld at a time of war. "My dear friends, I know you are scared, but everything is in control. My Peculiars' Senate has a plan. It is already in play. You have nothing to fear. Make Wildwoods your sanctuary. We are well prepared. You will find food and drink in the geography cabin. There are blankets and pillows in the history cabin. There will be stories and activities for children in the library. Sleeping quarters for families with children under ten are in the Latin and Aramaic cabins. Families with older children in the planetarium. Remaining adults in the herbology cabin. Those prone to accidental bursts of magic under stress should go to the spells cabin, which is already equipped with containment zones. The sanatorium is ready to tend to ailments. Those of you with healing skills may sign up for shift work there. Stay away from the bestiary unless you want to get bitten. The Bestiary Master tells me there is an outbreak of venomous spiders in there. Please inform the quill at the exit of your name as you leave the vaulted cabin so that we may be sure who is on the premises."

A wave of murmurs spread through the crowd. Murmurs of worry and confusion that only needed a match to ignite. Or a dissenting voice.

"We can't just leave our neighbours to fend off the dead. We want to help," said an ageing werewolf.

"I want to know what we're going to do about our city being overrun," said a fierce selkie. "Phinnaeous Shine wouldn't have taken this lying down."

Lavinia's voice cracked like a whip. "You have no idea what you are talking about. Phinnaeous Shine would have let this city burn. He's part of the rabble of immortals that has brought this about.

"We want to hear from her. From the eternal girl," shouted a flower fairy with a babe in arms.

All eyes turned to me, expectant with hope.

My palms grew clammy. I opened and closed my mouth like a goldfish, but I didn't have any resourceful ideas or any comfort to give. I was caught in a vortex of godly anarchy just like them. My mind whirled through all the pieces of the puzzle we had: the gods I had defeated, the ones I couldn't stop from spilling blood, the one I convinced to rediscover his faith, the weapons and skills we had won, my shattered faith in the Earth goddess, the relationships that had deepened and the love that had grown. I had done so much, but they still expected me to solve it all.

"She's a fraud," said the werewolf with a growl. "She can't help us any more than the senate."

I bumped up against the lie I had told myself all my life, that if I tried hard enough, I could control the world and other people's reactions to me. If I stayed out of the way of the mean girls at school. If I listened to those who demanded respect. If I over-delivered to my boss. If I kept the house clean. If I had the perfect family. If I stood taller or had whiter teeth or perfect skin or great hair.

Not knocking a good blow-dry. Those put a spring in a woman's step.

Why are you thinking about blow-drys? Say something, woman, said Orpheus. *Say anything. Give them hope.*

Ezra locked at me, concern on his face.

There in the vaulted cabin, as the dead ravaged the city and sun rays illuminated dust motes drifting across the crowd of peculiars, I understood an essential truth. My generosity would never be enough. I could only do my best. Critics would speak, even when they had no skin in the game. All I could do was out my best self into the universe and accept what eventually shook out. Like a cosmic slot machine.

Though I was scared standing before the crowd—the ones I inspired, the ones who shook with fear, and those waiting for me to fail—I shed my self-doubt and the judgement of strangers. Gossipmongers and enemies became meaningless. I could speak my piece and withstand any toxicity.

"I'm a latecomer to this Otherworld." I looked at Ezra. "But if you know my family, you know what we stand for. Before the night is out, we may ask a lot of you. But we won't succeed without each other."

Calypso stepped forward to join me, her attire and

bearing immediately commanding attention. "Think about that before you spout rubbish at those who save your arse."

Lavinia arched a thin eyebrow. "Well said, Custodian. Now. Go, see to your families."

They dispersed, reluctantly at first, then in a flood, reciting their names to the inky quill and scroll that hovered above them. When they had gone, a small group of senators remained in the morning light beneath the soaring rafters and stained-glass windows.

Rob came forward. "I have surveillance teams on the ground. The dead are coming from a ring of seven graveyards built around the capital in the 1840s in response to the booming population. I'm getting reports of hundreds of the dead flowing into the city from each one, with famous residents cracking up their graves, too. Christina Rossetti, Emmeline Pankhurst, and Daniel Defoe." He swore. "Even the East End gangsters, the Kray twins. Let's bloody hope that in death, they are more placid than in life."

Margola pulled a pencil from her red chignon and flipped open her notebook. "It's quite the story. This is going to keep me busy for weeks."

"We need to shore up this place," said Erelim. Since falling from heaven, he'd been incapable of taking a stand, just in case he made the wrong call. "Those of us who can fly can retrieve food supplies. The yew tree will keep out the city. The dead will disintegrate with their shoes. We should wait it out."

Ezra bristled. He lit a cigarette and took a drag. Rings of smoke curled out of his mouth as he spoke. "I love this city and its people. We can't abandon them. My seekers and I can cover a lot of ground. We are strong, fast and fearless. Alisha has told us that the dead are not difficult targets. The blue goddess intends to bring chaos and blur the line that separates reality from the afterlife. But we can hold that line. We can put the dead back where they belong."

"Like the Justice Minister, I am used to covering large geographical areas, but I cannot see how it is possible to round up all the dead. The area is simply too vast. Unless we strike from above," said Calypso.

"The coven has umbrellas, and we could enchant more," said Isadora. "Some pupils are already proficient at riding them. It might take a week or a month, but we could pull it off. The fairies and angels could help."

Cillian shook his head. "Even with all the luck in the world, it would be impossible to strike from above without harming innocents. The plan is just too imprecise."

The kernel of an idea formed in my head. "We have an asset I think we can lean on. Pan isn't allied with the other gods. He found renewed belief when I confronted him after the tremors. He helped me locate the Rejuvenation Pool at Shakespeare's Globe. What if we can convince him to shepherd the dead with his pipes? Then the elves with their black hole magic could strip their brogues off, and the dead would just be a pile of old bones and skin again."

Ezra nodded slowly. "That could work. Pan could help us contain them."

"I'll coordinate with government labs to return the dead to the right graves," said Rob.

"It's a huge operation," said the Prime Sorceress. "The coven can round up stragglers in Otherworld taxis. We'll need a large contingent of vampires to roam the city and wipe humdrum minds. Vampires who can be trusted not to feed on the innocent."

Orpheus gave a curt nod. "It's a short list, but I'll see to it."

"We'll spread the usual story for international outlets." The chance of success infused Rob with renewed energy. "It was a training exercise, etcetera. The world already thinks Brits are eccentric. A little retrospective doctoring of footage, some deepfakes, and we can take control of the narrative again."

"Excellent." Lavinia frowned, looking around at the nine senators gathered. "Where's Flinar? Where's the Defence Minister? His elves will need to retrieve the brogues if the plan is to work."

A swirl of doubt in my belly. "He must be caught up at the elf settlement. Leave Pan and Flinar to me and Ezra."

Delving into my pocket, I slipped my engagement ring back on my finger.

Lavinia's hazel eyes met mine. "As you wish, Alisha Verma. Happy hunting."

FIFTEEN MINUTES LATER, after a tip-off from Rob, I sped across a city in carnage in Ezra's arms. The dead had taken over the streets, driving humdrums to take shelter wherever they could, in homes, shops and office blocks. We didn't stop to help. It would have been useless, like cutting off Medusa's snaking tendrils of hair rather than her head. The guilt balled in my stomach as our bodies compressed and jolted through the monochrome swirls before we emerged, disoriented, in the hallway of a block of posh flats off Richmond Park. A coat stand stood outside a simple door marked with the number 111, topped with a hat I recognised as Pan's.

I rapped my knuckles on the door and listened to a grousing and grumbling on the other side of it.

"He's not going to let us in." Ezra reached out for my hand and whisked me inside.

The god of shepherds, goats and pastures cast us a look of utter disgust. His pale green eyes sparked with anger as he wagged a finger at us from the comfort of a tartan armchair. His pipe lay across his strong thighs. "First, you add me to a group chat, and as if that wasn't the ultimate sin, you then break into my home. A home I was forced to move into after you put me out of favour with the rest of the immortals. I've only just got home after defending my flocks from the hungry dead. What do you want?"

I took a deep breath, unsure of whether his half-divine or half-animal side would be dominant today. "The game of gods is coming to a head, Pan."

He shook his mop of thick, brown hair sadly. "I thought as much. Demons and the dead walk side by side with the living. The world is unbalanced. My goats are bleating incessantly. The deer are cowering in one square mile of the royal park. Worst of all, Gaia is not making me laddus."

"How about you go down fighting?" said Ezra. "Take the pipes. Help us shepherd the dead. You could stay here and play a sorrowful tune, or you could make sure this city hears your song."

Pan tapped his pipes, pale green eyes assessing. "What's in it for me?"

Cautious hope filled me. "A ride on a dragon and the last batch of laddus Gaia made."

"The dragon you nearly scorched me with? At least a dozen laddus?" A slow smile spread across his lascivious lips at my nod. "It's a deal." He heaved himself out of the armchair, straightened his straining shirt across his pot belly, put on a tweed jacket and slid his panpipes into a silver-lined pocket. Then he fetched his tatty top hat and offered his arm to me. "Shall we?"

I took it and reached for Ezra, linking us all together as we tumbled through the universe towards the wintery woods where the elves and dragon dwelled and the book hid.

20

The day was bleak and full of pain. Human wails and police sirens met our ears as we teleported between the worlds. Our purpose burned in my mind: brief the elves, ride the dragon, herd the dead back to the graveyards from which they had come in all their gruesome glory.

We emerged in a clearing, senses alert to trouble, yet all was normal. Ezra put in a call to the farmhouse to brief Maximillian to arrange for the wolf packs to gather in the cemeteries while I kept an eye on Pan. The atmosphere at the settlement made me uneasy. Elvish parents played frisbee with their children in the dim light, disappearing into black holes and then re-emerging with gleeful delight. Some tended to their oak, pine and thatch homes, replacing weathered materials or adding insulation to their walls. Others shared fresh bread with their neighbours. As if nothing untoward happened across the city. As if they were oblivious to how the curtain of normality had been pulled back across the city to reveal the horror beneath.

Disconcerted, I turned to Ezra when he hung up the phone. Vapour clouded from my mouth in the wintery air. "Why has nothing changed here?"

Pan called out with gusto. "Dragon, oh dragon, come out to play."

Ezra rolled his eyes. "What an idiot. And that's without the tweed."

"I heard that," said Pan. "I'll have you know I shop at the same tailor as the werepigeon."

I ignored their griping, foreboding stirring in the pit of my belly. "Why hasn't Flinar reacted to my text and Lavinia's call to attend the senate?"

Copper burned in his grey eyes. "I agree. Something doesn't feel right."

He shrugged off his jacket and unbuttoned his shirt before undoing the clasp of his belt.

Pan gave a throaty chuckle. "Oh, goodie. Is it orgy time already? A bit of debauchery is just the distraction we need as the world ends." He scanned the elves. "That one's mine. And that one—"

I whipped out Transcender from its baldric and angled it at Pan's crotch. "You've had centuries to learn about consensual sex. Keep that baguette in its wrapper, you hear me? Or I'll show you a helicopter move I've been learning."

My gut twisted as a surge of whispers overcame me as if the black hole hiding the Book of Names had opened. Sword in hand, I spun in a slow circle to the clearing beyond the settlement, where Flinar had hidden the book and the dragon that guarded it.

My friend stood there, his milky eyes wide and his full lips quivering, dejection evident in the droop of his shoulders and dull grey head.

He caught my eye and mouthed to me, *Sorry.*

Sharp pangs of disappointment and pathos mingled in me.

Behind him, two goddesses interacted, not yet wise to our arrival. Death wore a blackened cuirass, a gorget, medieval leg harnesses and gauntlets. Gaia wore her simple cuirass and sturdy boots over a Punjabi suit in rusty red as if an afterthought. Ready for war. Death locked tongues with Gaia, her arms travelling over Gaia's body with reverence. With no skirt of rotting arms or necklace of thudding skulls, she almost looked normal. Almost capable of love. The Earth goddess locked her arms around Death's neck and stroked her cloud of hair back from her face. A gesture of tenderness, not duress.

My knees buckled as the world tilted on its axis. How long had they loved each other? How long had they buried their affection for one another? Was it destiny that they found each other at the exact moment in time that it would cause the world to blaze?

Gaia had said that I was her champion.

I had just been another pawn in the games of the gods.

My heart was a desolate wasteland. The whispers in my head crescendoed as Death and Gaia pored over the Book of Names. There it was, a notebook made from cowhide and covered in stardust. They lifted out the black, internal ribbon and thumbed through its ancient, crumbling pages, where sapphire ink spelt out the deepest secrets in the universe.

Its power called to me, a relentless pull. I craved it like an addict.

Pan stepped behind a chestnut tree and slanted his tatty top hat to shield his face. "Oh boy, oh boy. This relationship didn't work so well the first time. Somebody's getting laid, at least."

Ezra grasped my chin, stark naked, his voice harsh. "We have to hold it together. You hear me?"

I shook, my sword limp in my hands. "They have the book."

His jaw clenched. "Call the dragon, take the shepherd god, herd the dead. I'll take care of the book."

He took one last look at my face, then teleported to the Book of Names, teleported to where the two goddesses read, their heads dipped together. And I suddenly understood why he was naked, that he meant to fight two goddesses using all his advantages: his wolf and teleportation abilities.

I understood that he was doing his duty.

For the Otherworld. For the city. For me.

I ran towards them, my feet crunching on twigs, releasing a peaceful, damp woodiness that contrasted with the horror in front of me as Ezra emerged at the goddesses' side and reached for the book.

In agonising slow motion—or so it seemed to me—Death took Ezra by his neck and lifted him off his feet into the crystalline air. She raised an eyebrow at his manhood and flung him like a bowling bowl across the clearing.

Ezra bounced on the ground, once, twice, his body grazing the earth as a cry left my mouth.

Gaia stood still, her cherubic face inscrutable.

Flinar sank to his knobbly knees, his head in his hands.

I reached Ezra, my breath bottled in my chest. He lay winded at my feet, the body I loved so much developing mottled bruises from a single clash with Death.

The sky was cold, blue and empty above us. Grass curled on the floor like singed, tattered cat's whiskers, and I thought of Echo and how I needed him. But Mirabel needed him, too. Was this how it ended, here in this lonely clearing, with the elves averting their gazes nearby? How ironic that my grandmother had also fallen at the hands of the elves. Was this how Mirabel lost another set of parents?

Next to me, bones cracked as Ezra shifted into his wolf.

I rose, fury burning in every cell, stronger with him by my side.

Death's dark eyes flashed in warning. "There's no point, Alisha. I've already won."

I held my sword aloft. The sword she had made for the lover at her side, from a heavenly cloud.

"Oh, very well then." Death raised her twin sword and thundered towards me.

She was larger than me in both weight and height, and with her momentum, I would have no chance if I remained rooted to the spot. I ran at her, finding a kernel of belief in myself, eager to test what would happen if my sword met hers. The Martin Luther King Jr. quote swam in my head about the arc of the universe being long but bending towards justice.

Maybe it would all work out. Maybe I'd fell Death, and Gaia wouldn't be in love with her anymore. Maybe I could save the city and go back to playing happy families. My trainers pounded the ground.

My breath came fast. Maybe. Maybe. Maybe.

A blur of copper-brown fur as Ezra stormed past me, grey eyes fixating on me for a moment before he leapt through the air, at Death or at Gaia, taking them both to the floor with winding heft.

But Death's obsidian twin of my sword was still raised.

"No!" My breath left my body as it pierced Ezra above his left forelimb, inches from his heart.

He didn't even whimper. Grey eyes widened as he slumped over it, and his body jerked—just once—as Death pulled it out. Blood gushed over his copper-grey fur.

The blue goddess moved away, her face painted in disgust, accepting a handkerchief Gaia silently offered her. She wiped her sword clean like an inanimate object mattered more than the man I loved. The man I had pledged to marry, who now lay still and listless on the wintery ground.

They still had the book, so what good had his sacrifice done?

I didn't go closer to him. Not with my heart in my mouth and my mind a fog of all the things I could have done differently, all the paths that could have led to a happy ending. Not with the whispers submerging me, reminding me of my calling. I balled my fists and addressed the Earth goddess and Flinar, tears catching in my throat, thumbing the engagement ring on my finger, a bittersweet comfort.

"Why did you betray us?" I cried out.

The elf, still on his knees, crumpled like he wanted to disappear into one of his black holes. "Will you ever forgive me? The elves have been through so much. Death offered to spare this settlement if I told her where the book is."

The blue goddess crowed. "You didn't think you knew about all my little visits, did you, Alisha? It's like a chess game. All I had to do was plot a flurry of moves and box you in. It turns out the eternal girl is more of an eternal failure. What hubris to think you could outwit immortals."

A triumphant smile spread across Death's face as she pulled the Earth goddess closer to her and nuzzled her neck above her armour and the shawl of her Punjabi suit.

The Earth goddess's body was pliant, her lips slightly parted, as she enjoyed the blue goddess's affection. As if her body remembered the rhythms from the first time they were together.

How could she go back to Death after all that had been wrought? How could she, after Death had commanded the sun god to twist the sword in her gut, leaving her as ashes until we had brought her back?

Watching her body language, I understood that the Earth goddess wasn't an unwilling participant. There was something dark in her, too. She gave as good as she got in the battle of their tongues, in her nails clawing down Death's arms, in the bruising pressure of her lips against the kisses that the belligerent blue goddess offered. Theirs was a toxic love reignited.

Death came up for air. "We've all had to do learning, haven't we, Gaia? Take you. You lost your appetite for Death. I'm enjoying giving it back to you. First, we'll take this melting pot of a city. Then the world is our oyster."

I loved this city. This city, where December heralded a time for families to pick out trees and open advent calendars. For lovers to dip into department stores for artisan chocolates and sparkly special editions of booze. For children wrapped in thick scarves to enjoy hot chocolate topped with marshmallow.

But not today. Today, the clock ticked down to the apocalypse.

Today, unsuspecting Londoners confronted the dead with heavy-bottomed pans or feather dusters or a four-pack of baked beans or whatever they had to hand. At the blue goddess's behest, the dead scared the wits out of the living, in direct contradiction to the laws that kept mankind sane.

Death threw back her head and laughed, and the space she created was just for her and the Earth goddess as if Ezra didn't bleed onto the ground, as if Flinar didn't cower, as if I didn't have thoughts whirling around my head about how to defeat her.

"Do you remember, Gaia, how you tried to persuade me to remember the light? Tried to persuade me that He would forgive me? That I just need to confess my sins, say three Hail Marys, eight Our Fathers, bathe in holy water, and He'd accept me back into his bosom? Well, this is *much* more fun." The blue goddess glowered. "Isn't it, Gaia?"

"Yes, Kali," said the Earth goddess. Like a follower, not an equal.

Gaia's face was a hellscape of impassivity where there had once been wisdom and hope. There was nothing there when she looked at me. No humanity, no pity, not even recognition. It hurt me to see her so small.

But when I looked at Ezra's limp body, I saved my sorrow for him. I saved my sorrow for the humdrums dragged into this unholy mess.

Death looked between us, assessing whether she had, at last, tarnished the Earth goddess—conquered a soul that had been pure, that had seen beauty in small things and insignificant people—and twisted her inside out. "I have the book, so I will let your little pet live. I know how long it took you to search for her and how attached you get to your little lambs."

She really believed she had neutralised me, but the book called to me still, underlining my destiny.

My fists clenched, my nails making little moons in my palms. Heat flushed through my body. She had forgotten that middle-aged women might have froth and bubbles on their upper layers, but underneath, we were tidal waves. We might fizz along, but when our anger popped, we were unstoppable.

Death eyed me as she twisted her sword. "Gaia searched for you for centuries. She needed someone pure enough and strong enough to be trusted with the book. Someone who wouldn't be seduced by it. There are many middle-aged women who are pure enough—sagging skin and tired bones worn out by wrangling with the world—but no one strong enough. Until Rajika Verma. Until you. But without the Book of Names, you aren't a threat. You're just another disappointment." She turned her wicked face to Gaia. "I still need proof of loyalty, darling. You don't mind, do you?"

"Always so mistrustful, Kali," said Gaia. "You have the book, even though you won't tell me where He is. Isn't that enough?"

Death pouted. "Bloodshed is such an aphrodisiac." She swung hooded eyes to Ezra. "Kill him. I'll let your little lamb live if you kill the wolf. Finish him off. Put him out of his misery."

My stomach twisted, but I was ready.

I'd felt the pull of the dragon the moment we arrived. It didn't matter where he was—a drawing on a page, in another country or in a black hole. We had been connected since the moment of his birth, since his conception. I called him, sending my need for the creature I had called into life through the threads of the world, through the hazy light and into the undulating dark, where they had imprisoned him, furious at the book that had been stolen from him and me.

My voice, authoritative and clear. "Now, Tielbu."

He burst through the canvas of the woods, nostrils smoking, bony wings beating. He dwarfed the goddesses, dwarfing me. Flashing, amber eyes, tombstone teeth, fiery breath, black talons sharpened. An ancient creature prone to vengeance and ire.

Death and Gaia pivoted in his direction, tensing.

I propelled myself onto the dragon's turquoise back, a command hovering on my lips to light the immortals on fire if that's what it took to keep Ezra safe. Tielbu's body rumbled with pleasure at my presence, ready to do my bidding, ready to be unleashed. My breath hitched at a sudden movement of Flinar.

Milky eyes pleaded with me to trust him.

"He is my friend," shouted the elf on the wind.

Sprightly, unfaltering, his lips set in a determined line, Flinar disappeared and then reappeared next to Ezra before sucking him into a black hole with a strange, birdlike call. One by one, the elves in the distance vanished into black holes, too.

The Earth goddess shrugged. The Earth goddess, who could feel the vacant spaces and the full ones. Whose talents allowed her to sense where the petals fell, and beehives lay empty, where tectonic plates shifted and volcanoes formed.

"I guess the wolf lives another day," said Gaia.

Death's inky eyes narrowed as she leapt towards us, but I didn't flinch.

I leaned into Tielbu's scaly neck as his bony wings lashed the air, our minds and purpose one. He swung towards the oak where the third immortal quaked in his tweed, pipe in hand. I lassoed lily-livered Pan to us, and then we were skyborne, the whispers of the book ebbing with every metre. As the dragon turned towards the first of seven graveyards circling the city, Death's cry of wrath followed us up through wisps of clouds. I risked a look at the goddesses below.

Death railed at the sky, her armour clanking.

Gaia held up her fists, wrists upturned, then opened up one hand, followed by the other.

Pan's tatty top hat whirled off his head as he clung to the dragon and plopped onto a bare branch far below. "Perhaps I was too hasty. That was a high price to pay for a dragon ride and a batch of laddus. Death is going to enjoy killing me over and over again. She always was too macabre for me." He shook his head. "But it's Gaia that saddens me. A cook like her succumbing to darkness. What a waste. It's possible that the Lazarus pit mixed her up. Maybe it brought old feelings to the surface. It's been known to happen, and the Earth goddess has always had many faces. Rage. Love. Revenge. Nurture."

I nodded. My heart was a hollow hole at my centre as we left Ezra behind.

21

———————

Ezra wouldn't have wanted me to give up, so I didn't.

The dragon flew across the city, leaving our enemies, lover and the elf settlement—now empty of elves—behind. His amber eyes searched for the dead, never tiring. He discerned the dead by their putrid smell and unnatural movements, the trail of bodily fluids and the drag of their feet in the brogues made by the blue goddess. His wings stretched out, and his scales rippled beneath us.

He had been waiting for this moment. He lived for these moments.

I whispered against him. "No fire, Tielbu. This is strictly a clean-up mission."

We flew from Abney Park and Highgate in the north of the city, to Kensal Green and Brompton in the west, to West Norwood and Nunhead in the south and finally to Tower Hamlets in the East, the cemeteries known as the Magnificent Seven. Graveyards that housed angel statues, stone mausoleums and gothic architecture, where in the modern world, open-air gigs, wood-carving courses, storytelling sessions and forest schools took place.

Where today, the dead rose.

166

The living had, for the most part, deserted the streets after looting supermarkets and convenience stores. No double-deckers chugged along the streets, and those with cars had hot-tailed it out of the city or as far as fuel would allow them to go. Others barricaded themselves in their home, and we spied pale faces behind twitching curtains. It was every man, woman and family for themselves. Leaders had gone to ground: government officials, local councillors, the police and even Neighbourhood Watch. Only the odd priest, imam or rabbi remained, having clambered on top of an abandoned emergency vehicle or wheelie bin from where they made grave pronouncements from their holy books.

I roped Pan to the dragon's back with a loop of wind as best I could, although sometimes he slipped and slid between Tielbu's wings. At a sighting of the dead, the dragon swooped downwards, flying level with the Victorian housing stock or sometimes a metre from the asphalt while the piper played sleepy tunes that made the dead crave their graves.

He wasn't a courageous god. Maybe he had been once when the devout had worshipped him, when men had worn their Sunday best and participated in lynch mobs, and the executioner's axe had swung in town squares. The modern world had made him soft. Or perhaps his softness stemmed from the submissive deer herds in the Royal Parks or his cushy job on the board of Battersea Dogs Home. In any case, he trembled when the dead loomed closer. If I hadn't been there to coax and coerce him, he would still be hiding behind the chestnut tree.

The god played the bamboo pipes in a way that transcended the panpipe recordings played in the lifts of Mediterranean hotels or the treatment rooms of slightly sticky spas. According to mythology, his simple instrument had been made from a nymph's body who had escaped his amorous attentions by being turned into a reed by river nymphs. On it, he produced a symphony of crystal-clear high and deep bass tones.

And the dead followed.

I gagged at their foul stench. Desolate, protruding eyes, sacks of diabolical longing and sedated energy, infernal madness and dripping flesh. Stringy bodies and spiked bones, oozing wounds and stunted flesh. Concave skulls and seeping bulges, grotesque grins and serrated mouths, grime and dirt and ash. They loped in groups, mostly at ground level, though we found some caught in gutters and climbing drainpipes, low moans and grunts, and nightmarish voids that I pitied rather than feared.

In Tower Hamlets, a fleet of Otherworld taxis swerving all over the street caught my attention. With a nudge from me, Tielbu hovered in the air for a fraction of a second before a thumping landing, heading off their charge.

I slid off the dragon's back, leaving Pan to catch his breath.

The Prime Sorceress emerged from the driver seat of the first vehicle, swinging her trusty umbrella like a baseball bat. Her silver curls frizzed from hard work. She'd been leading a fleet of taxis that had cleared the Eastern part of the city of the dead. She ignored the dragon and the shepherd god and got straight to the point. "What of my nephew?"

Tielbu stuck his head into a butcher's shop twenty metres away. I ignored him, haunted by the memory of Ezra's blood pooling on his coat.

I voiced the meagre comfort I had been telling myself over and over. "Flinar is keeping him safe. He has his thistle charm."

An audible release of air. "That should keep him from Death's door. The elf will pay for his betrayal."

"Flinar acted out of love and fear. Everything he does is for his people—I can't hold that against him. I believe him when he says he won't harm Ezra."

"He will not live if he does." Her expression was pinched, the look in her eyes lethal.

I shook my head, remembering the cigarette butts in her office, the same brand as the ones we had seen the blue goddess smoke.

"Death knocked on lots of doors. One of them was bound to open." I was so tired of lies and subterfuge. So tired of the quicksand beneath my feet, not knowing who was an ally and who a foe. I looked into the depths of her irises, searching for the truth. "The blue goddess visited you, didn't she?"

The Prime Sorceress stilled. Spots of colour entered her cheeks. "Yes, she did, Alisha. She visited me not long after you found the Book of Names in the Celestial Library. She offered to make the coven more powerful than any that had ever existed if I handed the book over to her."

My pulse quickened. "What did you tell her?"

Frosty pink lips curved into a smile. "I told her I didn't have the book. But I had already made plans for us to be the most powerful coven in the world. That I had done it without her and that Wildwoods would hold together. I told her that not everyone uses power for ill."

"You should have told us. Ezra never doubted you, but I would have trusted you sooner. We could have helped." I massaged my temples. If I'd known that Death had been making the rounds, I could have gotten there first. Stopped her from whispering in Flinar's ear. Stopped her from taking the book. "She asked something else of you, didn't she?"

"Yes, she wanted to corrupt me by asking me whose blood she should spill in the room where Mirabel recovered from the dream god's attack. She warned me to stay away, or she would have massacred you all."

I shuddered. "You are the reason Rayna is dead."

"No, Alisha. Death wanted her pound of flesh. I didn't know who she would target in that room, but I was willing to bargain for Ezra's life. And yours and Bel's because Ezra cares for you. And because so much rides on you staying alive."

"What did you have to do in return for our lives?"

"Ferry thirty souls of the dead in my fleet of Otherworld Taxis to the River Styx, which has a tributary off the Thames." A sigh. "You think of me as transactional, over-ambitious, manipulative maybe. You doubt whether I care for my loved ones. But we both want what's best for this world, Alisha." She twirled her umbrella against the pitted ground. "Are you ready to trust me now?"

She wasn't an easy woman, but now I understood, I did trust her. "I am."

A ruckus sounded in the back of the taxi, where three of the dead pummelled the windows. In the front passenger seat, Ignacio the rat flicked through a tattered copy of an A-Z, his movements frantic.

"Then let's get this show on the road." Lavinia glared at her passengers. "The sat nav failed half an hour ago. Possibly a side effect of Margola trying to bring down comms to stop the horrendous images from this out-of-control city from igniting global panic. It doesn't help with ferrying this lot back to their resting places, though." She turned to me, her eyes strangely pleading. "The book?"

My stomach quivered. "Gone."

"The Earth goddess?"

"In thrall to Death."

"Then perhaps we have reached the end times after all." The Prime Sorceress softened. "I was starting to think you could pull this off. Still, the least we can do is clean up the streets one last time. To think, all that green juice I've been drinking and all the youth potions I've been taking, and it's all going to end today anyway. Well, let's get on with it, shall we? One last adventure."

I didn't hide my engagement ring when her eyes flickered to it.

"So what my rat spies reported is true. That jewellery is proof that pledges of marriage always end in disaster: boredom, affairs, illness or death. There really is no other way out, which is why it always surprises me when people enter into it. I mean, really, Alisha, there are other ways for both sexes to service themselves without having to walk down the aisle *for love*. Haven't you heard of sex toys?" Another sigh. "Still, maybe the memory of love is all we have when everything else is taken away."

We parted ways. Me on my dragon, she at the head of the fleet of taxis.

By nightfall—which in wintery London was teatime—our work had been done. The dragon, Pan and I shepherded the dead. The coven drove the Otherworld taxis, rounding up strays. In the absence of the elves, Maximillian and the wolf packs circled the cemeteries, pulling off the brogues, ready for Tielbu to light his seventh bonfire. Margola used her comms contacts to obscure the truth. Rob led the state operation to take control of the narrative and reunite graves with the right remains, although, with the time constraints, there was a significant margin of error. Orpheus's vampires wiped humdrum minds. Even without Ezra and Flinar fulfilling their roles, Wildwoods and its allies pulled together. Some whooped for joy at our shared efforts, a light in the darkness. Though the operation was slick and fruitful, to me, it was like sticking a plaster on a chasm of gloom.

Afterwards, I dropped Pan off at his Richmond flat. "Thank you for helping us."

He devoured a laddu, pale green eyes on mine. "It won't make a difference. You might have won the battle, but the war is not over. Still, it is godly to try. Goodbye, Alisha Verma. Don't call on me again."

The heavy door of his building swung shut, and I ventured out to the dark streets, where humdrums questioned why they couldn't remember the previous twelve hours.

I knew in my bones that Pan was right.

Death wasn't finished yet.

22

———

It was the winter solstice, endless night and snuffed-out light.

Gaia had told me I would feel alone. At least she hadn't lied about that. There was no time for sleep, even though my body craved it. Even though the Jericho necklace lay heavy at my neck and my arms ached from clinging to Tielbu as he tore through the skies and from slashing at the grasping dead with my sword.

I couldn't sleep without knowing Ezra's fate anyway.

So we flew, the dragon and I, across starless skies, over the black depths of the Thames and quaint English gardens and the remnants of gore strewn across them, to the woods, where I had last seen Ezra and the elves. The dragon knew the lines of camouflaged elvish dwellings, the trees twisting up like cathedral spires, the inky blue shadows of bark, and the clearings in between. He landed, his mammoth body slumping with shuddering release after the day's exertions.

When I leapt from his back, my knees buckled. Righting myself, I sheltered against his throat column for a moment. We shuddered on the eerie ground, the cold penetrating our bones. All light fled.

My voice was thin. "I'll gather some wood. We can make a fire and look for Ezra."

"You must not lose hope." The dragon's ancient voice rumbled through his scaly body. His hot breath thawed my cold hands. "It is no coincidence that the wolf was hurt in the very woods where he has run with his pack and arranged sanctuary for the elves and me. The land looks after its own."

Dragons were wise and mysterious creatures. Maybe he knew the end of our story, or maybe he could simply discern and judge things in the wind that remained hidden from me.

I heaved myself up to hunt for firewood. A shuffling and a surge of whispers rooted me to the spot. I blinked as a flashlight appeared out of nowhere, blinding me until my eyes adjusted to the glare. The heavy silence dispersed as happy-go-lucky elves, armed with torches and makeshift weapons, emerged from dozens of black holes, chattering excitedly.

Flinar pulled at his jogger with twitchy hands. "We've been waiting for your return, Alisha."

The surge of whispers in my head became a background noise to our exchange.

"Where is he? Where's Ezra?" The ball of fury at my centre melted into joy at the sight of a halo of pink-and-purple-and-turquoise hair. I crashed into Marina, hugging her. My words garbled about Ezra and the Earth goddess and the dead and the book and how, as the apocalypse neared, Londoners had stolen bloody loo roll. I scowled at Flinar. "We need to find Ezra, Marina."

"Slow down." My best friend swatted me. "When were you going to tell me about his marriage proposal, you cow? I'd better be a bridesmaid. Your wolf is fine. Flinar called me in the nick of time, just before the mobile networks went down. I have no idea how they called emergency care in the Dark Ages. Anyway, he would have been a goner without the thistle charm. That sword of Death's is no butter knife. A win for men who wear jewellery, eh?"

"Christ, woman. Let her see her man." Two strong hands —Rob's—physically moved Marina aside.

Ezra, weak and pale, sat partially clothed on a stack of blankets, with Marina's medical bag next to him. A jolt of electricity as his eyes met mine. "Hi, hellfire."

I dropped next to him in a crouch, not daring myself to speak until my hands had found the wound between his left shoulder blade and where his heart ricocheted under my palm. "You're okay."

He nodded, but I noticed he held his body strangely like he'd been through the wars. "I'm okay."

My throat was tight. "I was scared."

"So was I. Come here." He pulled me against him and rested his chin on my head.

I drank in the feel of him like a woman thirsting in the desert. "You were right to trust Lavinia. You need to let her know you're okay. She loves you and was on a warpath for Flinar."

Ezra raised an eyebrow. "You two have an understanding now?"

"Something like that." Whispers clamoured in my head, urgent, emphatic.

His brow furrowed. "The elves kept me hidden and arranged for my care. Don't be too hard on him. No lasting harm was done beyond a scar or two."

I nodded and stood to address Flinar and the elves. "I don't blame you for trying to save yourselves. I don't blame you, Flinar, for leading Death to the book." The whispers grew stronger. "In fact, I think the Book of Names is still here."

Rob swept his torch across the settlement with the practised air of a police officer who had conducted night-time woodland searches before.

Marina twiddled the crystals in her bra. "The gemstones the foxes gave me really are helping me connect to my visions. I saw a snippet of one earlier, of Gaia looking up into the sky and unfolding her hands one by one. Like this."

She demonstrated.

Flinar piped up, his voice small and tentative. "Like her magic trick at the cottage Christmas party with the tulip bulb and the jagged rock."

"She did that today. That wasn't a vision of the future. It was a vision of the past," I said. Adrenaline chased away my exhaustion, making me alert. "She switched the Book of Names. Don't you see? The chess set in her Tooting flat, the centuries of planning. Gaia has planned for all of this. She isn't really on Death's side. She's on ours."

Ezra grimaced as he got to his feet, supported by Rob and Marina and an uncertain, hovering Flinar.

The elves scattered as I followed the whispers to a hovel. My mouth was dry, senses heightened as I stooped and reached inside. Beetles scuttled, and my fingers found the slimy squishiness of a slug and then the surprising softness of petals and silk beneath.

The whispers crashed like the tide against the shore of my mind. Holding my breath, I grasped the silk and pulled it out, eyes widening at Mum's paisley scarf. A clutch of begonia and gerbera daisy petals that had no place being in a hovel in the woods at the height of winter but that I had seen in Gaia's garden came out with it, as well as a smattering of cardamom pods and cloves that the Earth goddess enjoyed in her chai.

Fingers trembling, I unfolded the scarf to reveal the notebook made from cowhide and covered in stardust.

Ezra whistled low and long while Marina hugged Flinar.

Rob, glimmering in his puffer jacket, pumped his fist in the air. "Finally, glad tidings for the Prime Minister."

Gaia knew my strengths and my weaknesses, even that I needed little signs to see me through the night. *Hold together, despite the fault lines,* she had said. *Remember that kindness wins the war.*

I stood up in the darkness, an expanding feeling in my chest, and gave the book to Flinar. The power wasn't all mine; the power was to be shared. We were stronger that way. "I trust you. Keep it safe with your black hole magic."

Flinar's sail-like ears billowed with emotion. "I touched the book when I took it from the dragon and handed it to the Earth goddess. It makes me greedy for power."

"That's why your black hole magic is so important. You can lock it away until the time comes. We'll need Orpheus's bell to call Death and the remaining rogue gods. Then I'll ask for it, my friend."

His milky eyes shone with a film of tears. "Thank you for your forgiveness. I'm not a great leader, but I promise to be a great friend."

"You are a great leader, Flinar. I think you come from a long line of great leaders. The elves have survived despite everything society threw at them." I turned to Ezra. "I think it's time for us to forgive a prisoner in the dungeons under the Ritz too."

He grew still. "Meriel Naehorn?"

Rob cursed. "You want to show her mercy even though she killed your grandmother? You can't just let lunatics out on the streets of London."

Marina shrugged. "To be fair, the city has seen worse recently."

I bit my lip. "She saw the Otherworld more clearly than many of us. She instinctively rails against the dark. I don't know if I'm making any sense. A gesture of reconciliation, maybe. Or maybe I don't want the world to be snuffed out with her still down there. Flinar, you'll keep an eye on her?"

He nodded, eyes shining. "I will. Our queen will be a great asset on the battlefield."

Ezra gave a deep, weighted sigh, his brows drawing together. "I'll get it done."

178

23

———————

Where did you go when darkness swirled around you? Not to the cottage and my love nest with Ezra, not to Wildwoods where Mirabel and Echo waited out the storm with the rest of the peculiar community, but home to our three-storey, red-bricked house overlooking Tooting Bec Common.

Dad hadn't obeyed the summons to go to Wildwoods. Neither had Sahil. If the world was ending, it was here they wanted to hole up, in the house of our childhood, with its pretty sash windows, peeling shutters and walls lined with books. Here, where Mum had pottered happily in the garden and koi in the pond swum in oblivious circles. Here, where Mum's shrine loomed in the hall, and Dad's studio overflowed with paints. Here, where he'd found a renewed lease of life with Alma.

Streetlamps flickered as I walked up the block-paved drive with Ezra and Marina. The front door lay ajar. No need to lock the door when the end times were coming. Inside, the heat was on full blast. Anxious voices came from the dining room.

"This is important information. You have to tell her," said

Alma. "Gaia said every bit of the jigsaw contributes to the whole, and nothing the Earth goddess says is ever hot air."

"She didn't even tell me she is a falcon. She's way above me in the pecking order," said my brother glumly. "And the phone lines are down. How are we supposed to reach her?"

"My mother could animate birds." Dad's slurred speech told me he was stoned. "There was a nest of attacking birds in our garden. And now my children are birds. But my mother could also animate hippos. So I give thanks my children aren't hippos. And that there wasn't a hippo in our garden."

"Get a grip, Dad," spluttered Sahil.

Ezra, Marina and I rounded the corner to find flour had been liberally sprinkled all over the mahogany table, but rather than wafting with freshly baked cakes, the dining room ponged with weed. Alma and Sahil fell into stunned silence at the sight of us.

Dad, dressed in a Spiderman costume, pulled off his mask and rushed to embrace me. "Alisha? Oh, thank goodness. Alisha is here. Sahil, she is not a bird. Stop with your werepigeon envy."

Sahil groaned. "Can you just tell him that I'm not making it up? It was you on the roof in Soho, wasn't it? The peregrine falcon? It took me a while to piece it together, and then the dead started roaming the streets of London, and comms went down. So I ended up here, and Dad got out his bong."

"Alisha, love," said Alma in a cloud of flour. "Leave your sword by the door, will you? I don't like weapons in the dining room."

I did as I was told, realising how this was now Alma's home more than mine, and I didn't mind at all.

Dad pinched my cheeks. "Thank goodness you're all right. Although I knew you would be. The dead were hardly a match for you at your Mum's graveside, were they? Even I could handle them." Dad giggled sheepishly and gave a little wave to Ezra and Marina before slumping into a chair. We really had to wean him off the bong, but I feared without it right now, he'd be a nervous wreck.

"We're fine, Dad. With the phone lines down, I was worried, so we came to check on you." I took a deep breath. "But you should know, Sahil isn't lying. I learned how to wild in the Celestial Library."

Marina grinned. "And I've got visions now."

"Have you had a vision of us being together in the future?" said Sahil.

"Sorry, no." Marina blew out her cheeks and settled into a chair next to Alma.

"Worth a try." My brother shook his head woefully. "You saved my life up on that Soho rooftop, sis. Those crows had it out for me."

Ezra pulled out a seat for us both.

"What are families for?" I slid into mine and gave my brother a small smile before turning anxious eyes to Dad and Alma. "I doubted Gaia when she had been true all along."

Alma, who had been making snowflakes in the flour using doilies as templates, dusted off her hands. "Never mind, dear. The goddess knew she was asking a lot of you. She practices what she preaches, you know. She's very forgiving. That's why she likes middle-aged women. She's a great believer in second chances. I should know. When she first came across me, I was selling pesticides for a living and spending my free time watching Julio Iglesias music videos. She convinced me that baking, tending to stray souls and making doilies was my true calling. She's very wise."

Sahil cleared his throat and cocked his head, and I saw again that he would never be as handsome as he had been prior to his werepigeon days. But perhaps he was kinder now. "I've been trying to wrack my brain about what point you turned up. I was so focused on waiting for human you that my mind is all muddled about it. Although I'm pretty sure being a werepigeon is causing some brain shrinkage. I mean, you saw Phinnaeous Shine weasel his way into the gods' favour again. You saw the Earth goddess, but Alma says there's no way she's rotten. You saw Hermes send the crows to exact their revenge on me and how Death planned to up the ante on her plan with some visits."

I chewed the inside of my cheek, impatient. "Yes, yes, I know all of that."

His brown eyes glowed. "But you weren't there before, were you? You didn't see Morpheus."

A pain in my chest. "Morpheus is alive? I killed him in the Celestial Library. We did it together."

"Did you, though?" said Sahil. "Aren't we all still dreaming? I saw him, Alisha. I saw him with my own eyes, but he left before Gaia did. You see, Death still doesn't fully trust her. It's all still to play for. But I'm not as beautiful or as remarkable as a peregrine falcon. A werepigeon blends into the sooty roofs of London. They were distracted by Phinnaeous's arrival. I'm pretty sure they didn't realise how long I had been eavesdropping. Maybe I called attention to myself with a poor landing after I called you from the phone box; who knows? But I was listening before. I heard what they had to say."

Ezra leaned forward, a growl in his voice. "The clock is ticking, bro."

Sahil hiccupped up a werepigeon feather. "Not only did I see Morpheus before Gaia arrived, but I heard the blue goddess tell him that the reason he was alive is that killing an immortal requires a holy trinity. The sword, the book and the presence of the entombed one."

"The entombed one." My gaze flitted about the room, blearing. "You mean the Father of the Gods?"

A vein throbbed in Ezra's jaw. "This is a clue, Alisha. He's entombed. We just have to find him. Don't you remember what Gaia told us?"

Of course, I remembered. *God is pure love. Pure love doesn't go away. It's always with us,* she had said. *He's merely napping. What fools the rogue gods are to believe God is dead. They failed the test He set us all. To keep an open heart in the face of disappointments.*

I looked around my loved ones' faces.

So this was it. This was how we faced down Death.

I reached out for my brother's hand, and for the first time in our adult lives, there was no awkwardness between us at the unbidden sign of affection. "Sahil, you don't know how much you have helped today."

He squeezed my hand. "I've been speaking to pigeons about town. Learning their language and all that. It's surprisingly complex. They seem to make the same sounds, but when you listen hard and pair the sound with the look in their eye, there's a richness to the conversation. Anyway, after they were turfed out of Trafalgar Square, they've had eyes everywhere. I think I know where we can find the big guy."

Dad beamed at us.

I closed my eyes in the safety of the circle of my family and tuned into the natural world, finding a deeper consciousness and reaching for the web of life. I deepened my breathing, remembering the Grove of Tomorrows, remembering Rayna's teachings and Orpheus's encouragement. With every inhalation and exhalation, with every stretch of my toes and emptying of my mind, I felt the vibrations of the ecosystem we were all part of.

Maybe if I'd listened harder to the universe, I would have found the answer before. Maybe if I hadn't buried my nature, then none of this would have happened. Maybe Mum wouldn't have died. Maybe Nita would still be doing her baking soda experiments and would have grown up to be a world-renowned scientist. Maybe Fei Yen would still have her arm. Maybe Mirabel would still have her parents.

Maybe Rayna would still be tending to her plants in the sanatorium.

I had made mistakes, but I wasn't responsible for the suffering of my friends and family.

Life was sometimes unfair. All we could do was be there for our loved ones.

A woman in her midlife knows that learning takes time. Change doesn't happen overnight; it is incremental. It builds. Though my learning had been slow, the changes had been deep and hard-won. I had walked away from my gambling ex-husband. I had unravelled our family history and found out that Echo was more than a Bengal cat. I had learned to love again by opening my heart to Ezra and Mirabel. I had mended my relationship with my brother. I had discovered that I was a night-class teacher and so much more. That I could raise dragons and face down terrors. I had met a chai-drinking, laddu-making goddess. I had taken a stand against unhinged immortals. I had tested my limits and flown as a falcon.

Incrementally, I had uncovered my true self. It was never too late to listen.

I focused on the nebulous pink of my closed eyelids, my heartbeat, then branched outwards, sensing the old beams and creaking floors of our family home and, beyond, the frosted lawns, the wintery breeze rippling through the boughs of bare trees on the road outside, the gentle swell of the earth beneath the city asphalt and the undulating currents of the river Thames. My thoughts slowed, and I followed their meanderings, past tube stations and bus depots, past rubbish dumps and estates where young men watched their fighting dogs compete, past glowing art galleries and empty bridges.

There, under the stars and the city lights, I found the song of life and, with it, the threads of connection to my creations. I found the place they converged on when I released them from their purpose. A woodpecker, ravens, butterflies, vampire finches, a red-tailed hawk, waxwings and hornets. All in one place, not in the natural environment but a built one with pearlescent masonry. A dome—no, an abandoned, airless crypt in central London that thrummed with life.

The very beginning of life.

I opened my eyes. "I see it, Sahil. I see it, too."

He gawped. "Well, I haven't seen it. I drew my conclusions from pigeon gossip. Just once, I wish you'd not raise the bar."

"We're going to need Lavinia and Orpheus to plan this right," I said. "We'll need to send a message to the Celestial Library for Calypso to come back. We'll meet at Wildwoods."

Dad took another puff of his bong. "Oh, let's all go to Wildwoods. I've missed Bel. She's been busy recently with all that training they've been doing. She doesn't come here enough, does she, Alma? I hope she's not embarrassed by my superhero wardrobe. I can be plain old granddad if she wants me to be."

My brother nodded. "We'll have our meeting. Then Alisha and I can strip and shake a tail feather. It'll be like that time Mum and Dad took us to a German sauna thinking they'd have English sensibilities about nudity."

I cringed at the memory. "It's going to be beautiful."

Marina frantically rubbed the lucky clover tattoo on her wrist, as she always did when she was nervous. "We shouldn't go to Wildwoods tonight. We should stay here. We can have the meeting here."

I frowned, craving a hot water bottle and bed, craving being lulled to sleep by the rise and fall of Ezra's chest. Rest would come later. "Why would you say that? Bel and Echo are at Wildwoods. Our friends and allies are there. Of course, we have to go there."

Marina dropped her voice into a whisper. "You're going to die. I don't want to lose you."

I hesitated, scared to ask. "What happened in your battlefield vision, Marina? The one where you saw Calypso?"

"There was all-out war at Wildwoods. I saw Calypso, Orpheus, Ezra—even pupils—fighting against the gods. Against Ra and Mami Wata and Hermes and Cardea. Wildwoods itself was getting involved. I could barely breathe." Marina chewed her lip. "I've never seen anything like it. I felt this immense sense of loss. And that loss was you, Alisha. You were gone."

Sahil let out an involuntary squawk. "The Ouija board at the cottage Christmas party spelt out the Verma name."

I shook my head. "Those things are a bit of fun. A jump scare. They're not reliable."

Ezra gripped my hand, urging me to take the warning seriously. "We'll find another way."

The overheated, carpeted dining room, with its hazy cloud of flour and marijuana, became oppressive. I floated above my body. It wasn't that I didn't believe Marina, but her vision didn't make sense to me. I dug my hands into the pocket of my jeans and closed my fingers around the cardamom pods and crushed petals that the Earth goddess had left for me to find.

The odds didn't matter. I really believed we could do it. I was fine about putting myself on the line to fulfil the prophecy.

Every moment had led here, from the moment of my grandmother's death.

I brushed off the foreboding that seethed in my stomach. "I have to finish it. I have to try."

Dad flicked his lighter, dipped his head to the mouthpiece of the bong and exhaled a cloud of marijuana. It was like being in a 1990's dorm room. His overprotectiveness of me had been a feature of his parenting for so long, but the weed made him less cautious and more trusting. "A child doesn't die before their parents. That's against the laws of nature. We have the Earth goddess on our side, and she made Rosalie a promise. I believe in you, Marina, love, but I have experience of living with a seer, and it's more miss than hit."

Marina and Ezra exchanged worried glances.

"I've had quite a good success rate so far, actually," she said.

"You're going to have to buy me a huge bouquet of flowers to make up for that, Joshi," said Alma tartly. "And not ones from the petrol station either. They wilt quicker than your—"

Dad interrupted. "Have a bit of weed, won't you, love? You know what they say…those who smoke together stay together. And I do love my life with you, my Spanish omelette."

Striking that sentiment from my mind, I stood up and set my shoulders back. "That's settled then. I just need a coffee and a paracetamol. Then we'll head to Wildwoods to get all the pieces on the board."

On the way back from the kitchen, I lit a candle at Mum's shrine. A peaceful resolve filled me.

When we were united, nothing could go wrong.

24

Prompted by me, the Prime Sorceress declared war on the gods.

We arrived at Wildwoods to find floodlights on, the arena jam-packed full of peculiars of all ages and abilities, choosing weapons to defend themselves and fight for the future.

Lavinia's coven sister Morgan, the midnight-skinned witch with slender curves and icy blue eyes, led some pre-battle stretches. She lifted her striped golf umbrella above her head, circling her shoulders and then forwards again in a flash of candy pink and white. "Five rotations, that's it. Everyone, please. Lunge to the left and hold. And to the right. Hold. Straighten up, grip your ankle, feel the stretch across your thigh and calf. And the other side. And release."

This time, I had brought my family with me. With grim faces, we pushed past the throngs of peculiars to squeeze into Lavinia's office. There, the senate plus a few choice additions had gathered: frayed tempers, worry warts and the battle-ready.

The Prime Sorceress embraced me and Ezra with genuine warmth, and I realised what a disservice I had done her by comparing her tenure as Prime Sorceress to her predecessor.

How unfair of me to expect her to be transparent when Phinnaeous never had been. I had wanted explanations of her motives when she didn't owe me any.

I was lucky to have such a formidable person on my side.

She still liked to flex, though. It wasn't Lavinia's style to wear power lightly.

Having showered Ezra with affection, the Prime Sorceress sat at her Ikea desk, her manicured fingers steepled together and glowered at Flinar. On her left, Ignacio the rat trained his gaze on the elf, black beads of intent, like that was his sole job. At her right, her sister Isadora rode an exercise bike, a trickle of perspiration on her brow. Orpheus—a small, bronze bell balanced on his knee—Cillian, Helio and Erelim sat wedged onto a pink futon, although the angel's wings expanded and contracted as if they demanded more space. Calypso, Margola, Flinar, Rob, Marina, Dad, Alma, Sahil, Ezra and I made up a semi-circle on the outer rim of the room.

The Guns N' Roses rucksack with my grandmother's armour in it clanked as I set it down. I dropped my mental barrier so Orpheus could enter my thoughts. Then I crouched, sharpening Transcender on a whetstone next to Lavinia's umbrella stand, earning an approving nod from Calypso.

I can hear your heart pounding from here, said Orpheus.

That's not fear. That's adrenalin, I said.

His voice in my head. *As it should be. You are fearless. You are divine. You are woman.*

I snorted. *Are you quoting an Emmy Meli song? You've been spending too much time with Echo.*

The vampire sighed. *Chanakya Gunbir Hredhaan of Maharashtra has been taking his duty of care to your daughter very seriously. Like a babysitter, a bodyguard, a weapons instructor and a tribute band all in one.*

The Prime Sorceress raised a cool eyebrow at her sister.

"Off the bike, Isadora. I know you miss the gym, but your bottom hasn't suffered for the change in your priorities. It's still as flat as a pancake."

Isadora flushed. "Sister, please. I'm aiming for Kardashian buns, as you well know."

Lavinia straightened her backbone. "Tonight is the winter solstice. The longest night of the year. The night when it is inauspicious to go outside in case we are whisked away with the souls of the dead. The night we would usually slay and feast on animals. We would burn yule logs and ward off misfortune with the ashen remains. We would shun work and spend time with our families." She stood up, imparting her energy to the room like a preacher in a pulpit. "But this solstice marks a change. This solstice, we will work. We will pull together. Tonight, we find out whether the Chameleon Tale is fact or fiction. We find out if the eternal girl will stop the coming dusk. But Alisha won't be alone. Alisha has us. The Custodian has left her post to fight alongside us. We have our covens, our packs, our clans, our legions of angels, our bands of leprechauns." She sighed. "Plus a mischief of elves and a pair of *hu hsien* foxes."

It's enough to write the chorus of a new Christmas carol, said Orpheus.

"Don't forget three selkies," said Margola. "Although we are better fighters in water."

Isadora nodded. "Wildwoods is primed. The sphinxes are ravenously waiting for the command to be freed from their stone bodies. Our students and parental cohort stand ready. We have opened the vaults of the school and the Celestial Library to retrieve legendary weapons. Poseidon's trident, Brahma's arrow, the sword of Zulfiqar and Odin's spear. Let these weapons bring pain to our enemies. Let our pupils not impale themselves."

I sheathed my sword, my heart clamouring in my chest. "Our plan is a good one. We have the power to overcome the rogue gods once and for all. Until then, it will be your job to weaken them, to hold them at bay until we can strike a fatal blow."

Even if we succeeded, was that what I wanted? Did we want a world without gods?

"You say you know where the Father of the Gods sleeps," said the Prime Sorceress.

I darted a glance at my brother. "We know."

A sharp intake of breath from those gathered, particularly Erelim, who pulled out a rosary from his leather trousers and prayed like he was at mass.

"The rogue gods are formidable enemies, but if the battle happens here, we'll be at an advantage. Here on home turf, with the building mobilising to help us," I said. "You won't be able to kill them, but you can slow them down. Clip their wings. Work together to ambush them and diminish their power. A temporary measure until I can get the rogue gods to His resting place." I took a deep breath. "If we achieve that, we won't need to fear them any longer. Some of us may get hurt, but by the end of this long, dark night, we will have vanquished them."

Lavinia's gaze probed Flinar, her expression sour. "You have the book?"

The Prime Sorceress appears to want to quarter the elf with laser vision, said Orpheus. When this is over, I must take him to my tailor. I find a well-dressed individual is bullied less than those in rags.

Flinar knees locked together. He wrapped his stringy arms around his core. "I do."

"See to it that it stays that way," snapped the Prime Sorceress. "We shall have words about your position on the senate later. And your wayward elf queen."

"There is no need," said Ezra firmly.

Lavinia's helmet of hair-sprayed silver curls jerked up as the school shuddered as if the sphinxes had torn their stone bodies from the earth just outside the grounds. There was only one situation that allowed them to do that unbidden.

We all sprang up.

Wildwoods had been breached.

"The gods are here," cried the Prime Sorceress. She lunged for her umbrella. "Hurry."

Our eyes widened as a haunting siren blared across the school. A tidal wave of cries reached us from the arena. Through the window of Lavinia's office, the rope bridges retracted as the school responded to its attackers.

In a flash, Orpheus was at my side. He pressed the bronze bell into my hand. "You're going to need this."

A frown as his dark eyes flicked to the engagement ring on my finger. *I take it that is Neuhoff's?*

It is. I accepted the bell, my hand lingering a moment on his cool ones, and slipped it carefully into my jeans. *I am sorry.*

I knew the score. One day, you can tell me where I fell short. His smile was bleak. *Good luck, Alisha.*

Then he was gone, striding out of the cabin with the rest of the senate to lead his clan of vampires.

Dad tapped me on my shoulder. "Me and Alma might stay in here a moment if that's okay, love. I'll look after your rucksack."

"I won't be far. I'll stay close in the battle." Flinar trembled and raised his voice over the still-blaring sirens. "For when you need me."

I nodded as hands at my waist spun me around.

Ezra pulled me hard against his chest. "Stay alive, you hear me?"

I wanted to take refuge in the musky scent of him: mountain air and earth and the tang of roll-ups in the air. He teleported us to ground level before running into the fray, stripping as he went. A moment later, the copper-grey wolf bounded through panicking peculiars towards danger.

His howl pierced the air, mingling with the siren, attracting answering calls from his pack and other packs that had come from across London.

I sent a wish up to the stars that his wound knitted itself together to withstand the strains of the night and that he would be able to defend himself and others. Then I searched for Mirabel and Echo, hoping to at least get them on the outskirts of the battle, where she could feel useful but be safer.

Using my wind powers, palms flat against the sawdust of the arena, I rose, hovering in the air to scan the battlefield.

Everywhere was carnage.

Pools of artificial light vied with expanses of shadow. Students and parents armed with swords, spears, clubs, and umbrella ends dipped in poison. Wings and teeth and claws. Crystals and wands.

The witches—oh, the magnificent witches—bending and twisting and twirling their umbrellas as they readied themselves for fierce acrobatic excellence. The vampires glowered, ready to box with their fists and tear with their fangs. Helio rode a gigantic lizard from the bestiary. The leprechauns dusted our fighters with luck. The angels, wings extended, held shining blades aloft. The roaring sphinxes shook the restlessness from their fleshy bodies.

The shifters raced to circle the unseen enemy, formidable in appearance: wolves but also a lumbering bear, a panther and my werepigeon brother, firing out gloops of pigeon poo with abandon, his beaked teeth at the ready. Meriel Naehorn, still in her prisoner garb, swung a cricket bat with wild abandon as elves looked at her in disbelief. The foxes were there too, though they feared this community, already in their six-tailed *hu hsien* form, never an inch apart from each other.

Alongside them, Rob held a 9mm in one hand and a Taser in the other. Marina straddled soaring Nightfall, clutching a dominatrix's whip and a can of pepper spray, an upgrade from the deodorant bottle she usually carried to deter attackers.

Clenched jaws and roiling panic. The scent of sweat and urine. The atmosphere was heavy with adrenalin, pride and have-a-go heroism.

And Wildwoods, beautiful Wildwoods, protecting its own. Trenches, barriers and mists appeared around the most vulnerable. The trees readied their branches to pluck the enemy off the ground. The cable car rail ripped free of its fixings to become a monstrous weapon in its own right, sparking and hissing in the night.

I lowered myself to the ground, heart pummelling my chest. Why couldn't I see Echo and Mirabel? Where was the enemy?

The warning sirens lapsed, and peculiars held their breath in the silence.

My scalp prickled as a gnawing, churning sound replaced the siren. Drawing my sword, I gritted my teeth as stifled cries broke out all around me.

The gods came.

They came, ripping a void in the sky.

They crashed into our sanctuary in a row of chariots drawn by foul-smelling, gore-dripping demons. Demons reconstituted from the shrivelled sacks of meat from the skip outside Shanghai Moon, harnessed like huskies. Not one but four chariots. The Wild Hunt repurposed for their own ends.

Morpheus, risen from the dead, rode in the first. The dream god didn't appear as his shimmering disco diva self but had chosen his nightmarish true form: an unclothed mass of fiery bones and sinewy flesh, stunted wings, horned head and a thick, twirling tail. Next to him, Phinnaeous Shine—whose shapeshifting ability meant he could have chosen any two-legged form—appeared as himself, revealing his utter lack of shame about what an utter imbecile he had been. His chin was raised, his robes newly dry cleaned, his midnight skin smooth. With a heart as dark as his, he should have looked like an elephant's arse.

The second carriage carried Cardea and Mami Wata, the first in armour of rose gold, the latter in her customary dress made of fisherman's nets, their faces shining with glee. Hermes and Ra came next in a chariot shining like the sun, a murder of ravens with them.

But it was the last carriage that made me gasp.

Terror made my heart slow.

The last carriage, grander than the rest, with the longest chain of harnessed demons, carried four: Death, Gaia, Mirabel and Echo.

Death, in her blackened cuirass over her skirt of rotting arms, medieval leg harnesses and gauntlets, holding the twin of my sword. Her necklace of thudding skulls encircled the gorget, and her coal eyes were wild with malevolence. She was no longer capable of love. Behind her, Gaia's plaited hair was limp and open. She still wore a simple cuirass over a red Punjabi suit, but her fortunes had changed since we'd seen her in the woods. Her mouth was gagged with her shawl, and her hands bound in front of her. In her arms, against her chest, she carried my limp leopard.

Even in the face of the greatest obstacles, he had tried to protect my daughter. My Mirabel, whose tear-stained face in the demon-drawn carriage, made me want to crumble.

Red-hot hate seared through me as the three carriages raced through the peculiars, shaping a channel for Death and her prisoners to face me alone. The minor gods held back my family and friends, though Ezra surged forward with his pack, snapping at Morpheus and Phinnaeous. Orpheus boxed his way to Cardea, contemptuous of her diseased fingers, and my werepigeon brother tussled with the crows. Lavinia somersaulted through the air with her coven, eager to be the one to take down Death.

None of them made it through, despite force, courage and passion. Despite love.

Battles broke out on either side of the quiet tributary in which Death approached me. A white noise skirted to the periphery of my mind as she brought her carriage to an abrupt halt alongside me.

Mirabel's eyes were skittish and wide with horror, auburn tendrils drenched against her forehead.

The blue goddess turned her hooded gaze on me. "I was wrong to let you go, little lamb. It turns out I should have slaughtered you back in the woods. We could have made you into our yuletide feast. You see, I thought I had the Book of Names, but it was just a cheap magic trick. One that literally fell apart between my eyes. Poor Gaia was dismayed."

She kicked Gaia's knee with her spiked boot.

The Earth goddess buckled, spilling Echo's limp, golden body onto the floor of the arena. When Gaia straightened, Death kicked her again, this time in the teeth, dislodging the gag in her mouth.

"Looks like kitty's seventh life is well and truly gone," said Death.

Gaia panted, but her brown eyes were defiant. Fire and promise raged in them as she spat out enamel and blood. "You'd think after centuries of practice, you would have become adept in the language of love and learned to be a generous lover, Kali. But as ever, it was all me, me, me. You didn't make me one cup of chai."

Death rolled her eyes. "Chai, chai. It's always chai with you."

I clenched my sword, begging Mirabel with my eyes to hold on.

Death scanned the battlefield, sensual lips curving into a smile. "So this is where we're at, little lamb. I want the book. The real book this time. Or the girl dies. You can thank Phinnaeous Shine for that tip. He was very forthcoming about the girl being your weakness. He's someone who knows how to fight dirty. It's always so satisfying to have a good piece of leverage, don't you think?"

She leaned over the side of the carriage to pull a tethered demon towards Mirabel.

Mirabel flinched, terror building in her like a wave.

"Leave her alone." A note of cold fury in my voice.

"Do you know what the funny thing is? I didn't even have to find the girl. She came to me. Just a little whisper in her ear that your life was at stake, and she came to me. She was overwrought about losing another parent and really thought she could take me down herself. When the leopard couldn't stop her, he followed. Loyalty. Such a tricky thing." She glared at Gaia and then reached out her hands. "The book, Alisha. Or the girl dies."

Behind her, Flinar appeared at the edge of a swell of elves, wrestling Mami Wata's snake.

I shook my head at him, the slightest movement. We couldn't give it to her.

I looked into Death's inky eyes. "Take me. Take me instead of Bel."

Death tilted her head and gave me a hard smile. She drew out an excruciating pause while our lives hung in the balance. "Yes, maybe I will. It took Gaia centuries to find someone who wouldn't be corrupted by that damn thing. Who could handle its power. And I want Gaia to suffer. There is nothing more debilitating than hope. Taking you will buy me a few centuries to establish the new world order."

She pushed Mirabel from the carriage with a flick of a hand.

Mirabel landed with a thump and sprang back. "No! Please take me. Not her. Not my Mum."

Mum.

How I had hoped to hear that little word.

Her screams gutted me, and though they tore me apart, I

raised my palms and called the winds, holding her back, though she railed at me and cursed and cried her heart out. Too cruel for life to deal her another blow. If I left her here, at least she stood a chance of surviving. Ezra was a good man. He would take care of her. My family and Wildwoods would rally around her, whether it was a day or more. Whether the world was at peace or in chaos.

"It's my fault. It's my fault," said Mirabel. "Please, Mum. Don't do this."

"None of this is your fault," I shouted over the top of the wind that pinned her back, over the top of the battle that raged around us, ignoring the slobbering demons grasping at me. My voice caught in my throat. This felt like a goodbye. "I've been so busy trying to live up to expectations that I underestimated the toll it was taking on you. We all get things wrong, Bel. That doesn't mean there's something wrong with us. You are my perfect girl. I couldn't have wished for more."

"Motherhood. Such a well of endless pain." Death strode from the chariot and grabbed me by my hair, tossing my sword into the sawdust.

I didn't regret my choice, even as she dragged me behind her. I didn't regret any of the choices that had made me who I was. I kept my eyes wide open as Death bundled me next to the bound Earth goddess, and the demon train pulling the carriage gathered speed. As we jolted off the ground, I witnessed Mirabel lose control and unleash her fire fairy powers, a fireball of sheer anguish. She blew a limb off Morpheus before vomiting in the sawdust. My eyes were wide open as a copper-grey wolf leapt through the air and landed next to Mirabel. A werepigeon picked up my sword in his beak and flew skywards, cooing a sad song of pain.

Only when Death's carriage tore open a new void did I close my eyes and wonder if it was finally time to rest.

25

———————

Heavy darkness wrapped around us. Not the darkness I waded through en route to the Celestial Library, laden with surprises. Not the darkness at night, when my cold feet sought Ezra's warm calves. Not the darkness of the winter solstice, shrouded in the promise of renewal. The darkness of the void was silent and without end, without even the fires of hell to illuminate the dark.

I listened, reaching for any respite to quell my rising dread, and found the rise and fall of the Earth goddess's breath. It was a balm. The demons dragged us deeper into the void, and we couldn't speak because the blue goddess stood inches from us. Even so, I dared to reach out to touch Gaia and free her bound hands, expecting her to seize the opportunity to overcome Death.

But she didn't. She remained still, inhaling and exhaling.

When my eyes grew accustomed to the dark, I found her hands in a prayer pose, so I mirrored her because, quite frankly, I had nothing else to do at that moment. It didn't matter if I was an atheist or agnostic, or a believer in gods or paired socks. All that mattered was reaching for a little comfort.

Even though I would have preferred a bucket of Malbec or Dad's bong.

I mirrored her prayer pose, and the Earth goddess's wise, kind voice filled my head.

Gaia was a little peeved off. *I had it all planned out. Centuries of planning. Of allies and manoeuvres and sleight of hand and waiting. Oh, all that waiting. And I go and fluff it by having the fake Book of Names disintegrate in front of Kali's eyes. In all my immortal life, I'll never live it down. It was hard to hold that little trick when I spent all my energy pretending to enjoy Death's amorous attentions.* She sighed. *Maybe she would have come to know anyway. Even when nature duplicates things, there are always slight differences. Nothing is precisely the same.*

It's over, isn't it? I said. *I just wish we could have snatched victory from Death.*

A wistful note filled Gaia's voice. *Gods are complicated, just like people. There was hope for her once.*

Had her relationship with Death enjoyed high points, or had the passing of time made the Earth goddess view it through rose-tinted spectacles? As we plunged deeper into the darkness, it was clear that I'd never find out.

Are you disappointed you chose me as your champion? I asked.

Oh no. Nothing ventured, nothing gained, as they say. Your grandmother gave up power to do right by everyone. I had a hunch you would be the same. She grumbled. *Although I was rather hurt to see your doubts multiply the further apart our paths took us. It wasn't just the cardamom pods and the petals I left to buoy your faith. It was how I blessed the boundary of your cottage the night of your party so that you would have a safe haven. And how I planted pansies on your mother's grave to save you from the sight of her awakened body.*

I didn't apologise. I had given enough. Instead, I took a deep, pained breath as the chariot stormed closer to its destination. *Couldn't you have saved Mum?*

A soft breath of release. *How I wish it worked that way. I have observed the butterfly effect for many years. If she had lived, Alisha, you wouldn't have become who you are. You're wearing the wonderful piece of jewellery she envisaged all those months ago, aren't you? The one made of science and love.*

I am. I touched my index finger to it in the dark and rolled my thumb over my engagement ring, but her question rubbed salt in the wound because everyone knew that the dead had no business wearing jewellery. Wealth didn't follow us into the afterlife, if there was such a thing.

You know your sacrifice isn't wasted? said the Earth goddess.

I thought then of the people I had left behind and the world with its wonders. Its mountains and rivers, meadows of blooms and thunderous clouds, the music that made us dance and the books that made us think, the leopards who zoomed and the love that held it all together.

There's a wonderful statue of Millicent Fawcett in Parliament Square, and the engraving always makes me smile. 'Courage calls to courage everywhere,' it says. She chuckled. *Did you see the werepigeon pick up your sword? He's a clever boy, really, despite appearances. It's the key to everything.*

I frowned. Why was she talking as if we still had a chance?

Death whirled around and backhanded Gaia. "You're doing it again, aren't you? Will you ever just sit still and do as you're told?"

"Oh, Kali, you wouldn't be so in love with me if I was boring," said the Earth goddess.

Death smacked me in retaliation for Gaia's retort.

As my grip on the chariot slipped and I blacked out, I wondered if I'd fall like a stone into the nothingness or if I'd ever hear Gaia's voice again.

I woke, disoriented, calling out for Gaia. She didn't respond. The acoustics of my voice spooked me. I was on my back in a tight space, my breathing shallow and strained. I was motionless, inert. No demons pulled me into the darkness. Grit lined my eyes. A wretched, clawing cold pervaded my bones. My heartbeat accelerated as my hands traced the space, and my legs kicked out. I was in a box. I pushed upwards with all the force I could muster, and a smattering of a wet, cold substance fell into the box: sand or soot or soil.

I opened my mouth to taste the substance. Soil. Chalky, gravelly soil.

A box in soil. A scream ripped from my throat.

Death had buried me in a coffin.

I balled my fists and pummelled the lid of the coffin, panic rising. How long had I been trapped? Even now, the air thinned as if there were only a few pockets left. The Jericho necklace lay hot on my neck.

Had Death buried me while Gaia watched, just to torment her? I grew delirious.

Maybe I could kickbox my way out. But the space was too tight to get a large enough swing, and the oxygen too thin to squander on wasted effort. It was so easy to succumb to despair in the darkness. I called the winds, but they wouldn't come. Not where I was. No one looked for me. I would die here, alone, scared, until the last sliver of breath left my body. In an unmarked grave, or worse, a stolen one. I jumped at the thought of sharing the casing with its original owner. How Death would laugh for devising this torment for me and Gaia.

Though I had accepted my fate serenely, as my last moments neared, I railed bitterly against the dark. My heart pounded. My hands searched in vain for a tool, anything to help me. I had so much to teach Mirabel, so much love to share and experience, so much of the world to explore in Ezra's arms, so many friendships to deepen, so many books to read, so much to learn, so much change I still wanted to make to myself and for my loved ones.

Dammit, I had so much laundry to do that I would be ashamed for anyone else to touch. And if I had known I was going to die, feminist or no feminist, I would have had one last wax. Because last impressions counted as much as first ones, and my muff looked like a grizzly bear.

Could death be a release, or was it always a tragedy? What had Mum felt when she passed away? The moment of death was a let-down, really, deep in the earth in the coffin that shouldn't have been mine. There was no blinding light, no deluge of rain, no eviscerating lighting, no reel of memories from a well-lived life. I had expected more. A little grace. Or someone to accompany me in my final seconds. A guide. An angel, maybe. Or a family pet. Or someone recognisable from an insurance commercial.

No such luck. Nada.

As my eyes fluttered shut and I gave up, the necklace so hot at my neck that it seemed as though hell was my destiny, a voice filled my thoughts. Or maybe the coffin. A voice that I missed dearly. A voice I had last heard when using the spectral sword in Streatham Cemetery when she had told me and Dad to run.

Was it an echo of her in my imagination, or was it really her? I sank into the fantasy.

"What did I tell you about giving up?"

Like a candle in the dark. "Mum? I miss you. Come back."

"We live, we give, we die. That's the beauty of it," said Mum.

Tears mixed with dirt on my face. "I'm not going to make it."

"The Jericho necklace won't work indefinitely. Do you remember how you stole Mami Wata's breath? You have to use your own breath to tunnel out."

My body was slack. I could drift off like this. I wasn't alone. Mum was with me, like when she read me bedtime stories as a child.

"Alisha! Now."

"What if I suffocate myself?"

"Just a little more courage. You can do it."

I held my hands above my mouth. A hot tear trailed down my face as I wrenched the breath out of me, wringing it out like a washcloth, stealing every last drop of oxygen from my lungs before flinging my hands upwards. I turned the breath from my body into a gust of twisting wind, brief but strong enough to make a crack in the lid of the coffin and funnel up through the soil.

Air trickled downwards into the coffin, a dribble rather than a gush, but it was enough. Enough for me to take advantage, despite my delirium, despite my choking need for oxygen.

I held on, turning the trickle of air into a stronger gust that ruptured the integrity of the casket around me, and then I clambered out through splintered wood, pebbles and soil into the graveyard.

Filthy, panting, my nails and hair caked with grime, I swept my gaze around my surroundings for clues about my whereabouts.

I wasn't in hell or the void. I was south of the river in Blackheath, home of wild heaths, yummy mummy cafés and stately Georgian homes. The village was storybook beautiful —apart from being buried alive—until I remembered the rumours that plague victims were buried in mass graves here in the seventeenth century.

What a lark the blue goddess was. Always finding ways to be even more despicable.

The odd night bus chugged along the main road, but I didn't need transport. I had my own wings. I plucked the bronze bell from my jeans and set it on a tuft of grass beside me. Stripping off, I tossed my clothes into the open grave. I meditated in the nude, in the company of crumbling angel statues in the Blackheath graveyard, under the solstice moon, shaking the shackles of the night's experiences.

Against all odds, I was still breathing.

That made me think I stood a chance.

I reached for the bell to summon Death and rang it with a sense of calm.

Standing, I found my place in the ecosystem of all living things and then shifted into my peregrine falcon form. Tilting my head, I admired the gleaming universe ring on my foot. Then I launched into the chill air, shook off the graveyard dirt and dipped into the Thames to drench my feathers before soaring across the city towards St. Paul's, where the entombed one slept.

I was ready for our rematch.

Death could come and find me.

26

The dome of St. Paul's Cathedral glimmered, a beacon in the night. The medieval lines of the cathedral contrasted with the sweeping modernist lines of the Millennium Bridge. I landed on the cross at the dome's summit, a slight shiver in my bird bones, my feathers damp from the river.

Animation created a bond. That connection to my creatures guided me here.

I'd been here once as a child when Mum insisted we spent our weekends as tourists in our city. She'd marvelled at the Baroque architecture achieved by Wren, spoken in hushed whispers about how the cathedral had many incarnations. It had been looted, destroyed by the Great Fire of London and bombed by suffragettes. Then she harried us up the steps of the dimly lit spiral staircase to the Whispering Gallery, where we thrilled at the acoustics. Afterwards, we'd lit a candle at an altar and made secret wishes for an ice cream lunch.

A calm confidence radiated through my breast. I spread my wings and glided across the building, searching for a way to access the interior. Spotting a section of a broken stained-glass window, I hopped through without difficulty.

Steep shadows and radiant silence cloaked the interior of the cathedral. I flew over a black-and-white diamond floor down the nave, past imposing sculptures and religious paintings of saints in gloomy blues and red, under cupola frescos in muted palettes, towards the choir stalls. I pressed on, eager to reach my destination, veering past the pillared high altar and glittering mosaics down the steps to the crypt that encompassed the footprint of the cathedral. Famous Brits—Wren himself, Admiral Nelson and Alexander Fleming—lay buried or memorialised here. But I didn't seek the grand tombs and sarcophagi.

A flare of joyful recognition as I landed outside the Artists' Memorial, startling my naked brother.

"What the…" He did a squeaky fart. "Alisha? It's creepy down here. I confused you for a ghost." His brown eyes shone as he crouched down to me. "I didn't think I was ever going to see you again."

I bounced lightly with happiness before shifting into my human self and grabbed a velvet drape from a nearby altar. "How long have I been gone?"

"An hour, maybe two." He pressed my sword into my hand.

"Thank you." Its familiar weight comforted me. "Is the battle still going?"

His cheeks were hollow with worry. "Yeah. A dozen or so losses. All adults but a few kids are seriously wounded in the sanatorium."

Grit in my throat. "Is everyone we know okay?"

"For now. Ravynne took a serious knock and one of Ezra's pack. The smallest wolf, I think. I'm not sure how long everyone can hold out. Our strength is in our numbers, but we're cannon fodder. They have stamina and strength, and if Death returns…" He shuddered. "That's why I came here."

"I should tell you. I rang the bell to summon Death."

He looked at me, aghast. "Damn, Alisha, we're not even wearing any armour. We're like a pair of plucked chickens waiting to be roasted."

"Let's get cracking and see if whatever's in there can move the dial." I looked down at his pecker. The air in the crypt was chill. "You left your boxers at Wildwoods, eh?"

"My boxers are all over this city." His grin contorted into a grimace. "We can do this."

We stepped in, side by side, into the Artists' Memorial. My stomach fluttered as I swept my gaze across arches upon arches, memorials and inscriptions from psalms. Our bare feet slapped the ground, past artists and sculptors laid to rest in close proximity and over prominent ones whose burial spots were marked by ledger stones. The austere, monochrome feel contrasted the work of those who rested here, like J. M. W. Turner, who had painted worlds steeped in noise and colour.

I knew there was life here still, though the cathedral was empty of clergy, worshippers and tourists.

A kaleidoscope of butterflies welcomed us, and I sucked in my breath: red animals, painted ladies, small tortoiseshells and holly blues. A green-veined white settled on my shoulder, its tiny legs and fluttering wings tickling my skin. My eyes searched in the dark, and I found them: the ravens, the woodpecker, the red-tailed hawk and the waxwings. They grouped around a granite chest about the size of a milk crate. It had a rounded top and was elevated on an altar adorned with an unlit iron candelabra.

A rush of energy came over me.

"There," I breathed.

Sahil's straggly brows drew together. "Are you sure? When they said entombed one, I was expecting an imposing granite casket, not that."

I squeezed his arm. "I'm sure."

We inched towards it, and to me, it seemed like the flagstone floor had become a frothing sea. My doubts surged. We should have been fighting alongside our loved ones at Wildwoods.

What if we'd got it all wrong? What if the police discovered us stark naked siblings with a load of animals in the crypt of St. Paul's? What if everything after Mum's death had been a fever dream? What if all we had to do was to go home to Tooting Bec to find Mum batch-cooking into Tupperware containers?

I gripped the drape, the sword, and my brother's arm.

All we had to do was put one foot in front of the other and not overthink it.

I shushed the whistling, shrilling and croaking birds, my pulse thrumming in my throat.

Sahil stared at the smooth chest in rose granite. "You touch it."

"Coward." The word tripped off my tongue, but I knew it wasn't true. He'd been as brave as me through all this and less supported. "Let's do it together."

"He can't be in there anyway, can He? I mean, the Father of the Gods can't be teeny."

We counted aloud like we'd done when we'd wrestled as children. "One. Two. Three."

My stomach roiled as we tried to prise it open, digging our nails into the seam between the lid of the chest and its base.

It was stuck fast. No amount of pulling and shoving winched it open.

Sahil's minty breath tickled my ear. "That's a bummer. I haven't brought my chisel. Although I've come to realise there are some things that can be smuggled in a werepigeon anus. At least we won't get struck with a thunderbolt."

I leaned closer to the granite, squinting in the dark. My

fingers found gold plating. "There's a lock there. It's too big for a key."

A memory tugged at me, twisting up from the recesses of my mind. I frowned at my sword.

The sword is the key to everything, Gaia had said.

"Sahil, you don't think…" I inserted the tip of Transcender into the keyhole and eased it in. A third of the obsidian blade disappeared into the chest. I twisted it with care, heart hammering.

The lock popped.

I leapt back, pulling the sword and my brother back with me.

Teal green spiralled over the vaulted ceiling, like the aurora borealis, although we weren't in the Arctic or the Antarctic but in the basement of a London cathedral, hardly a place of geological wonder. A wash of blinding light prompted us to squeeze our eyes shut. Every single nerve ending zinged with life.

"Hello, Eve. I see you are wearing your birthday suit and have discarded those ridiculous fig leaves." The deep, sonorous voice filled every crack and crevice in the crypt. "You can remove the drape. There is no need for shame in the kingdom of God."

Sahil and I clung to one another as if we were each other's lifeboat.

I shielded my eyes, shaking like a leaf, and considered strategically spouting falcon feathers if He disintegrated my drape.

"Adam, why do you resemble Eve?" said God.

"This is my sister," said my brother. "We are Sahil and Alisha Verma."

A pause. "So what Gaia and I discussed has come to pass. She fulfilled her promise to free me."

Acute thirst made my mouth dry. "She did."

"She is as reliable as the seasons." The crypt juddered

with His booming voice. "When the heavens crumbled, and I sent the gods to Earth on my last breath, not all of them repaid me in kind. They became faithless as their powers and standing dwindled. So Death imprisoned me in my weakened state in a rundown South London church used as a skate park."

"That sucks, man," said my brother.

I elbowed him in the ribs. We weren't in the hood talking to our mates.

"Thank you for your empathy." God's deep timbre brimmed with affection. "Gaia almost found me in that first church, but she got distracted by an errant skater who needed her help. That was two generations ago when Rajika was the Custodian of the Celestial Library. I see now that you are her kin."

Even though my eyes were closed, the warmth of His light spooled over my face.

"Death moved me here to St. Paul's." A hint of exasperation in His voice. "It's the sort of place that attracts drama. Churchill's and Thatcher's funerals took place here, as well as Charles and Diana's royal wedding. We knew how that went downhill. It's quite peaceful here amongst the artists. They are always a special kind of human. Dreamers. Outsiders. Empathisers."

An echo of Gaia in my head. "Love never dies. She couldn't kill you."

"Death never even worked out how to open the chest," He said. "That was Gaia's work. She is as good with flowers as she is with stone. She was in on the whole charade from the very beginning. It was a teaching opportunity. I am very patient."

"You knew," breathed Sahil. "You knew the rogue gods would betray you."

"Of course. Gaia and I placed our bets aeons ago. We even divvied up the planets like marbles. I only lost one in this solar system. Pan could have gone either way. But Pluto's a dwarf planet, so I didn't lose any sleep over it." God chuckled. "It was the laddus, wasn't it?"

"Gaia didn't know where Death took you. And Death didn't know how to open the chest." Goosebumps chased up my skin. My sword hung heavy in my hand. "But Death had the key from the very beginning. She was the one who fashioned it and gifted it to Gaia."

"The heavenly sword," said God. "But Death could barely bring herself to look at it, let alone use it after Gaia's rejection of her love. Gaia had given *her* gift to a *mortal*. To you—a fledgling warrior—who was brave enough to wield the sword. Death's ego was wounded. So she made a twin of it."

Awe filled my voice. "But that one wasn't the key."

My brother piped up. "Because she made the first one with love. And the second one with hate."

"Isn't clarity of understanding a beautiful thing?" He said. "I want you to return to the battlefield. When the time comes, the twin swords will clash. Then I will come."

I wet my lips; eyes still squeezed shut, our vulnerability laid bare. "That's it? Can't you tell us how it ends? Can't you tell us whether our friends will live and if the balance will be restored?"

"No, my child," said God. "There's never any surety in life. Surely, you know that from reading the sacred texts. Teachers don't give students the answers. We just shine a light on the path."

I kept stumm about my atheist beliefs. Maybe I didn't need to put a tentpole in the ground. Maybe I could be spiritual without being religious. Maybe I could choose to navigate my life by the customs and beliefs that resonated with me and just be true to myself.

God probably heard my questioning, but He didn't shame me.

My brother muttered his disappointment. "Plucked chickens, I tell you."

It was Gaia I thought of, her bound and gagged body on the back of the demon-dragged chariot. "What about the Earth goddess?"

"Death needs an invested audience. She will drag Gaia with her to witness her crowning glory. It's one of the perverse ways she gains enjoyment," He said. "I tried very hard to persuade her to enjoy more wholesome pursuits. But alas, she always preferred wreaking havoc in mosh pits to joining choirs of angels. Do you have anything further you wish to ask me?"

I pressed Sahil's hand as the light spun across our crossed eyelids. "Can we speak to Mum?"

"No," He said.

Next to me, Sahil slumped. "That's crushing, man."

My chest tightened. "But I want to tell her I love her."

"You still haven't learned that lesson." The warmth of His light in the crypt was an embrace. "She knows. The love you share didn't disappear with her death. Isn't that the message of this time of year? Now go. The battle awaits, and so do two bottles of water at the cathedral ticket counter to quench your thirst. And hurry. I've been shielding your presence here since the moment you freed me, but that bell you rang at Blackheath means Death is already on your tail."

27

———

His light faded as we turned our backs on the Artists' Memorial, making us shiver with loss. I ventured a look over my shoulder, and though the room lay in shadows, the iron candelabra next to the open chest burned. With a sigh, we stumbled up the steps to the main cathedral, blinking to reorient ourselves to the bleak darkness. Waxwings, crows and butterflies swept past us in the direction of the broken stained-glass window. They no longer had any reason to remain in the depths of the crypt.

Only once we passed the high altar, our feet squelching against the floor, did my eyes acclimatise.

I grabbed Sahil by the shoulder. "Your hair."

He faced me, eyes widening. "*Your* hair."

I picked up a lock of my thick, curly hair and found it had turned silver, just like my brother's. "That was His doing, wasn't it? Some sort of reaction to His divine light."

Sahil gulped. "I think so."

"He did me a favour. Colouring my roots has become the bane of my life."

"With all this going on, *that's* the bane of your life?" My brother gave a wry smile. "He did me a favour too. One by one, He's taking all my vanity away. That's got to make me less of an arsehole, right?"

I burst into laughter, and he did, too. We found the bottles of water on the ticket counter and quenched our thirst. Then we shifted into our bird forms, and just like my big brother had carried my bag on the way to school, he carried Transcender in his werepigeon beak on our way to Wildwoods.

As I whooshed over the wintery London rooftops ahead of my werepigeon brother, I convinced myself that everything would be okay despite the depth of the night.

WILDWOODS LAY IN RUINS.

The yew tree recognised my brother and me, even in our bird forms. I trained my falcon gaze on the battlefield. Every muscle and sinew strained to be part of the fight. Floodlights vied with shadows. Pools of blood spilt under burnt husks of trees. Lavinia's barricade of inverted umbrellas hung twisted and useless above the arena. A crater smoked at the centre of the vaulted cabin while smaller cabins dangled precariously in trees. My bird heart drummed at the sight of the obelisk— no longer piercing the clouds—warped and folded over as if it were origami, not steel. The candy-striped cable cars puddled in the soil, now molten glass and metal. Cinders danced over the now flattened curve of the reading nook. Library books sodden with blood lay strewn across the battlefield.

Peculiars suffered and struggled. Howls of anguish drifted skywards, and broken bodies stretchered from the crimson ground. Witches clung to their umbrellas, chanting flurries of spells. Growling shifters leapt across the terrain, vampires blurred, and elven black holes popped. Last ditch attempts under the canvas of the velvety night.

At the centre of it all, the minor gods waged war—Ra, Hermes, Mami Wata, Cardea and Morpheus—covered in gore and glory. They revelled in the pain they inflicted on us.

To them, this was a game.

To them, this was a small moment in eternity.

Yet, as Sahil and I flew ever closer, I found pockets of hope. The pack of wolves led by a grey-copper alpha. The armoured leopard next to the fire fairy. The rainbow-haired empath on a black pegasus. A vampire with alabaster skin, his fists raised. Two old artists on a turquoise dragon.

My relief at their safety was tempered by the enormity of our challenge.

I dove towards the battleground, the familiar sawdust arena which had long been a place of learning and now stank of death. Just before hitting the ground, I shifted into my human form, silver hair loose and free over my shoulders.

The werepigeon grunted above my head, dropping the sword into my hands. "Stay alive."

I gripped it, a neat catch, already scanning the battlefield. "Find Flinar. We need the book."

My brother flashed his teeth in a gruesome appropriation of a smile, then, in a puff of scruffy feathers, headed towards Hermes and his unkindness of ravens.

Tracking the battle from the arena was impossible. Thick darkness encompassed us with only small pockets of relief. My senses went into overdrive. The iron taste of blood in the air. Cries and panting. The clash of swords and whizz of umbrellas.

Fallen angels left me breathless as they swept past, flying low and hard. The coven—minus Lavinia—stormed past, pursuing Phinnaeous Shine, whose wizardry meant even against five witches, he stood a chance. A hair's breadth away, the snarling foxes fought a mix of demons and djinn, backed up by a troupe of teenage fairies and magical pangolins. They alternately lashed their sharp-edged tails and curled into scaly balls when threatened. Faeza's green-violet *hu hsien* eyes softened at the sight of me, her foxy scream piercing the air. Next to her—together in love and strife—Fei Yen's six tails fanned out as she sank her teeth into a demonic glowing skull.

I slashed left and right, driving my sword into two demons on the periphery, boobs bouncing in opposite directions, but I didn't care.

I pressed on, searching for Morpheus, the strongest god on the battlefield.

A silent scream gathered in my throat as Cardea portalled behind a leprechaun three metres away, strangling him with her diseased fingers. The leprechaun's body slumped to the floor. Calypso was already there in a beautifully pressed suit, metallic eyeshadow painted in war stripes on her tawny skin, flanked by the sphinxes. The portal goddess created confusion by creating doors at ground level and in the air, her movements unpredictable, a peekaboo of horror. But the Custodian had the powers of the Celestial Library, even though it lay thousands of miles away amongst the stars. They portalled, and when the goddess paused a moment too long, Calypso whirled towards her, dreadlocks flying as she flipped in the air and brought down her blade runners on Cardea beneath her.

Calypso flashed me a victorious smile, slipped the Guns N' Roses rucksack off her shoulders that she must have retrieved from Lavinia's office and tossed it to me. "Walking in your grandmother's footsteps, I see. You're going to need this."

Stomach fluttering, I unzipped it and threw on my grandmother's chainmail and boots.

A sense of destiny surged through me. I could almost see the finish line. I sensed the chain of my ancestors through my sword, the sway of the trees, the rotation of the planets and the flicker of an iron candelabra in the crypt of St. Paul's Cathedral.

Calypso gave me an approving nod. "Go get them."

Then she turned back to meet the portal goddess's spear with her knives, her brown eyes gleaming with deadly intent.

I pushed on. The battle was too chaotic to unleash twisting winds. At the edge of the arena, the dragon breathed his fire in short bursts, bonded to me, neither of us willing to risk harming our own side. Instead, I felled enemies in my way: djinn, demons, helping those who needed me. I called out for Flinar. My eyes raked the dark for Morpheus. For Ezra, Mirabel and Echo. Hoping with fervour the bodies that tangled at my feet weren't my leopard's.

That he still lived. That they all still lived.

My arrival hadn't gone unnoticed. The sphinxes roared and circled the battlefield to spread the word. Euphoria rippled across the arena. Flagging spirits revived.

She lives. She lives, came the whispers.

As if they had already somehow mourned my death. As if their belief had been restored.

I passed Orpheus and his vampire clan battling the leathery sun god in a pool of molten light. Ra's liquid amber eyes glittered in his swarthy face as he shot the vampires with arrows of searing sun. The vampires wore yellow electrician's gloves that Wildwoods ejected from the ground. Orpheus had commandeered sparking cabling from the cable cars as whips, his clashes with the sun god a dazzling display of strength and speed. An unknown vampire fought at his side, sultry and strong. He whipped her out of harm's way before he noticed me.

You escaped Death. Relief coloured his every syllable.

A sense of calm settled over me, knowing that our friendship was still intact, that his awareness of my engagement hadn't somehow broken the bond we shared. Even if he had wanted more.

She's on her way, I said. *Who's the sultry vampire?*

Dark eyes held mine. *Seskel's cousin.*

The one who'd been at the club when he'd watched Mirabel for us. *You like her.*

The sultry vampire ran towards him, fearless, determination written all over her face.

Orpheus braced himself and propelled her towards the sun god. *Maybe I do.*

I'm happy for you. Keep your eyes on the enemy, okay? I used my wind magic to steady a non-witch zooming overhead on a coven umbrella. *Can you manage the sun god?*

He laughed and tightened his grip on the sparking cable. *You no longer need a teacher, Alisha. That makes me your equal, not a damsel in distress.*

Further along, Meriel and a group of elves battled Mami Wata. My palm tingled as I called a winter wind, sending a twister to floor the water goddess. No sooner had I hit her than I stole her breath, buying the elves a moment of respite. The elf queen grinned at me, blue eyes no longer vacant but full of purpose. Matted, grey hair flew out over bony shoulders clad in her sack-like dress as she called forth elven magic, harnessing Mami Wata's snake with the ease of a snake charmer. With her, the elves would have mastered more than black hole magic.

"Where's Flinar?" I needed the book, but its whispers were silent.

"He has the tome I desired." The elf queen's cackle was wild and joyous. "The world is indeed changing, Rajika. But can it change fast enough to save us all?"

The elves surged, and I spotted Morpheus at last.

My stomach hardened at the sight of his opponents. There was Ezra and the pack with Mirabel and Echo.

The leopard—who was never more than a step from my

daughter's side—bore new scars but was conscious again, majestic in shining armour commissioned by my grandmother. Mirabel flamed a trio of djinn with the nonchalance of a kid playing computer games. Tufts of fur. Strips of flesh in teeth. Snarling mouths. A thick, coiling tail. The dream god disappearing and reappearing in clouds of hellish smoke, the limb Mirabel had exploded dragging behind him. The grey-copper wolf, distracted, searching the battlefield for me.

Taking off at a run towards them, I leapt over a trench and into the fray.

"He's mine," I shouted, scattering loved ones and allies with a channel of wind. I barged the dream god with my shoulder and boxed his gaunt nose with my left fist.

Morpheus recoiled. His injured limb made him unstable, but he wasn't cowed. All physical pain was temporary for an immortal. Primordial power dripped from his pupilless eyes.

"I have dreamt of this," he hissed, his ridged tongue nightmarishly long.

Somewhere in the background, Echo had broken into a rendition of the *Ghostbusters* theme tune.

I was done playing games.

Transcender was the perfect weight in my hand, an extension of my body. The obsidian blade was short, and I had to get in close. But it didn't matter. I didn't need a shield when I could manipulate the winds to be a perfect buffer. Smoke billowed, but I'd sussed out his patterns, and hubris made him underestimate me.

I spun and pierced his stomach, withdrawing quickly to re-engage with a diagonal cut to the dream god's shoulder.

He bellowed in pain, but the injury wouldn't slow him down for long.

My eyes locked on Ezra, a frisson of understanding between us.

The grey-copper wolf—his fur matted with blood—

howled, and his pack responded to his call under the glowing moon of the winter solstice. They formed a ring around me, Ezra, Mirabel and Echo, buying us a precious few seconds together while they tore at the dream god's sinewy black flesh.

Mirabel sobbed, her face and hands blackened with soot. "You're here. You're really here."

I hugged her. Even as I did, the pack struggled to contain the dream god as he dissolved into smoky nothingness before solidifying elsewhere, his thick, twirling tail threatening to gut those who dropped their focus.

I turned to the three of them. "We have to end this. I don't want to send them to hell one by one, only for them to emerge anew from a Rejuvenation Pool. We have to control them long enough for the Father of the Gods to get here."

The grey-copper wolf's growl rumbled in his throat.

I pressed my forehead to his, and as I did, the whispers of the book surged. "That's right. Sahil and I found him. It's nearly over." I squeezed my daughter. "I trust you, Bel. I'm not going to tell you to get to safety. You are a formidable warrior. But Echo's staying with you. Now go."

The grey-copper wolf's eyes softened. Then he gave a growl-like bark and broke the ranks of his pack to take the brunt of the dream god's ire, leaping and twisting, tearing a strip from Morpheus's protruding wings.

Mirabel and Echo followed, fairy and hunter, fire and tombstone teeth.

I looped my thumb and forefinger in my mouth and catcalled. Experience of walking past building sites told me that the sound would attract Marina's ire wherever she was.

A flash of pink hair as Nightfall veered in my direction, whites of eyes and chomping teeth, a stallion thrilled by battle, as if this was his natural habitat and not the gleaming corridors of a library amongst the stars. She rode him bareback, without a saddle or reins, her pole dancer thighs clinging on. With her leather bodysuit amongst thick plumes of black feathers, she evoked a burlesque dancer, not a war-waging vet from South London.

When the horse neared, Marina simply leaned over and pulled me up behind her. She squeezed my thigh as Nightfall powered upwards, working hard to achieve momentum with my additional weight.

"Love the new look, babe. My vision was all wrong. Well, not wrong, but it stopped too soon. When the void closed, I knew you were okay." Her skin glistened with perspiration, and she nonchalantly sprayed pepper spray at a passing crow and slashed a winged demon with her whip. "I love you."

"And I love you." I wrapped my arms around her waist. "Take me to the vaulted cabin."

28

Nightfall landed through the crater at the centre of the vaulted cabin, snorting and tossing his mane in warning. The embers flitting over the ashen rafters didn't frighten him. Nor the stained-glass fairy tales blown out from the windows that crunched under his hooves. His eyes rolled at the stage: of all the books housed in the library amongst the stars—the ones that amused, thrilled, educated and comforted—this was the one that heralded loss.

With a hand of comfort on Nightfall's shuddering flank, I jumped down from his back. Marina followed suit. It only seemed yesterday that we'd discovered my childhood Bengal cat was a leopard from the plains of India. A sour taste pervaded my mouth, and dread mushroomed in my heart as we picked our way across the vaulted cabin towards the Prime Sorceress and Defence Minister. As the sounds of turbulent battle snaked across Wildwoods, I understood that sometimes beasts were kinder than people, and sometimes people were beasts.

We reached the stage, our breathing shallow, five feet between us, and looked up.

Lavinia and Flinar sat side by side on austere, high-backed chairs in a crescent of glowing pillar candles. On a table between them, pillowed on my mother's scarf, the Book of Names waited for someone to claim it.

My muscles tightened in readiness.

Death heard its call, too. Of that, I was certain.

Flinar's ears quivered. "I knew you'd know where to find me."

"The whispers called me." I turned to Lavinia. "You weren't with the coven on the battlefield."

"The elf came here because it is the seat of power and where he's always wanted to be," said Lavinia. "I've been playing chess while you've been playing with my nephew's cucumber. I did try and warn you, Alisha. Wildwoods revealed his location to me when he emerged from his black hole."

Flinar quaked. "I came here to keep the book safe and because my presence on the battlefield destabilised the queen. She thinks she is still our leader."

"I believe you." I meant it.

Marina's cotton-blue eyes assessed Lavinia's aura. "It's the Prime Sorceress who covets the book."

The witch's eyes flicked to the Book of Names.

"I know it calls to you, Lavinia," I said softly. "It creeps inside our heads, promising power. But it corrupts. The prophecy says only I can wield it."

I inched closer, locking eyes with the Prime Sorceress. A battle of wills.

Behind me, Nightfall reared up on his hind legs.

Grief etched lines on her face. "The prophecy doesn't say if you'll survive. I couldn't save my nephew from the loss of his parents. Gunnolf and I played tug-of-war over him after their deaths. I schemed to gain his teleportation powers. But I can save him from the loss of you. Let me undo all the times I've wronged him. Let me do my duty as Prime Sorceress and as Ezra's aunt."

I picked up the scarf and the Book of Names. Its whispers were a sigh in my head as if it was finally back where it belonged: with me.

The resolve in her eyes wavered. "It's my duty."

I shook my head and placed my hand on hers, remembering Ezra's words. *She's a link to my mother that I don't want to give up.* "Ezra needs us both."

"As you wish, Alisha." She drew in a shuddering breath, for once seeming older than her years. "I'll follow your lead."

"As will I," said Flinar.

Nightfall delivered Marina and me back down to the blood-soaked arena. His feathered wings retracted as he landed. We dismounted, and he cantered off, whinnying in Calypso's direction.

Rajika's armour hung heavy on my body. My mother's paisley scarf fluttered at my neck.

"I have to do this part alone," I said.

Marina—my sister, my support—readied her pepper spray and whip. "No, you bloody well won't."

A well of love flowed between us, though danger menaced all around, and we walked through the battlefield. I opened the notebook made from cowhide and covered in stardust. Then I read aloud, power tingling from my head to the tips of my toes.

Sapphire ink and crumbling pages. Words in a language I didn't understand—Aramaic, Hebrew, I couldn't know—but could instinctively decode. Words the elf queen had sought long ago. Not the given names of the gods, the ones in stories and engraved on altars; rather, their true names, bestowed by the Father of the Gods when the universe first dawned. Names that allowed me to control them. I turned the vowels over in my mouth, feeling the click of my tongue, rugged consonants and guttural rolls in the back of my throat. A raw, primeval power. A harsh grace.

Just ahead, Orpheus and his clan battled Ra, drenched in sweat.

As I read, the sun god faltered.

"It's working," said Marina. "His light is dimmer. His arrows slower."

The battle is turning. Read, Alisha, said the vampire. *There are already too many dead.*

I walked on through the pressing dark, but I wasn't alone. There was Marina. Then Mirabel and Echo joined the other side of me. Next came the foxes, each on one of the outer edges. A red-tailed hawk, waxwings and butterflies from the crypt at St. Paul's soared overhead. Thundering through the sky on Tielbu's shimmering turquoise scales came Dad in his superhero costume and Great-Uncle Rajiv.

"I'm coming, Alisha," shouted Dad above the din of the dragon's wings. "Never fear."

Rajiv drank in the sight of me in my armour and flowing silver hair. "I mistook you for Rajika."

"Easily done, Uncle. A battlefield is no place for bifocals." Dad handed a sheet of paper to a leaping Echo, black and yellow smudges covering his fingers. "You go do your thing, love. No need to squint in the dark."

I animated the fireflies from the illustration Dad had painted for me, and they lit my way. Tears of gratitude prickled my eyes. The burden of the prophecy had never been just mine to carry. My friends and family bolstered me with their belief, their wisdom, their love and their physical acts of courage.

The fireflies danced, a reminder of how even the smallest of us could have an impact on the arc of the world. As I read, the raging of the gods quieted, and their blades stilled as though I had pulled a noose around their necks. The gods— once unbeatable—strained against the binding of the ancient words.

With every syllable, the momentum of the battle tipped in

our direction. The vampires coiled cables around seething Ra. My brother released his bowels on Hermes as the fallen angels encircled him. The elf queen taunted Mami Wata as she trapped her in the tank once used for Kraglek. Calypso roped Cardea to the crumpled obelisk, and Ezra's pack overcame Morpheus, pinning his wings and limbs down with their snarling jaws. And the sphinxes encircled Phinnaeous Shine, who'd had trapped them in their stone forms for countless years.

"We are victorious," announced Margola's voice across the arena.

The woman is a fantasist, said Orpheus. *We have to be vigilant.*

He was right. I knew it before Echo's growl and Tielbu's roar. I knew it before Ezra bounded to my side. I knew it by the surge of whispers in my head that the night's ordeals weren't yet over.

I closed the book and addressed Wildwoods. "This is the eye of the storm. Death is coming."

Too late for good sense. Too late for intuition.

Margola's announcement had tipped the mood in the arena into heady relief verging on ecstasy. Peculiars laid down their weapons and looked in horror and hope at the scenes around them. They embraced each other, daring to hope that the long night might soon be over. That it might be time to tend to the sick and grieve the dead.

The hair on my neck stood on end as time slowed. The kind of stillness that happens just before a car accident, a plane crash or the passing of a loved one. When all hope is suspended and the inevitable follows.

Death came, knowing that we'd let our guard down, from behind the blanket of the starless sky.

She came in skeleton form with a garland of poppies and lilies around her head, her eyes hollow, her hand of bones holding Surrender's obsidian blade aloft.

She came through a yawning breach in the night, riding her chariot of sulphurous demons with the Earth goddess sallow and chained alongside her.

"To arms! Secure the gods," called the Prime Sorceress.

The Wildwoods battalion responded. The coven teleported to the minor gods in a flash, chanting protection spells. Marina coaxed Mirabel back while the remainder of the senate joined Ezra and Echo at my side. We stood as one, just as we always should have.

The arena grew quiet as a tomb.

Shadows lengthened as Death stepped into sawdust, reeking of blood and piss and animal dung. Her skull turned 180 degrees, taking in the fate of the minor gods. "They are not immortals. They are embarrassments. I had such high hopes for the vampire, but he gave you my summoning bell. Where did you go after you rang it?"

My pulse was a butterfly in my throat.

Death liked the sound of her voice. "Coffin entrapment usually reliably snuffs out life, but no matter. Why should I waste centuries when I can destroy both you and the book here?"

Her skeletal smile could have splintered the moon.

Beside me, Ezra let out a growl of warning.

With trembling fingers, I opened the crumbling pages.

Death turned her eye hollows on the book. "If you read, you condemn not just me but the Earth goddess. We will rise again and take what's ours. Is my vision of the world really so bad, Gaia?"

My stomach clenched. The Earth goddess deserved to be in her Tooting flat, her cascade of hair oiled and plaited, or at her favourite café with a cup of chai. She deserved to potter in her garden and while away hours with her latchkey children all around her. She deserved to bask in the light Sahil and I had experienced in the crypt of St. Paul's.

But in the deepest mountain browns of Gaia's eyes, in the

flecks of ocean blue and verdant meadow greens, I saw acceptance.

So I read, knowing it might be her undoing.

I read Death's name and Gaia's name.

I cycled through the names of the gods, like a rosary, over and over.

The gods jerked. The gods raged. Even the ones that we had already trapped, as if Death's arrival had given them one last spark of courage, one last window of opportunity to mould the world in their sinful image. As if they had truly forgotten what it meant to be good and kind and the light in the world. As if this was the most dangerous moment for us all.

Death slowed, meeting resistance as if the air thickened as she came towards me.

Still, I read.

I read as chaos reigned.

I read, hungering for more power, a craven pit of desire.

I read as a silver-white werewolf with piercing blue eyes, medium in size, sprang through the air—a wolf I recognised and Ezra loved.

Death's skeletal arm cut through the air. She sank her gleaming blade into the pit of the werewolf and twisted the hilt. Maximillian slumped as his guts poured onto the dust. Torn flesh and jutting bone.

I read as Ezra pounded towards Death to exact revenge, and Orpheus slammed him to the ground, recognising his attack as futile. Saving him for me, though the grey-copper wolf persisted, and the vampire bled. I read as Isadora teleported to a group of students targeted by Cardea and her diseased fingers, neither the first nor the last Wildwoods headteacher to use her body as a shield for her pupils. I read as Echo fended off demons freed from the harness of Death's chariot, and Mirabel, Dad and Tielbu joined him as if they were barbecuing meat. I read as the cackling elf queen dragged Morpheus into a black hole, glee in every spell and glint of her blade. And as poor Flinar carried his queen's lifeless body back out, a smile still on her face.

I read, even when horror snaked up my spine, and Ra's arrow of sun ignited the Book of Names with searing heat. I read while he lit another, and Calypso spun through the air to protect us and paid with her life. Her beautiful eyes became glassy even before the book had fallen in a burning heap from my hands. Nightfall's ears flattened, and his eyes rolled, and he reared up in grief. I couldn't look. It hurt too much to see her there, her body cooling in the sawdust, her uncreased trouser suit charred by Ra's hand. Hot tears stung my eyes and burned my throat. She was so clever and courageous and so utterly beautiful. It wasn't fair for her to be cut down in her prime. Why couldn't it have been Rashida or Helio instead? Why did the good and kind die first?

My nails dug into the palms of my hands—anger, hot and righteous, churned in my stomach. I wouldn't give in to sadness. Not yet. I needed to pull on my big girl knickers and make Death pay.

That was what Calypso would want. That was how I could honour her.

I lifted Transcender and met Death in the centre of it all, though she was a goddess and I was just an ordinary woman. Because I was extraordinary in some ways, and I believed in myself.

Our twin swords clashed: one stone blue, the orange, shaped like the elliptical pupil of a snake. All else blurred into nothing. Death's skeletal arms whirled, and it took every ounce of skill and focus for me to counter her.

At times, she branched out to oncoming threats: a grey-copper wolf, a tall vampire, a rainbow-haired woman bringing a cloud of pepper spray, an armoured leopard, a fireball-throwing fairy with moss-green eyes, a somersaulting witch on a dull brown umbrella, a scraggly werepigeon leading an army of pigeons ejecting pellet turds from above, a superhero Dad and the weakened Earth goddess freed by a coven of witches.

Though all that unfolded on the periphery, there was only me and Death, her skeletal arms whirling, the pounding of our feet, clouds of sawdust and clumpy earth, trees spouting from the arena to protect me, the ringing of our swords, the swell of my tornado, the clatter of my heartbeat, the pulsing Jericho necklace entwined with the paisley scarf at my neck, my anger at Death mixed with compassion for the living. She had compromised the balance of the world. She played dirty yet expected to win.

Not on my watch.

Though my feet were tired, my eyes blurred, and I was impatient for the light from the crypt at St. Paul's to fill the arena, I used all my skills and talents to stay alive. Though the book was gone, and Death had almost won. Though I couldn't possibly hope to best a warrior as accomplished as her. Though when Transcender hit her body, her skeleton held, and when Surrender hit mine, my flesh bled.

Still, I fought because middle-aged women don't give up, even when the universe delivers them a dump truck. Middle-aged women dig deep and try harder, and they make every moment count.

A sharp pain overcame me as Death's sword struck a vein in my thigh.

Cold and wetness spread across my body, though I wore my grandmother's armour.

Though I was the prophesied eternal girl and Gaia's champion.

My sword fell from my hands, but Ezra's arms caught me. He wasn't a wolf anymore. He was himself. Though I loved every part of him. The scent of mountain air and earth and roll-up cigarettes, of blood and sweat and fear. He was hurt too—an oozing gash on his arm, under his eyebrow and in his side—but his concern was me. He called out to someone, Marina or Dad, about taking me to St. Georges Hospital or the sanatorium. The Earth goddess counselled him.

I hated goodbyes. Wretched partings that tore at the soul.

I fought to keep my eyes open, though white spots filled my vision, my thoughts became disjointed, and my body no longer responded to what my brain told it to do. The Jericho necklace pulsed at my throat or maybe my heartbeat. As a radiant, blistering light chased away the winter solstice and a familiar booming voice filled my head, I sensed my connection to all things. To the ground, the sky, the roots that wrapped themselves around me, like they had once wrapped themselves around the dying witch Elvira.

He had come. He had come, like a partygoer timing his entrance for the best impact.

As if he had a sense of humour or a whole host of priorities and we were only one.

The light was blinding, but I wanted to see. I wanted cocktail sticks to prise open my eyes. Was that the gods on their knees? Death stripped of her garland of flowers? Gaia, serene and renewed at His right hand. The gods, gone, taken from the arena as if they had never existed. As if they didn't deserve to exist.

A booming voice saying *thank you* in my head.

Damn, I wanted to drink celebration pinã coladas with Marina. I wanted to tell my dad that I appreciated him. I wanted to have a lazy Sunday on the sofa with my daughter and our leopard. To go to dinner and the opera with an old vampire. To have the foxes read my tarot and dance at a K-pop concert with them. To soar over fields in my falcon form with my werepigeon brother telling me to slow down. To have celebration sex with Ezra and get married and fight over whether we should keep the old sofas and grow old with him.

I wanted it all.

"You did it." Ezra cradled me to him. "Rest now. It'll all be okay."

My consciousness slipped further away as though I had become submerged in a lapping river.

Somewhere, in the depths of a South London park, peculiars prayed and cheered.

29

I woke disoriented at the edge of the arena with a tangle of boughs around me. A dull ache permeated my thigh. The Earth goddess sat on a small mound by my side. Her armour was gone. She wore a fresh sari in cobalt blue with an olive-green border and sipped from a flask of chai. The night had ended, and the skies were bright. But the moon glimmered in the cerulean sky, and the sun was nowhere to be seen.

My throat scratched. "What time is it?"

"Oh, not yet 3 a.m." Gaia's cherubic face dimpled. "He tends to do this when He comes. Delivers some razzle dazzle then disappears, leaving everything out of sync. I'm always cleaning up after him."

I sat up and took in my surroundings. We were at Wildwoods, a stone's throw away from the arena. The battlefield had all but emptied, and I wondered if this wasn't Wildwoods at all and maybe the waiting room for the afterlife.

"Am I dead?" I asked.

Gaia laughed with delight. "Of course not, Alisha, although with the blood loss, it was touch and go for a minute. Still, your mother's Jericho necklace and my root magic did the work. And He would always have sent you back to the living after all you braved for us."

I remembered the radiant light. "He came."

Her eyes twinkled. "To think, all the dilapidated churches off the beaten track I checked, and He was in St. Paul's all along. Kali definitely got me there."

The memory of Death chilled me to my core. "The gods?"

"Gone," grinned Gaia. "He's giving them a moral spanking right now. It will be a long time before He gives them free rein again. The minute they felt his light, they grovelled for forgiveness, but as my latchkey children know, forgiveness isn't automatic. It only comes with true repentance and a change in behaviour." She took a final slurp of her tea and fastened the lid of her flask. "I loved her once, you know."

"I know." Love was like that. Sometimes, it broke your heart.

"A few fallen angels begged to return to heaven with Him, too, just in case you're wondering why you can't find their bodies. He said it's up to you what to do with the shapeshifting wizard. You'll find him in the arena under some demon goo."

"Oh." I felt no malice towards Phinnaeous Shine, only pity. A pause. "I thought God might stick around to have a word with me."

Gaia rested her hand on my face. "It's like that for me too. However much time I spend with him, I always want more. But then I remember how much I have."

I bit my lip. "Goddess, I'm an atheist."

Her brow furrowed. "Words. They have such meaning, and sometimes they mean nothing at all. All you have to know is that faith doesn't solve everything. Humans still have to do the work. You know how it goes: improve every day, help the weak, care for the earth, keep your ego in check, write a gratitude journal, yada yada yada."

I frowned. I couldn't remember the last time I had slept soundly. I craved fresh sheets and a plump pillow, and Ezra's calves for me to warm my feet on, but something niggled at me. A gap in my memory. Words I had spoken but had drifted away like kites on the wind. A book I had once held that had entwined with my very cells.

Gaia picked out a cardamom pod from her tongue. "Oh, you won't ever remember *those* words again. It's best that way. You're wonderful but not perfect, Alisha. We wouldn't want you falling prey to baser instincts. But if you must know, you're one of my top humans ever. It's a very small list." The light in her eyes warmed my cold bones. "You really were very brave, you know. I might have found you, but your decisions were all your own. You made your ancestors proud. You made me proud. I haven't felt so free in a long time."

She heaved herself to her feet, dusted off her sari and picked up her flask. Then, with a smile that melted icebergs, she walked away. Strapped to her back were the twin swords, crossed.

A tidal wave of desolation crashed over me. "Will I see you again?"

Gaia glanced over her shoulder. "Who else is going to make laddus for your wedding? I've been practising all these centuries, hoping we'd have something to celebrate."

I didn't respond. Instead, I drank in the sight of my family approaching. Dad with his arms outstretched. Marina kissing her lucky clover. Mirabel with blue crescent shadows under her eyes. Ezra, his arm bandaged and stitches under his eyebrow. And my golden leopard, his fur matted with blood and his tail hanging perhaps a little crooked but his majestic head high with pride.

As I stumbled up and scampered towards them, I knew everything was going to be okay.

Phinnaeous Shine waited for justice to be served. His robes were torn, his feet in demon goo, the gods he had long courted hauled away to the heavens.

"I did this for Wildwoods," he said.

The Prime Sorceress cast her eyes around the wreckage of the school and the bodies covered in blankets. Her usually exemplary posture buckled with exhaustion. "You did this for yourself. A decision you made over and over again."

His mouth was pinched. "Send me to the Court of the Wolves or the Ritz."

"Oh, we tried that. I may be many things, but I'm not stupid. You know what the definition of stupidity is, don't you?" The Prime Sorceress was going to need more than a few youth potions to smooth out the lines on her forehead. The night had taken a toll on us all. "It's a lesson we all learn."

Ezra lounged against a tree, a roll-up hanging in his mouth. He took a drag, stubbed it out, and offered me his hand. "Doing the same thing over and over again and expecting the same result."

"That's right, nephew. That's why this poor excuse for a man is not going to the Court of Wolves." Fury simmered in Lavinia's voice and manifested in the tight curl of her fist on her umbrella. "How should we punish him, Alisha?"

Tielbu, grazing on some Marks & Spencer beef Dad had bought him, snorted with excitement.

"It's enough to know how far he has fallen. That he will never have power over anyone again." I pulled my silver curls over one shoulder. "Talent is nature. Character is a choice. You could have been so much more, Phinnaeous, but beyond that, I have no feelings to waste on you. Not anymore."

The Prime Sorceress twirled her umbrella with glee. "Step

forward, my coven sisters. We will determine a fitting punishment to accompany a long life."

Phinnaeous's sneer fell away as the coven stepped forward.

"May your bus seat always feel suspiciously wet," said Chandra.

"May your tea never be the right colour," said Ravynne.

"May you always run out of loo roll when you most need it," said Agatha.

"May your mattress always be lumpy," said Isadora, who hadn't yet recovered from Cardea's attack.

Lavinia nodded with satisfaction. "May you be haunted by what you enabled. May the memory of your sins never fade."

As Phinnaeous looked on in confusion, Dad lurched forward on Tielbu's back. "If nobody else minds, I just wanted to make it clear that your predatory pursuit of my mother, Rajika, was unwelcome, and I should let the dragon nibble your chipolata."

Tielbu's amber eyes hooded, and he swooped down, his jaw wide open and smoking.

Phinnaeous's blanched, his arms dropping to his side.

The dragon swallowed him whole and spat out his robe and shoes, and though he didn't speak at that moment, I read the meaning in his eyes loud and clear. *He had it coming.*

"Oops." Dad reached for his bong. "Animals will be animals."

Copper flecks danced in Ezra's eyes. "I guess the Marks & Spencer beef didn't stave off his ravenous hunger."

WE REBUILT WILDWOODS.

We rebuilt it, although two dozen peculiars had perished

on the battlefield, and we reeled with shock. Our clash with the gods had shaken the school to its very foundations, but our community was unbroken. We tended to the sick and injured, made preparations to honour the dead and consoled one another in our grief. Slowly, our physical ailments healed, although the psychological trauma took longer to process.

It helped to keep busy. Many hands made light work. We cleared debris scattered in the sawdust and tree canopy, mended the school with graft and magic, salvaged books, and planted seedlings.

New shoots of growth sprung up. We marvelled at how the prophecy had come to pass.

Margola's article in *The Otherworld News* was typically dramatic.

Druid Heir does it again in Wildwoods Showdown

But I knew the truth: the story hadn't been mine alone but a tale of friendship and uncommon allies, of love lost and love renewed, of second chances and hidden depths.

After a few weeks, Orpheus created the Rayna Willowsun Memorial Garden in a quiet meadow within the grounds of the school, where slits of sunlight stole through ancient boughs. We buried our dead in oblongs of carved elm. Sandstone headstones made by the Earth goddess marked their graves, each one remarkably varied in sediment and composition, a labour of love. The leprechauns added a final touch, inscribing epitaphs in molten gold. We honoured them with wreaths and incense, poems and stories, and splashes of water and wine. When spring arrived, the crocus and daffodil buds would blossom, and their names would always be spoken.

When the crowd at the last funeral had dispersed, and those still in need of care in the sanatorium returned to their beds, the core of us came together at the foot of an ash tree, our chests tight with loss.

My thigh hurt from standing too long at the service, but I ignored it. "The cruelty of losing loved ones is that the chances to say their names dwindle, and they fade from our futures. Maybe if we name all the people we have lost, we can conjure up a moment when they are here with us and part of our victory." My voice shook. "I'll start. My mum, Rosalie Verma. Her best friend, Melissa Ramsay. My student, Nita Mubarak. The Custodian, Calypso Archer, whose name we honour here but also in the library amongst the stars where she made her home."

The Prime Sorceress sighed. "My sister by birth, Morena Drach. My coven sister, Elvira Crane."

The scar by Ezra's eyebrow was fresh and pink against his skin. "My father, Levi Neuhoff. My uncle, Gunnolf Zev. Our friend, the white wolf Maximillian."

"My parents, Juniper Elmstorm and Briar Elmstorm," said Mirabel quietly.

"My father, Sohail Verma," said Dad. "Whom my mother trapped in the crotch of a saddle."

"My sister, Rajika Verma," said Rajiv. "Who was brave beyond her years and gender."

The crookedness of Echo's tail gave him a debonair, approachable air. He'd had a lot of luck with his pussy harem, regaling stories of the battle. "Suki, the only poodle I regret killing and whose beauty deserved to be captured in a portrait."

Orpheus's piano player's fingers still bore the mark of Ra's arrows. "My friend, Rayna Willowsun. And my clan member, Seskel, a brute who could recite Victorian poetry with exquisite tenderness."

"The elf queen, Meriel Naehorn," said Flinar. "Who believed in the possibilities of Wildwoods, even when it didn't believe in her. And who died on her own terms."

The leopard's emerald eyes glinted. "Lucky, murderous her."

Sahil smoothed down his suit. For the first time in months, he looked more like his old self, as he'd reached an inner peace that reflected on the outside. "I'm feeling the pressure here and can't think of any more names apart from the former Prime Sorcerer. But that would be intellectually dishonest because I enjoyed the story of the dragon crunching his bones. And I've been trying hard to be honest."

"We've not lost people," said Fei Yen and Faeza. "We've found family."

"Yeah, we've got nothing." Marina patted her belly and locked eyes with Rob.

Ezra hugged me and Mirabel close. As Echo slinked around our legs, I looked up at the marshmallow skies over Wildwoods.

Tufts of pink cumulous clouds. Cascading light spilt over the memorial stones. A column of white birds. The scent of honeyed almonds and mulled wine drifted over the treetops from a Christmas fair in Crystal Palace Park.

The promise of new beginnings.

30

When spring arrived, our wedding took place in my childhood garden at Dad and Alma's house. The old ladies at temple said we shouldn't have waited. Over forties shouldn't waste time planning a wedding. They should sign on the dotted line before eggs and sperm shrivelled any further. As though the sole purpose of marriage was to a) host a party for strangers and b) to have babies.

At our age, we'd learned not to people-please.

On the morning of the wedding, I did my own makeup in my old bedroom, with a pop of blush pink on my eyelids and lips. Marina arranged my silver tresses in a half-up-half-down style. Then I slipped on the vintage lace dress I'd rented from a higgledy-piggledy wedding shop in Wandsworth, with cap sleeves, scoop neck and flared ankle-length skirt.

Marina buttoned the back of my dress, and her face crumpled when I turned to face her. "Don't mind me. I'm just so thrilled to see you happy."

Tears mingled with laughter as our foreheads rested against each other.

I dabbed at her face with a tissue. "We're ruining our makeup."

Marina blew her nose and shimmied to reposition her growing breasts into a knee-length purple velvet dress worthy of Dita von Teese. "I'm a wreck. All those losers behind the bike shed, at uni and on dating apps, and you finally found the one." She fixed a sunflower behind my ear with a bobby pin. "Are you ready?"

I nodded, my belly fluttering, and she left me at Mum's shrine, where Ezra waited.

We lit a candle there, his hand on mine, and when he turned to me, the world spun.

His tousled, chin-length hair was damp and curled at his ears. His tuxedo had been immaculately fitted, emphasising his muscular pecks, broad thighs and peachy bum, but it was his eyes that were my undoing.

His gaze was soft, and the growl in his voice promised passion and protection when he said, "I'm a lucky man."

"Yes, you are." Echo padded past, a bowtie made by Alma around his golden neck. After much persuasion, he'd agreed to let us tie our wedding rings to it.

"Echo?" I bent to caress his ears and laid my arms around his neck. "Ezra and I have been thinking about going to India on honeymoon if you and Mirabel would like to come."

His green eyes stilled. "You'd take me to the land of my ancestors…"

I swallowed the lump in my throat. "Only if you want to go. Of course, you could stay there if you wanted to. You've more than fulfilled your obligation to this family."

His face flattened. "Oath or no oath, my home is with you."

Ezra grinned. "She was hoping you'd say that."

Echo purred. "I thought she was discarding me like a used condom. Would I have to go in the cargo hold?"

"No, mate," said Ezra. "The three of you will be travelling there first class in my arms."

Emotion glistened in his eyes. "In that case, I accept. Come on. Let's get this over with. This ring bearer will not be happy if the buffet gets cold." He sighed. "Soppy stuff is so hard."

"Go ahead. Gaia's waiting for her wingman." I kissed him and turned shining eyes to Ezra. "Shall we?"

Ezra led me to the back door, where Dad waited. He shook Dad's hand and, with a wistful smile, strode out into the garden without me.

A small blotch of yellow paint marred Dad's newly trimmed moustache. "You look beautiful, love. Gaia said to give you these."

He held out a bouquet of sunflowers and daisies.

I accepted them and reached up to give him a kiss. "Thanks, Dad."

My heart pounded in my chest, but I wasn't scared. Not this time.

Dad offered me his arm. I smiled, and we walked through the garden, arm in arm, to the whistling of waxwings in Mum's favourite tree. We hadn't needed a chapel or a temple or a synagogue. We hadn't needed a trousseau or a dowry. We didn't even need a flower girl or boy, although Marina and Rob had a baby on the way, and I fizzed with such joy for her that I had been tempted to wait.

Though our guest list was small, it was perfect. They sat on white benches diligently repainted by Dad in preparation for the day: Lavinia in pink taffeta, with Ezra's other two aunts, Isadora and Chandra; Ezra's pack, including Rashida, who had once loved him but who he didn't give a second glance to, even though she wore skin-tight white; the foxes, beautiful in matching peach *qipaos* embroidered with pink blossoms; Orpheus, in a top hat and tails like he'd walked out of Edwardian London, together with the sultry vampire he'd been making eyes at during the battle; Pan, in his customary tweed; Flinar, in a shiny, black tracksuit with a penguin front; Alma in springtime pastels with a sachet of flour on one hip; Sahil smiling broadly, with designer stubble and not a fleck of pigeon poo in sight on his Saville Row suit; Rob and Marina, their hands entwined; and Mirabel in a dotty blue skater dress holding a bowl of coloured rice.

When I reached the front of the congregation, Dad transferred my hand into Ezra's, shook his hand and cracked a joke about losing a daughter but gaining a wolf. But it floated over my head because the moment had finally arrived, and my heart couldn't have been fuller.

We turned our gaze to Gaia as she created an arch of wildflowers under the azure blue sky, and our guests gasped. As the Earth goddess gave us her blessings and the leopard beside her purred, all I could think of was how this was where I was supposed to be, with Ezra's hand laced with mine and the sweetly rising heat in this city of shadows and possibility.

When Gaia invited us to share our vows, I looked up at him from beneath my lashes. "You are all I want. I'll walk beside you for as long as you'll have me."

His voice jittered, but his heart had always been steady. "I won't ever try to tame you. I'll honour your wildness and match it with my own."

We exchanged the simple platinum wedding bands carried by Echo.

With the Earth goddess officiating, the union wasn't strictly legal, but Rob had some contacts who could pull some strings.

"I pronounce you husband and wife." Gaia beamed. "You may seal your promise with a kiss."

"Keep it clean," called Sahil.

The guests tittered, and our kiss was sweet and filled with longing. When we pulled apart, Lavinia brought a glass inside a cloth bag for us to shatter, as was the Jewish custom, to show that marriage holds both sorrow and joy and that we would stand by each other in hard times.

But we already knew that.

Then Mirabel leapt up and threw the coloured rice as Ezra and I ran back down the aisle and stole more kisses until we were hot with need.

As twilight fell and a curtain of stars descended over my childhood home, we dined at trestle tables decorated with fairy lights and potted plants, feasting on chicory and kumquat salad, buttered sourdough, sliced meats and stacks of roasted aubergine. We chatted across the table, drinking water and wine and devouring a pyramid of Gaia's laddus interspersed with edible flowers. Dad found a Tupperware box tucked away in the freezer. In it was Mum's last fraisier cake, with layers of sponge, almond paste and cream topped with strawberries. As if she had left it behind for our wedding. As if, somehow, she was with us.

Snippets of conversation drifted over to where Ezra and I floated on a cloud of bliss.

"I'll get you the number of a good dentist, Gaia, to help with the teeth Death cracked," said Sahil.

"No need, werepigeon," said the Earth goddess. "These teeth are the perfect disguise on a South London estate. It's time for the gods to blend in for a few centuries again."

"Can you take the net off the koi pond now, Joshi?" said Echo, bored after devouring his allocation of meat.

"No," said Dad. "This is my daughter's wedding, and the koi deserve to enjoy it too."

The leopard's lip lifted in a snarl. "In that case, I will sing Madonna at you whenever you are constipated. And I know, at your age, it is a frequent affliction."

"Don't let him bully you, darling," said Alma. "I'll stock up on cranberry juice."

"I hear you are into K-pop music," Orpheus leaned across his date to speak to the foxes.

"Oh yes," Fei Yen's eyes glistened happily, anticipating an offer of tickets.

"We are very much looking forward to our next concert," said Faeza. "It is our favourite way to relax. We are relieved the danger is now over, and we won't have to refurb Shanghai Moon again."

"Indeed," said Orpheus. "Perhaps I can interest you in accompanying us to the opera?"

So it went on, our messy, oddball family, and we had never been happier.

After dinner, Lavinia retrieved her umbrella from under the table and spun fireworks in the sky. Coaxing particles of exploding light into darts and whirls, in pinks and deeper pinks and tiny flecks of blue. Tielbu flew past, drawing an E and an A in the sky like a Red Arrow, his heartbeat one with mine. On a whim, I pulled scores of butterflies and bees out of my head, delighting the foxes and the Earth goddess. The insects settled on garden flowers and the potted plants on the table, where Gaia gathered a crowd about her to explain their intricacies.

When Echo broke into "Celebrate" by Kool & the Gang, Lavinia came to find us.

Her hazel eyes flicked to Mirabel, who, together with Echo, led a conga across the grass. "The girl looks happy."

"She is. Before the night ends, we're going to ask her if she would like to make our family more permanent." Ezra looked at his wedding band. "We don't know what she'll say, but it feels right."

Lavinia chewed her frosty pink lip. "I told you once that family complicates things, nephew."

My husband met her eyes. "It's worth it."

"Yes. It is." Lavinia raised her champagne glass. "To you, Alisha. The eternal girl who drove back the dark. To think, how I doubted you when you were in Kraglek's tank and mooned the spectators. And to you, nephew, who didn't give up on love despite my miserable example."

I clinked my glass with hers and wrapped my arm around Ezra's waist. "The fireworks were gorgeous. Thank you for your thoughtfulness."

"I was softening you up for a pitch," said the Prime Sorceress. "Isadora's not been the same since her run-in with Cardea, and she was rather hoping for a quieter life. Are you interested in the role of Wildwoods headmistress? I've never been in your night class, but you have all the markings of a wonderful teacher. You already inspire young peculiars."

I shrugged. "They see my name in the paper. They don't know the real me."

"Never deflect a compliment. It's a sign of low esteem," said Lavinia.

"In that case, the answer is no." I bit my lip. "I have my eye on something else."

Ezra grinned at me. "She's in a good mood. You might as well ask her now."

A slow smile spread across Lavinia's face. "You see yourself as the Custodian. Of course, you do."

"With some minor adaptations." My voice was like a runaway train. It hurt to say my friend's name, but I pressed on. "I'll never fill Calypso's shoes, but the library accepts me, and I think I could be good at it. I'd like to be around while Mirabel needs me, but I have some ideas about how to make it work and a team of people and creatures who would love to be involved."

On the lawn, Marina desperately tried to escape the boisterousness of the werewolves in the conga.

"Come and see me in my office at Wildwoods on Monday. We can talk about terms. I'll need you to take some classes at the school and perhaps help me coax Orpheus into being Headmaster, but in principle, I think it could work."

Ezra kissed his aunt's forehead and mine, then headed off in the direction of Rob and some craft beers.

Lavinia raised an eyebrow. "It seems the empath is in need of your services. And I must stop my sisters from eating any more laddus before they go up a dress size overnight." A pause. "Welcome to the family, Alisha. Morena would be pleased with her son's choice."

I blinked as the Prime Sorceress wove her way towards her sisters. Then I plucked out my best friend from the chain of writhing bodies following the leopard.

Marina threw her arms around me. "Between your wedding and finding my favourite knickers this morning, it's been the best day. Even though I'm not allowed to drink alcohol or eat blue cheese." Her face fell. "For *months*."

I laughed. "It'll be worth it."

"The PM made Rob a commander." Her chin wobbled. "It's all so grown up."

"You are going to be a brilliant mum, Marina Ambrose." I pointed at my daughter, who appeared to be trying to teach Echo how to do the Electric Slide. "You have two babysitters right there for when you're ready. And I'll be over all the time with a takeaway and an effective baby burping technique."

We joined Sahil and Mirabel on the lawn, ignoring the tangled mess on the trestle table of half-empty wine and champagne bottles, remnants of salad, crumbles of bread and slivers of meat that Echo stole from the table. When Pan had wrapped Gaia's laddus in napkins and stuffed them in his pockets, he played the panpipes. Ezra and I danced with our guests in the moonlight, barefoot, damp-socked and wild, as if nobody watched.

When the night was over and the guests faded into the night, just a small circle of family remained.

I hugged Alma, my feet sore, my heart full. "Thanks for hosting tonight. It was perfect."

Ezra shook Dad's hand. "We really appreciate it." He glanced at Mirabel and Echo, who were sleeping over. "You two behave, okay?"

Echo's tail flicked. "*You* behave."

My husband grinned. His gaze softened as he looked at Mirabel. "We have something to ask you."

"Oh!" Alma's eyes lit up. "I read this in the flour."

"Shush," said Dad. "Don't spoil the moment."

I reached out for Mirabel's hand, and Ezra did the same. My heartbeat drummed in my ears. I'd played this conversation over and over in my head. "Bel, every day with you is a gift. We hope you feel the same way. We have something important to ask you."

Mirabel stiffened, her hand in mine tensing.

"It's nothing to worry about, Bel. We hope it's something to be happy about." Copper-grey eyes crinkled in the dark. "We would really like to adopt you."

Mirabel's eyes widened. She buried her head against us, and when she pulled back, tears stained her face. "You're choosing me to be part of your family?"

I cupped her face. "You're already part of our family."

The leopard roared with approval, loudly enough for the neighbours to switch on their lights and question once again if there was more to the Bengal cat than met the eye.

Afterwards, we tucked Mirabel into my childhood bed with Echo curled at her side and said our goodbyes to Dad and Alma. Outside, the whispering wind chased goosebumps up my skin, and I sensed Mum's presence: a letting go, gratitude and unending love.

I stepped into the circle of Ezra's arms, and he teleported me through the universe. It was calm between the worlds now that the balance had been restored.

We fell into our bed at the cottage, fumbling with each other's clothes.

When our skin was bare, Ezra turned on the lamp. He

pressed his chapped lips to where my braille-like scar had once been before we had known it was a map for the Celestial Library. "I miss it."

I nodded. "I do, too."

He pulled me closer. "Time to make a new map."

And it was. Our future beckoned.

ACKNOWLEDGMENTS

Inspiration is an elusive thing, prone to sing its song in the smallest moments. This idea for this—my first series—came about in a small moment while we were cooped up in the days after the pandemic first hit. A picture caught my imagination: a woman in nature in the process of wilding. Her eyelashes and hair were feathers, and a bird rested on her finger. That was the spark that led to Druid Heir.

Maybe I'll come back to this world someday. For now, it is time to say goodbye.

Thank you to my readers. Writing is mostly fun, but sometimes it is scary, especially at the point of sending stories out into the world. It means the world that you make the time for my stories.

To my brilliant reader group, thanks for your support and enthusiasm.

To Debbie and Sherry, my beta readers, who have made themselves indispensable in the course of a year and who read for me at the drop of a hat, thank you for your insights, constancy and friendship.

Thank you, Jeni, my editor, whose love of storytelling and the authors who create them shines through every interaction. Your clarity, wisdom and patience made all the difference. My gratitude to my proofreader, Toni, for your dedication and eagle eye and for polishing my words to a shine. Thank you, Maria, for your beautiful cover art, patience and grit, even when natural disasters made it difficult.

To my children, seeing the world through your eyes is like a tenuous link to a lost version of myself. I can't wait to see your dreams unfold. This Christmas, I don't have a pressing deadline, so we're going to read tangled-up in duvets, and I'll feed you Brussels sprouts like sweets.

To Jan, my husband, the best sounding board, first reader and doubt extinguisher. What would I do without your encouragement? And yes, the wolf is you: his strength, his sense of family, his courage. Let's go find a sunset.

SHARE YOUR READER LOVE

I hope you enjoyed *Midlife Battle,* the final book in the Druid Heir series. Thanks so much for being part of this journey.

Please take a few moments to leave a review online. Reviews are so appreciated. They tell authors which stories resonate and help readers discover our work.

If you are a book blogger and would like to feature my books, please get in touch at www.NilluNasser.com.

N. Z. Nasser

xoxo

STAY IN TOUCH & GRAB YOUR SHORT STORY

Come and be part of my tribe and join my facebook reader group at <u>Nasser's Book Nymphs.</u>

To receive free short stories and writing updates, sign up for my fantasy newsletter at <u>www.nillunasser.com</u>.

For a close lens into my world, you can get early access to work-in-progress chapters and other goodies by joining my exclusive community: <u>https://reamstories.com/nznasser.</u>

Here's a coupon for the first time you make a purchase in my online store (it's so pretty!) at <u>www.nillunasser.com</u>: NILLU15.

BONUS EPILOGUE

If turning the last page made you sad, you can stretch out the magic a little longer by signing up to my fantasy newsletter to receive a bonus epilogue, in which Alisha goes for dinner with Orpheus.

For a whole new story world (small town, hidden kingdom, sisterhood, witchy vibes and gargoyles) start my new series Majestic Midlife Witch today.

ALSO BY N. Z. NASSER

DRUID HEIR

Midlife Dawn, Book 1

Midlife Tremors, Book 2

Midlife News, Book 3

Midlife Drift, Book 4

Midlife Portals, Book 5

Midlife Eclipse, Book 6

Midlife Battle, Book 7

Druid Heir Collections

MAJESTIC MIDLIFE WITCH

To Save a Sister, Book 1

To Curse a Rival, Book 2

To Trick a Raja, Book 3

NEWSLETTER EXCLUSIVES

The Magical Grandmother, Druid Heir Short Story 0.5

A First Date in Paris, Druid Heir Short Story 1.5

Midlife Battle, Druid Heir 7 Bonus Epilogue

To Become a Witch, Majestic Midlife Short Story 0.5

Biryani Junction, a Majestic Midlife Witch Cookbook

ABOUT THE AUTHOR

N. Z. Nasser is a writer of fantasy fiction. Her stories are about women who charge the world, filled with magic and rooted in friendship.

A lover of barefoot walks along the beach, she is glad to have left behind her career in the civil service and to never wear heels again. Whether she is writing in her garden office or wrangling laundry, she is happiest with a cup of tea at her side.

She lives in London with her husband, three children, two cats and a fox-mad dog.